RIGHT CHURCH, WRONG PEW

RIGHT CHURCH, WRONG PEW

Walter Stewart

Macmillan of Canada
A Division of Canada Publishing Corporation
Toronto, Ontario, Canada

Canadian Cataloguing in Publication Data
Stewart, Walter, date.
Right church, wrong pew

ISBN 0–7715–9104–7

PS8587.T48R5   1990   C813'.54   C90–094440–4
PR9199.3.S74R5   1990

1   2   3   4   5   FP   94   93   92   91   90

Cover design by David Montle
Cover photo/illustration by Marcel Durocher

Macmillan of Canada
A Division of Canada Publishing Corporation
Toronto, Ontario, Canada

Printed and bound in Canada

For Heather Rowat

ONE

IT WAS ONE of those summer mornings when all of Nature smiles. The sun was shining, birds were frisking, a soft breeze was frolicking in the woods, and, in a tree just outside my bedroom window, a male robin was telling a female robin that he would too respect her afterwards. The sort of morning, in short, when a man of sense pulls the blankets up over his head and refuses to budge because he knows that on such a day something rotten is bound to happen. I paid no attention to the warnings of Nature. Leaping from my bed, I donned the bathrobe, slipped on the slippers, strode to the door, flung it open, and very nearly stepped on the body of Ernie Struthers, who was curled up on my front stoop.

I stared down at Ernie. He stared back, but you could see his heart wasn't in it. I slammed the door. This would bear thinking on. A fine thing, I was thinking, when a person goes to his front door to retrieve the morning paper and finds, instead of news of death and desolation in far-off places, a local body. Ernie was local all right. He ran the hardware store in town, but lived right here in Bosky Dell. He is — was — in his mid-fifties, a thin reed of a man with a mean face, although I concede that he was not, in his deceased condition, really looking his best. Ernie is — was — a bit of a character, but then, so are most of the people who live here. Figure it out for yourself: would you live year-round in a small cottage community with a name like Bosky Dell if you were normal? Present company excepted, of course.

I opened the door again, hoping that Ernie would be scrambling to his feet and explaining that it was all a big joke, ha, ha, and I should have seen the look on my face. Ernie liked jokes. Not this time, though; he lay there, dead as yesterday's news. I bent down and gingerly touched his cheek. Stone cold. That ruled out the possibility that he

1

had conked out while calling around for a morning cup of coffee. Why would he call round for a morning cup of coffee, anyway? The last time I had spoken to Ernie, on behalf of the paper, he had called me a needle-nosing son of a bitch. While I am no expert on etiquette, I don't think you can call a person a needle-nosing son of a bitch and then drop in for coffee. In any event, the cold, hard touch of his flesh showed that he had been deceased, as we say in the newspaper game, for some time. I slammed the door again; time for more thinking.

You will be saying to yourself, hey, this guy is a journalist; finding a body on the doorstep will be terrific for him. Not so. I work for the Silver Falls *Lancer*. The Silver Falls *Lancer* is interested in death, true, but only so we can crank out those warm-hearted obituaries that begin, "His many friends were saddened to learn this week that Thaddeus Fuddpucker has departed this vale of tears . . ." We are not one of those hairy-chested, hard-hitting papers that is never happier than when it is ferreting out all the dirt about the mayor, or digging into garbage pails behind City Hall. When the police chief of Silver Falls killed himself a few years ago — blew his brains out with a service revolver and, if the gossip had it right, barely beat half a dozen others to the job — we reported that he had "died suddenly at work." We're that kind of paper. "Mrs. Mildred Lumpen recently hosted a delicious luncheon for the Women's Institute in her commodious Warren Avenue home" — that sort of thing. The only reason Ernie called me a, what he called me, was that I had asked him, on behalf of the paper, when he was going to pay his advertising bill.

We are a weekly, anyway, and since this was a Tuesday and we publish on Monday, whatever news value there was in Ernie would not come into play for us until next week, when the story would be history. No, I was not going to get a big pat on the back if I phoned Tommy Macklin, the managing editor, and woke him up to a raging hangover and the news that there was a body on my front stoop. I opened the door again and bent over Ernie again and was just about to roll him over when —

"Yoo hoo!"

It was the Widow Golden. She lives across the street from me and likes to, as she says, "keep an eye on things." A lot of small towns sport those little signs that say, "This is a Neighbourhood Watch community"; ours, if we were honest about it, would simply say, "Emma on Duty." Emma Golden is a comfortable woman of about forty-five, whose husband expired about a decade ago. From that time on, she has lived on the insurance while keeping an eye out for prospects, but since most of the bachelors around these parts are as shy as shot-over partridge, no business has so far resulted. Although chubby, she is a comely woman, and friendly and nice, and if she weren't such a damn Nosey Parker, we would get along fine. She was walking out her front door now, and heading towards me.

"Oh, ah, Mrs. Golden."

"Is that Ernie Struthers passed out on your porch?"

This was not such a surprising question; Ernie had what was known locally as "a bit of a problem with booze."

"Looks like it," I replied, but of course, that didn't satisfy Emma. She came waddling across the road, wagging a large, jeweled finger at me.

"Well, my goodness, Carlton," she said, as she came right up to the porch and bent over Ernie. "I believe Ernie Struthers is dead."

"I believe you're right, Mrs. Golden. I suppose the poor old fellow had a heart attack."

"Heart attack, nothing," she shot back. "There's a whacking great knife sticking into him."

There was, too. How I came to miss it I don't know, except that Ernie was sort of lying on his side, and the knife was low down and towards the back. I gulped about seven times in rapid succession. The Widow Golden, needless to say, was as calm as a salamander; she waddled round the other side of Ernie, so she could get a really good look at the knife.

3

She touched his cheek once, gently, and sighed. You could imagine her mentally ticking off one more possibility on her Might Marry list.

"Why, Carlton," she said, "isn't this the funniest thing?"

"Funny?" I gabbled, "why funny?"

"This isn't a knife at all, Carlton. It's a whaddyecallit."

"A whaddyecallit?"

"It's a tool of some sort, Carlton, and it's one of your Dad's."

She pointed to the handle of the instrument, which I now recognized by its round shape as one of my Dad's set of pin punches. I told Emma this.

"Pin punch?" said Emma, "what's a pin punch?"

She had me there. It had something to do with putting holes into wood, but not, at least not usually, people. "Thing for punching pins," I told Emma.

"Well, whatever it is, it's got your Dad's initials on it."

So it did. There, in bold letters for all to see, were the initials "HCW" — for Henry Carlton Withers, my late father. He had burned his initials into all his tools because, as he used to say, "the thieving buggers around here would walk off with a hot stove if they owned oven-mitts." In fact, in the matter of lifting tools that belonged to others, my Dad always gave as good as he got — or, rather, vice-versa — but local tradition held that if you had actually burned your initials into the handle of something, chances were it belonged to you. So Dad laid a scorching path across every tool in sight and here was the fruit of his labour, so to speak, staring up at me.

It was hard to know what to say. However, just as I was trying to frame a suitable pronouncement, a police car drove up on the lawn, right over the tulips I had planted a few weeks ago, and out stepped Quentin "Quarter to Three" Winston, of the Silver Falls police. I knew this was going to be a rotten day.

TWO

PICTURE THE SCENE if you will. Over there, glimmering through the trees, we have the tranquil waters of Silver Lake, burnished gold by the summer sun and without a thing on its fat-headed mind. A narrow road wanders along the foreshore, a thoroughfare which our imaginative forefathers called Lakeshore Road. (This connects, in due course, to County Road 32 and meanders fourteen miles into Silver Falls, population 14,000, our metropolis.) Off Lakeshore Road, several streets run southwards into the woods; and cottages, many of them now converted into year-round homes, dot these streets. Along Third Street, my street, the third cottage on the right as you proceed up from the lake is a small, white, frame affair adorned by three brick chimneys, the product of my mother's determination to be a good citizen, and conserve oil. She had three fireplaces installed during the energy crisis of the early 1970s, and all of them smoke. When you get all three going at once, the cottage is cozy on the coldest winter day; it is also filled with smoke. So you open the doors, let out the smoke, and let in the cold.

The lawn, a stricken patch of greenery where moss and dandelions cavort among the tufts of grass, is now festooned with three people. We have, reading from left to right, one plump and tender Widow Golden, in a rosy dressing-gown decorated with pink kittens; one long and lanky journalist in a dun bathrobe decorated with ancient egg, jam, and coffee stains, and Quarter to Three Winston, who ought, by rights, to be out harrying the criminal element instead of flattening the remnants of my lawn in his size thirteen regulation boots.

I may say I was impressed, even while I was terrified, to find Quarter to Three so swiftly on the scene of the crime. His name comes from his habit of standing with his broad brogans planted heels together, toes out. He is normally to

5

be found in this pose on the main drag of Silver Falls, where his principal duties are to breathe in and out and, occasionally, hand out a parking ticket to some stranger in town. Locals, needless to say, do not get ticketed, or, if by accident they do (sometimes it takes Quarter to Three a while to recognize when one of the natives has purchased a new car), the tickets are indignantly torn up and strewn across the street. Quarter to Three doesn't get upset; his mind, such as it is, is normally occupied with thoughts of food or of the delectable Belinda Huntingdon, waitress in the O.K. Cafe on Main Street. Quentin does not possess one of those steel-trap minds you read about, and it was a puzzle to me how he came to bring me so swiftly to book.

"Morning, Carlton," he said. "Nice day." He smiled at the Widow Golden — you can get the effect of Quarter to Three's smile if you hit a cantaloupe with an axe. "Morning, Mrs. Golden. Some hot." (Quentin grew up in the Maritimes.)

"Oh, hello, Ernie," he added, "didn't see you at first."

Quarter to Three had fallen into the same error that Emma had embraced, in supposing that Ernie was supine as a result of the effects of Catawba, his usual tipple.

"I came to see you, Carlton," he went on, grabbing me by the elbow and moving me over to one side where we could talk confidentially, "about getting a write-up in the paper for my sister's wedding."

Well, he could have phoned me about that, of course, but that would have courted the danger of being overheard in the police office trying to square the press, or being overheard at home — he lives in Burnt River, one of the surrounding towns — by his wife, who can't abide any of his numerous sisters. Easier to drop in on me on his way to work. I told him I would be happy to do right by the girl, and would no doubt have eased the oversized flatfoot back into his car and on his way, but Emma Golden stuck her oar in.

"Quentin," she said, "somebody has murdered Ernie Struthers."

"It's my sister Clara," Quarter to Three rumbled on,

"she's marrying that fellow who works with the Hydro." He stopped, shook his head as if to clear it. Emma's words had penetrated the concrete and were trickling down inside his head, on the lookout for brain cells. They found some. He looked up.

"You don't say," said Quarter to Three. "What do you know about that."

He strode over to Ernie's body, glowered at it as if he had just caught it hanging a U-turn on Clarence Street, and reached for a notebook. He came up with his book of parking tickets, glowered again, shrugged, unlimbered his ballpoint pen, started to write, stopped, pushed the top of the pen down to produce the ballpoint, started to write again, stopped, shook the pen, gave the whole thing up as a bad job and stood there, looking confused and not unlike a bull worked to a frazzle by a matador, if the bull happened to be wearing a uniform that was several sizes too small for him and had emblazoned across the chest pocket, "Silver Falls Police."

Emma decided to be helpful. Helpful people — this is recognized by all the leading authorities — are the cause of most of the world's unhappiness.

"Quentin," Emma said, "shouldn't you call this in?"

"Right," said Quentin. "Call it in."

"You can use the telephone in Carlton's place," said Emma, being helpful again. "After all, that's Carlton's Dad's whaddyecallit sticking in Ernie's back."

Whatever made me think Emma Golden was friendly?

"It is?" said Quarter to Three, as he bent over Ernie and was just about to seize the evidence, when a deep, commanding voice shouted, "Well, good morning, all!"

Quarter to Three stopped. We all looked back towards the street where, striding purposefully over the weeds and looking, to me at least, quite a bit like the cavalry on a rescue ride, came my neighbour and friend, Hanson Eberley, with a coffee mug in his hand, and a light in his eye.

The coffee mug was evidence of the fact that Hanson, like many of the retired folks in Bosky Dell, had a habit of wandering around the little village after breakfast, for a chat. Cold coffee, hot gossip. The light in his eye came from the fact that he had spent most of his life on the Metropolitan Toronto police force, and had retained the policeman's habit of wanting to be in on things. My front stoop, with its recumbent body and confused cop, looked promising. Hanson is a tall, rangy, good-looking man, with steel-grey hair, piercing blue eyes, and a pencil-thin moustache. If David Niven had had steel-grey hair, he would have looked a lot like Hanson and the resemblance was heightened, although I am sure Hanson was unaware of this, by the fact that he is a natty dresser, and always wears a cravat to top off his costume.

My mother was not fond of Hanson. "What kind of a man, for God's sake," she would say, "wears a cravat in a place like Bosky Dell?" My father, on the other hand — it was not the only subject on which they ever differed — was a great admirer of Hanson's, and often pumped him for stories of his detecting days which Dad turned into flashbacks and sold. He was a freelance, for which read "starving," writer.

Hanson had taken early retirement from the Toronto force, where he had attained the exalted rank of Staff Inspector on the Homicide Squad, eight years ago and retreated to Bosky Dell with his wife, Nora. They were working, had for years been working, on Hanson's memoirs, which everybody guessed were really going to be something when they came out. Nora used to be Hanson's secretary, but they must have worked better together when they were both on the force than they did after settling in Bosky Dell, because no one had ever seen any actual writing result from their joint endeavours.

Hanson was one of my heroes, in part because my father admired him, and there were not many people Dad admired, and in part because he radiated self-assurance, a quality I have always yearned for. Once, I tried to grow a moustache like Hanson's and my mother, after handing me an SOS pad and advising me to wipe it off, asked why I thought I needed a moustache. I said so I would look like... and then, thinking quickly, substituted David Niven for Hanson Eberley, not wishing to provoke my mother's scorn.

"But, honey, you already look like David Niven," she said. "David Niven has a head; you have a head. He has two eyes; you have two eyes. He has a nose; you have a nose..."

I wandered off, and cancelled the Great Moustache Project, but my desire to be like Hanson Eberley never faded. When my parents were killed in an auto crash a couple of years ago, Hanson offered me, along with the sympathy that is never in short supply on these occasions, cold, hard cash, which is. While I didn't take it, the offer increased my admiration for Hanson, and to see him cutting across the lawn, alive with intelligent curiosity, filled me with reassurance. Hanson would fix things.

It took him about two minutes to "debrief," as he put it, Quarter to Three Winston. Ernie Struthers was deceased. Right. Apparently stabbed to death with that thing now sticking out of his lower back. Right. Which had Carlton's father's initials carved into the handle. Hmm, right. Quentin had been about to check out the weapon, sir, when you came along, sir, and...

"And just stopped you from making an ass of yourself by smearing your fingerprints all over the evidence. Well," said Hanson, taking charge, "get on your radio, Quentin, call the office, and have them send out somebody from the OPP."

"Yessir," snapped Quentin, and headed for his car, muttering, "The radio, why didn't I think of that?"

The obvious response, because you haven't got the brains God gave a golf-cart, sprang to my lips, but died there. Quentin was dim, but bulgy, and it couldn't all be fat.

While he was calling the Ontario Provincial Police and letting the world know that a murder had been committed in a quaint little Ontario village where, until now, our idea of crime was the time the municipal clerk was caught using public stamps on his private correspondence, Hanson walked around the body a couple of times, looking thoughtful. He stirred the ground around a bit with a length of stick he always carried with him on his walks — "in case of dogs," he said, but my personal opinion was that he substituted it for a swagger stick because it made him feel good.

He didn't find anything; in fact, the big discovery, when it came, was made by the Widow Golden, who was wandering around after Hanson, checking up on his technique, I guess.

"Why Carlton," she suddenly trilled, causing me to leap about six inches and bite my tongue, "this is addressed to you!"

"This" turned out to be one of those offertory envelopes they use in church so you can crackle a five-dollar bill in your hand in full sight of the congregation before palming the five, substituting a one, and sealing it in the envelope. It was lying under a small bush that grows in the shelter of my front stoop, about a foot from Ernie's body. Hanson's swagger-stick must have displaced it enough to catch Emma's eye and sure enough, when Hanson steered the envelope out into the open with his stick — he automatically kept his fingers clear of what might turn out to be evidence — you could see, typed on it in capital letters, "Carlton L. Withers" staring up accusingly.

"Hmm," said Hanson, "I wonder what this is all about?"

I wondered myself. Whatever it was, it was bound to mean grief for Carlton L. (for Lancelot, product of one of my mother's bouts of re-reading romantic poetry) Withers.

Emma immediately started speculating. "I thought you said Ernie hated your guts," she said. "Why would he come sneaking around at night to bring you a letter? Did he want to make up?"

"He didn't, I don't know, and I doubt it," I replied, taking her questions in order.

"Well, we'll soon have a better idea, in any event," put in Hanson, "the OPP should be here any minute."

THREE

HOWEVER, IT WAS close to an hour before the real cops, from the Ontario Provincial Police detachment just outside Silver Falls, arrived, springing Quarter to Three to go back to Silver Falls and spread his feet — and lies — all over town. Hanson searched around to the back of the cottage for footprints and so forth, while the Widow bustled off to make some coffee and Winston and I stared at the ground. There were two police in the OPP cruiser that rolled, inevitably, over my lawn: Sergeant Richard Moffitt and Constable Jack Jeffreys. Since the sergeant was built on the lines of a drinking straw and the constable on the lines of a fire hydrant, they remain in my memory as Mutt and Jeff. They didn't know what to do, much more than Quentin — murder is not one of the summer festivities in the Kawartha Lakes — and were happy to take gently proffered advice from Hanson, whom they knew by reputation. At his suggestion, a line was strung up along the lawn, to hold back the swarming mobs of twenty people who turned up in response to some unseen tribal signal, in hopes of seeing me hauled off in manacles. Many photographs were taken of the body, by Mutt, the tall one, who produced a camera from the trunk of the car. He also produced a fingerprint set and dusted the handle of the weapon, and the envelope. He called for a coroner, using my phone, of course, and at no time offering to pay the thirty-cent toll to Silver Falls, and in due course up rolled Morton Armstrong, known to one and all as Morton the Morgue. One of those brisk, outspoken doctors, he dreams of the day he will make it into *Reader's Digest* as an Unforgettable Character.

He poked at Ernie and pronounced.

"Dead."

A couple of minutes later, he produced the pin punch.

"Murder weapon."

11

The cops were all over me, of course, when I explained about the pin punch and Dad's collection. They didn't actually say, "Aha!" but it trembled there, unspoken. I took them over to Dad's workshop at the back of the garage, and ducked in to bring out the rest of the set. But it was gone. Vanished.

"Aha!" said Sergeant Moffitt.

"Now, gentlemen," Hanson said, "if anything, the disappearance of the rest of the set — you're absolutely sure it was here, Carlton?—" I nodded, dumbstruck, "— points away from this young man. He has been with a police officer since the body was reported, and you can easily check with Mrs. Golden on his story about the rest of the set being there."

This calmed down the cops, but not me. I never used my Dad's stuff, carpentry not being one of my strengths, but I had seen the set a few days ago. I had been looking for a screwdriver, with which to bang on the innards of my ancient Peugeot, *Marchepas*, an uncertain beast that will sometimes start if you hit the distributor cap a shrewd blow with a screwdriver. I hadn't found a screwdriver, but I had found, and used, a pin punch. It hadn't worked, but I knew the entire set had been on hand on that occasion. Now somebody had stolen it. But who? And when? And *why*?

Hanson pointed out that the most likely possibility was that it had been stolen at the time of the murder.

"But why?"

"There is no way of knowing, at the moment," Hanson said. "When we catch up to the killer, we can ask him."

He walked away to greet a couple of lugubrious-looking gents who turned up in an ambulance and, after a lot of backing and forthing and filling out papers and getting the cops to sign them, they carted Ernie away. Drove right over the lawn to get to him, too. I wondered if I could stiff the county for a few yards of sod when all this was over.

Meanwhile, I paced back and forth around the lawn, went inside, got dressed, ate a bowl of cereal, and, when Jimmy Swart finally turned up with the Toronto paper, read that. I learned that the usual quota of unfortunates in foreign climes had come to harm at the hands of typhoons and tyranny overnight, but I had no sympathy to spare for them. There were perils closer at hand. I wandered outside to watch Hanson waving a dismissive farewell to the departing ambulance and when he turned and called out sharply, "Carlton!" I gave a convulsive leap and bit my tongue again. Hanson beckoned; I came; he opened the door to the cottage and we went in, Mutt and Jeff, then self, then Hanson, who seemed to have taken over the role of host.

We sat down in the living-room. Not at once, of course; first I had to remove the top seven layers of coats, books, old newspapers, dirty socks, and decaying pizza from the sofa and two chairs. I offered the officers a cup of coffee, but Jeff, after retrieving a mug from the floor, examining its layer of scum with a shudder, and returning it, declined on behalf of both officers.

"Now, Carlton," Hanson began, "as a newspaper man, you'll understand that the officers here have a job to do, and I'm sure you'll want to cooperate."

I didn't, of course; but I made the conventional reply.

"Good," said Hanson. "Now, I have suggested to the sergeant here, and he has been good enough to agree, that, since this envelope Mrs. Golden found with Ernie was addressed to you, it might be as well if you open it."

"Can I do that? Isn't that tampering with evidence, or something?"

"I think not, in these circumstances," said Hanson. "It has been dusted, and only appears to carry one clear set of fingerprints. I'm sure we'll find they're Ernie's. If you just take it by the corner here, with a handkerchief, and open it carefully, without touching the paper directly with your fingers, I'm sure it will be all right. After all," he added, "there may be an important clue here, or something that needs clearing up quickly."

Oh, I know, I know, I should have refused to touch the thing, and hollered for a lawyer. But it was obvious that the person in charge here was Hanson, my friend and mentor, and if he said it was okay to open the envelope, I would open the envelope; just as, if he had said, "Take this knife and cut your throat," I'd have taken the knife and cut my throat.

Because my hands were shaking, it took me some time to worry the envelope open, and when I had accomplished the feat, I very nearly dropped the contents on the floor. I don't know what I was expecting — a scrawled, accusatory note, perhaps, or a letter of apology for cluttering up my doorstep. What I drew out was a newspaper clipping which turned out to be the account of the crash that had killed my parents two years ago.

Silently, I handed it across to Hanson, who said, "Harum, Hmph," and handed it to Mutt, the police officer closest to him.

"What is it?" asked Mutt.

Hanson looked across at me, and when I didn't say anything, he explained, "It's a newspaper account of an accident between a car and a truck, two years ago. Carlton's parents were killed in the crash."

Jeff chimed in, "I'll bet it was some bloody drunk."

"Well, yes, actually, it was," said Hanson.

"Knew it," said Jeff, "and I'll bet they never caught the bugger."

"As a matter of fact, they did," said Hanson. "It was Ernie Struthers."

FOUR

I HAD NEVER been in a police interrogation room before. I had been in the front office of the OPP station outside Silver Falls, picking up details on car accidents for the *Lancer*, but that was as far inside the place as I had ever been. I hadn't missed much; the room I now found myself in was about ten feet by ten feet square, with one window, up high on the wall, three chairs, a table, and a lamp on the table. That was it. Not even a wastepaper basket. It smelled, a combination redolent of ancient hamburgers, stale coffee, cold sweat, and hot fear. About forty minutes after Hanson had dropped his bombshell in front of Mutt and Jeff, they had me in there and they were striving, successfully, to reduce me to whimpering terror.

"You hated Ernie, didn't you?"

"Well, not exactly *hated*..."

"He'd killed your parents, hadn't he?"

"Well, yes."

"Loved him, did you?"

"Well, no..."

"Disliked him strongly?"

"Well, yes."

"Hated the bugger, in fact."

"Well, yes."

"Good, now we're getting somewhere. That was your father's thingummy, wasn't it?"

"Pin punch."

"Your father's pin punch, wasn't it?"

"Well, yes."

"Part of a set?"

"Well, yes."

"Now the set is gone?"

"Well, yes."

I kept thinking I should work out a substitute for Well,

yes, just for variety, but my mind didn't seem to be connected to my tongue anymore, as first Mutt and then Jeff — both of them sat backwards on their chairs, just as on TV, maybe it's a requirement — hammered questions at me.

"The person most likely to take the set would be the killer, wouldn't he?"

"Well, yes."

"So, Ernie came to see you and you just opened the door and stabbed him, is that it?"

"Well, no. I mean, no, nothing like that."

"Oh, I see. You met him somewhere else and stabbed him there?"

"No, no."

"So, you stabbed him at your place?"

"Yes. No. I didn't stab him. Say," the thought suddenly occurred to me, "was there a lot of blood around on my stoop?"

Mutt looked at Jeff. Jeff looked at Mutt. Jeff, almost imperceptibly, shook his head.

"Well, then, where was he killed?"

"We're checking on it. All we know for sure is that the weapon came from your place and the offertory envelope came from the Bosky Dell church."

I was impressed. Did they trace water-marks or something? "How do you know that?"

"There's a stamp on the back. It says, 'The Church at Bosky Dell.'"

I guess I missed that. Our church is non-denominational, which is very broad-minded of us. In the summertime, when it is busy, we have ministers from various faiths alternating, although our permanent cleric is an Anglican. My mother thought it sounded funny to call it just The Church at Bosky Dell. "It ought to be Saint Something," she contended.

"Sure," said my father, "St. Farmer in the Dell."

"Anyway," growled Mutt, "we know you killed Ernie Struthers, and we know why, and we know with what. Why don't you save us all a lot of time and make a statement?"

I was spared the necessity of a reply — thank God — by a commotion in the corridor outside the interrogation room, and in came the local OPP Inspector, Fred Burgess — him, I knew; I did a profile on him when he was appointed to the job — and, hard on his heels, Hanson Eberley.

"It's okay, Carlton," said Hanson. He nodded at Mutt and Jeff, just to let them know there were no hard feelings for what he was about to say. "The Inspector here and I have had a little chat, and we have agreed that perhaps these gentlemen, in their commendable zeal to get to the bottom of this thing, may have skipped a few steps."

Jeff gave him a glare. "Such as?"

"Such as instructing Mr. Withers as to his rights before beginning an interrogation, and giving him a chance to call a lawyer," Hanson replied smoothly. "And such as explaining why Carlton, if he did the killing, would either stab Ernie elsewhere, such as up at the church, and then drag his body home, or just stab Ernie on his own doorstep and leave him there."

"Ah," said Jeff.

"Um," said Mutt.

Inspector Burgess didn't say anything. He just looked at the cops, who suddenly jumped up.

"Well, Mr. Withers, thank you for coming in," said Jeff.

"We appreciate your cooperation," said Mutt.

"Your voluntary cooperation . . ."

" . . . and look forward to chatting with you again, when we have done some more investigating."

"Because, frankly," said Mutt, with a genial smile, "we know bloody well you did it, but we haven't worked out the details yet."

Jeff said that a statement based on our little chat would be ready for my signature later, and added a caution about not departing the district, or they would be forced to come and find me and jump all over me. I replied that I had no intention of departing the district. I told them I would be keeping a keen journalist's eye on their future investigation, but they didn't seem much impressed. Then Hanson and I got the hell out of there.

My car was parked outside the cop shop. Hanson — who seldom drives, and doesn't own a car — told me he had decided, after he dropped a brick in my living-room, and the rozzers had scooped me up, that his best course was to drive in and talk to the inspector, whom he knew from the old days. No doubt they traded fingerprint sets at Christmas. So, he had turned the key in *Marchepas* — no, of course we don't lock cars or put away keys in Bosky Dell — and, by golly, the engine had started, first time. Nervously — "I really hate driving," he said — he had come in to spring me.

We got in, I in the driver's seat, Hanson beside me, but I didn't turn the key, not quite yet. I asked Hanson, aggrievedly, whether it wouldn't have been better just to let the cops find out in due course that it was Ernie who had killed my parents.

"They probably wouldn't have got me into jail until this afternoon," I complained.

"It was bound to come up sooner or later, Carlton. In fact, it's better to have it out in the open now than to have that pair dig it up later."

I guessed that was probably true.

"After all," Hanson said, "it isn't as if you ever threatened Ernie or anything. Did you?"

"No. Never. To tell you the truth, when my parents were killed, I was in such a state of shock, it didn't occur to me to blame anybody. Ernie was a drunk. We all know that. He should never have been driving. But it wasn't as if he deliberately set out to kill my parents. He could as easily have been killed himself, except that his truck was a lot tougher than my father's Datsun. Hell, he and Dad liked each other; they were always stealing each other's tools."

"So you never contemplated revenge?"

"What was the point? I figured the law would take care of Ernie. When he only got three months in jail, I was angry, sure, but what good would six months, or six years, have done my parents?"

"There is just the chance that a stiffer sentence for Ernie might have deterred others from driving drunk," Hanson noted, mildly.

"It might have. I doubt it, though. You read these stories, but do they stop drunk drivers? Besides, there was another thing . . ."

"What's that?"

"You knew Dad. There wasn't a mean bone in his body. Revenge wasn't in him. It wouldn't have been right for me to go after it."

"You're right. Henry was a hollerer, but not a hater."

"Later on, I admit, when Ernie came into that money, I thought about suing him."

Ernie Struthers, for most of his career, stacked groceries in the Red and White store, and if he kept the peas off the corn shelves, considered that he had given good service. Then a rich and distant aunt, always the best kind, died, and for some reason, probably because she didn't know Ernie, left him quite a lot of money. He bought himself a hardware store, since this was about the time Freddie Burnside, who owned one, was getting ready to retire. Ernest Struthers, wealthy hardware magnate, was considerably more tempting as a target for revenge than Ernie, grocery-stacker, and Hanson wanted to know why I hadn't gone after him.

"Same reason. Oh, I thought about it. As you know, he didn't have any insurance, and all I got was a token payment from the Unsatisfied Judgment Fund, about enough to bury my parents, and not much more. So, I thought, when Ernie came into that money, I thought, maybe I'll sue the bugger and see how he likes it."

"But you didn't."

"No. What was the point? The lawyers would get the money, Ernie would lose his store, and where would that leave us? It sure as hell wouldn't do anything for my parents."

Hanson leaned over and patted my arm. "Well, I'll tell you, Carlton; there is a certain amount of incriminating evidence strewn about the place, and those two OPP louts obviously think you killed Ernie, but I don't, and I'll see you out of this if it's the last thing I do."

A lump, an honest-to-God lump came to my throat, and we sat there for a minute in a solemn silence.

Hanson broke it by saying, "Oh, I nearly forgot. You may as well have this." He handed me a copy of the newspaper clipping that was now part of the case of the late E. Struthers and explained that he had asked his old pal Fred Burgess to run off a copy for him before it was bagged and sealed. Two copies, in fact, one for him, one for me.

The one for me was pure swank; I wasn't going to be able to make anything of this.

"What am I supposed to do with it?" I asked.

"Read, heed, and inwardly digest, as we used to say on the police training courses. There may be something in this clipping that will tell us what Ernie was up to."

"Nothing good, I'll bet," I said and I leaned down to see if *Marchepas* would startle the world by starting twice in succession. She did, and I was just about to pull away from the cop-shop when I got an idea. A lulu, if I do say so myself.

"Hey, Hanson, what if you were to come out of retirement?"

"Pardon?"

"Well, think about it. Now, don't laugh. I remember a few years ago one of the Toronto newspapers brought a famous Scotland Yard detective over from the U.K. to help solve the mystery of a girl's disappearance . . . "

"You mean Fabian of the Yard?"

"That was the name. He was going to find . . . "

"Marion McDowell. I remember the case."

There was a thoughtful pause, and then Hanson said, "He never did find her, you know."

"No, but he had a good run at it."

"And you think I should try my hand at solving this case?"

"Why not?"

"Well, I admit the idea has a certain appeal. Certainly, I

was the one who put the notion into those fellows' heads that you did Ernie in. Perhaps it is up to me to help get it out."

"I could get a terrific story out of it," I pointed out, "and that would cover any expenses."

There was another pause, rather longer, while I looked out the window — at a fascinating view of the back of the OPP shed — and then Hanson asked, "Who would you write the story for, the *Lancer*?"

"Why not?"

"I thought the *Lancer* didn't go in for stories of this sort."

"Well, it doesn't, not normally, but in this case we'd have nothing to lose, would we? If you broke the case, we'd have an exclusive — even the *Lancer* would carry a crime story if it had a world exclusive — and if . . ."

"I fell on my face, nobody would be the wiser, is that it?"

"Something like that, yes."

"Well, perhaps it's worth thinking about. Is this the sort of idea that would appeal to your managing editor?"

"Tommy Macklin? To tell you the truth, the last idea that appealed to Tommy, really appealed to him, had to do with Dolly Parton and a whole lot of whipped cream, but I'm willing to give it a try."

Hanson nodded decisively. "Then perhaps you'd better get down to the paper," he said, "and give it a try."

FIVE

THE NEWSROOM OF the Silver Falls *Lancer* occupies the second floor of a building on Clarence Street, just off Main. The advertising and circulation offices are downstairs, for easier customer access. The building has seen better days; at a guess, May 1, 1901 is one of the better days the building has seen and, as a result, the newspaper office, until quite recently, was an appalling place to work. Too hot in the summer, too cold in the winter, and filled with dirt in all seasons. The only inhabitants who truly enjoyed the ambiance were of the four- and six-footed variety. In the days of hot metal type, when the words were actually set in lead on a linotype machine, we got into the habit of keeping a chunk of the stuff on our desks for heaving at the rodents and squashing the cockroaches. We used to hold a pool on the number of vermin exterminated on press day.

Then we got computers to replace the old typewriters — and, not coincidentally, to allow management to dispense with the services of typesetters — and they fixed the joint up for the sake of the computers. Computers don't like heat, or cold, or dirt, so all the improvements the peons had been howling for in vain, and which had been rejected on the grounds of needless expense, became affordable. The vermin, except for those actually on the payroll, disappeared. The newsroom is now quite comfortable, a long rectangle punctuated by the desks and terminals of the working stiffs and, across one end, the offices of the lordly — viz., Tommy Macklin, the managing editor, Harry Hibbs, the business manager, and Mrs. Sylvia Post, the publisher.

Tommy was sitting at his desk when I strolled in about ten minutes after two — the trip back to Bosky Dell to return Hanson to his home, added to the interlude with the OPP, plus ten minutes for an incinerated hamburger at the O.K. Cafe down Main Street, Silver Falls's answer to Maxim's, had made me a trifle late for work. I usually clock in at nine a.m., give or take half an hour, depending on the mood of *Marchepas*. Tommy looked up.

"Well, if it isn't the jailbird," he quipped. "I had a phone call from the Inspector," he went on. "He said something about you stabbing Ernie Struthers. You know what this means?"

"It means I'm fired?"

Tommy nodded, pleased with my ready intelligence.

"Wait a minute, Tommy." And I went into my spiel. I won't bore you with it here, because, frankly, it was a little sick-making. I appealed to Tommy's sense of justice — nonexistent — his spirit of fair play — ditto — the journalist's code that every accused person is innocent until proven guilty — actually, every journalist believes the opposite, but I gave it a try anyway — and the fact that, if he fired me right now, he would have to write the *Ramblin' John* column himself this week. At this point he appeared to reconsider.

"Maybe we should wait until you're actually arrested," he mused, "and then fire you."

I told him he was doing the fine, manly thing. Then, pressing home my advantage, I sprang the scheme about having Hanson work with the police on Ernie's murder, unofficially, of course, with self taking notes for a world exclusive if he cracked the case.

"We don't run that crime crap," said Tommy.

"But a world exclusive," I murmured. "We could sell it to the Toronto papers, maybe even syndicate a series."

Tommy looked thoughtful; which is to say, his eyes, already far too close together, seemed to compress even further, and he twirled the end of his quite disgusting moustache with his right hand.

"There's money in that," he acknowledged. "Of course, the paper gets the syndication fees."

"Certainly, Tommy." I wasn't giving up much. The series wouldn't appear unless the murder got solved, and I had no faith whatever in those two bozos from the OPP solving it. The way I saw it, Hanson was my best chance of coming out

23

of this without gyves on my wrists. Give me liberty or give me syndication rights, about summed up my view, and of the two I preferred the former.

"I'll think about it," Tommy said, and he pointed me out of his office.

I waved cheerily at him from the hallway. All the offices at the Silver Falls *Lancer* — like most newspaper offices — have glass walls. This is so the higher-ups can see what is going on at all times. Since there is generally nothing worth observing, the system may be wasted. Or maybe not. God knows what journalists would get up to if they weren't under constant observation.

I wandered over to my work-station. We used to have desks; since computers, we have work-stations. When I got there, I felt the way the smallest bear must have felt on that famous morning so long ago when Goldilocks dropped by. Someone had been sitting in my chair, and she was still there.

The intruder was a young woman and quite good-looking, if you liked the type. I didn't. She was long-limbed and slender, with brown hair, slightly curled and fastened at the back with a bandana. She cradled a Nikon 35-millimetre camera in one hand, and had a light-metre on a cord around her neck. She wore the uniform — scuzzy bluejeans, sloppy T-shirt, scuffed boots — of a news photographer. Nothing alarming, so far; but what alarmed me were her eyes. Black, they were, and lustrous, with a snap to them, the kind of eyes that keep sending out messages. Messages like, Watch it, Buster, or I'm onto you, Mac, or Just try something and see what happens. She reminded me of Mary Ambree. Remember Mary? She appears in the work of that outstanding poet, Anon, in a verse that goes:

They mustered their soldiers by two and by three,
And the foremost in battle was Mary Ambree.

Mary was a trouble-maker, and so was this one. I could see it at a glance and so, refraining from the natural inquiry — who the hell are you and what are you doing here? — I merely came to a halt in front of her and assumed a neutral expression.

To my astonishment, she thrust out her hand and said something that sounded like "Klovack." I shook the hand — it seemed the thing to do — and said, "Huh?"

"Klovack," said the girl again, and tapped herself on a highly interesting chest. Ah, I thought, her *name* is Klovack. Clearly, this was a foreign traveller visiting in town, without much English.

"Withers," I bellowed — it is always best, with foreigners, to turn up the volume — and tapped myself on the chest.

"Writer," I added, giving myself another tap. I pointed to her camera. "You photographer?"

"Christ on a crutch," said Klovack, "Tommy Macklin told me you were weird, but don't you even speak English?"

I saw that there had been one of those misunderstandings. The girl was not foreign, she was merely rude, one of the modern bunch who think that thrusting out a hand and rapping out a name constitutes an introduction.

"Um," I said, and "ah. Perhaps I should introduce myself. I am Carlton Withers, senior reporter here at the *Lancer*. You again are . . . "

"Klovack. Hanna Klovack, from Toronto."

"Nice to meet you, Hanna Klovack from Toronto," I said, which was a lie; this girl was going to be a pain. "What brings you to the boondocks?"

"I'm working here. For a while, at least." She raised the camera briefly, lowered it again. "I understand you've been taking most of the pictures up until now."

This was true, although I have never claimed to be a great photographer. When you work for the Johnson chain — the Silver Falls *Lancer* is one of the fifty-seven Canadian links in that glittering chain — you take pictures whether you can or not. That is, you point one of these automatic cameras at something and press the button. What comes out usually looks like a scene about half-way down the shaft of a coal-mine, but we print it anyway. It may be lousy, but it is cheap, and cheap is the second-favourite word in the Johnson vocabulary. "Free" tops the list.

"You mean, we've hired you as a full-time photographer?"

"Yep. I start today."

"Boy, you must be rotten." As the eyes snapped, the brows grew together and the mouth tightened, I realized that I might have put that better. "What I mean to say is, I'm sure you're a terrific photographer, but we don't pay . . ."

"No, you certainly don't pay much. But that's all right; I wanted to get out of Toronto and work in a small town for a while. I've been working for the *Star*."

The *Star*. The Toronto *Star*. That brought back memories. I had worked at the *Star*, soon after I graduated from journalism school, until management decided to relocate me elsewhere. Anywhere but here, is the way management put it, but the point is that I knew the *Star*, and if this girl had worked there, she knew her stuff. Trouble. I knew she was trouble.

"Well, we must get together and talk about the *Star*, sometime. I was something of a rising, ah, star there myself back in the dawn of time. But in the meantime, I wonder if I could have my work-station back."

"Sure. I was only sitting here because Tommy said you were going to be fired. Or jailed. Or both."

"Just one of those laughable misunderstandings," I said.

So Hanna got up, a swift, easy mover, arrogant as a cockatoo, and wandered off to read back issues of the paper while I fired up the old computer and rewrote a column of Neighbourly Notes from our contributor in Dunsford, one of the outlying hamlets. A tea and bake sale was recently held in the church hall to raise funds for Our Feathered Friends. Life in Dunsford is one damn orgy after another, all of them recorded faithfully in the *Lancer*.

I had tapped out about 500 words when I looked up to see that Hanna had returned. No doubt a few back issues were all the excitement she could stand at one time.

"Say," she said, "maybe you can explain something to

me. I've been looking through your stuff and," she reached over to my desk and plucked a copy of the current *Lancer* from it, turned to the inside and held up a piece carrying my byline. "You write this?"

I murmured a modest assent.

"It's all about the swell gang down at Barry's garage waiting to give you something called 'suave service.'"

"I made that part up," I explained. "In fact, the service at Barry's is more surly than suave. But everybody liked the piece."

Actually, Barry had come in the day after publication and bought an ad; for a brief moment there I could see that Tommy Macklin was contemplating giving me a bonus; but cooler heads prevailed, and I got a friendly nod, instead.

"This whole paper," Hanna went on, waving it in the air, "seems to be devoted to sucking up to advertisers and local bigwigs."

I nodded brightly. "That's it, exactly."

"And you approve of this?"

Approve? The girl must be mad. "What I approve of, young prune," I told her austerely, "is eating. We have worked out an arrangement whereby I do what I'm told, and the *Lancer* fixes it so I go on eating."

She rolled those luminous eyes. "Great. I'm here to get back to the real stuff of newspapering and I draw a spineless twit for a partner."

The "spineless twit" crack didn't bother me nearly as much as the "partner" bit.

"What do you mean, partner?"

"Tommy told me that if you weren't in jail, or didn't get fired, or whatever your little misunderstanding was, you and I would be covering some political dinner tonight."

"Ah, yes. That will be Orville Sacks, Silver Falls's gift to the world of politics. Our local member of the Provincial Parliament," I explained. "He's making a speech to the Rotarians. With an election in the offing, I guess the brasshats have decided to get behind Orville and push. No mean feat, the man must weigh 300 pounds."

"So, what will they want from me? Groups? Heads and shoulders?"

"Why don't I ask them, and see?"

But when I went back to Tommy Macklin's office, he was already closeted with Mrs. Post, the publisher, who was shaking her head in a dubious way as Tommy explained, I guessed, the advantages of the scheme I had sprung on him. Tommy saw me hovering and waved me in. Mrs. Post looked up and gave me a cool look. She is a handsome woman, if somewhat imperious, who inherited the paper from her late husband, Donald, and turned out to be so good at buttering up advertisers and putting the screws to the workforce, that when the Johnson chain bought the *Lancer* a few years ago, she stayed on as publisher, while salting the purchase price into the old sock. Nice work if you can get it. I met her mainly during Christmas visitations when, with Tommy Macklin at her side, both of them reeking of whisky and bonhomie, she circled the room, shook hands with all fourteen of the hired hands, and doled out the Christmas bonus, usually a munificent twenty dollars. She was looking speculative, and as I came into the room, she started in on Tommy.

"I don't know about this, Tommy," she said, "Oh, hello, Withers" — so much for me — "it sounds pretty dubious to me."

"Now, now, Mrs. Post, nothing to worry about, nothing at all. If it works, we have a great series, an exclusive; we can syndicate it through the chain across the country. And, if if doesn't work, we can just fire Carlton, and no harm done."

Mrs. Post still looked dubious. She gave me an up and down glance, and plainly didn't much like what she saw.

"Tommy tells me that you are in some difficulty right now," she said.

That was rich. I was staring at thirty years to life.

"But he says that Staff Inspector Hanson Eberley — of course, we've all heard about him, and the chain did that series on his famous murders when he retired — wants to help prove your innocence."

"If any," chipped in Tommy. "I don't suppose you actually did it, did you, Carlton? No, I thought not, too much of a wimp. Here, pick up your pen."

This last was because on the words, "I don't suppose, etc.," I gave a kind of convulsive twitch, propelling the ballpoint I had been fiddling with across the room; it narrowly missed Mrs. Post's elaborately coiffed hair. I rose, gibbered an apology, picked up my pen. Tommy went on.

"I gave Eberley a call," he said. "He says the local OPP aren't really equipped to handle a murder and will have to bring in somebody from Toronto. May take days. In the meantime, he has spoken to his old buddy the inspector, who says he has no objection if Hanson wants to do a little poking around on his own. In fact, reading between the lines, I gather the idea of having someone with Hanson's experience on the job right away, unofficially of course, strikes the inspector as pretty shrewd. And Hanson says it would be okay for you to hang around with him for a few interviews."

"I'll try to make the time," I said.

"He says the locals seem to talk readily to you . . ."

"The journalist's training," I interposed.

" . . . because, at least until now, they have always considered you harmless."

Mrs. Post jumped in, "So the proposal is that you would make notes on how the investigation is proceeding from Staff Inspector Eberley's point of view, and if he manages to crack the case . . ."

"We get a world exclusive," crowed Tommy. "If you don't, or if anything embarrassing comes out, why, we just dump you."

I said, of course, that I would be delighted to work with Hanson, I had every confidence in Hanson, and I knew he would see me returned to my former high position in the community.

This drew a quizzical glance from Mrs. Post, who didn't think much of my position in the community, and who still wasn't convinced that this was a good idea.

"The Silver Falls *Lancer* has a certain position in this town," she said, "a certain reputation."

This was unchallenged. I have already indicated that we were not famous for our robust reporting. There was the time a city alderman, driving home after a Friday night spent at the Legion Hall trying to answer that age-old question, is it possible to chug-a-lug twenty-one glasses of beer within five minutes and not throw up (the answer is no), took a short-cut between William and Main Streets via the front window of Elder's softgoods store. He was extracted from the wreckage by his brother-in-law, then second in command of the local constabulary. The accident was put down to "Sudden acceleration of the vehicle in question due to causes unknown." That was the wording on the Occurrence Sheet. There were those bold enough to wonder whether the matter should have been pursued further, but none of them worked at the *Lancer*. Other newspapers take mottoes like, "Truth Above All"; our is, "Curiosity Killed the Cat."

Mrs. Post didn't want to see us turning into one of those sensational newspapers, like the ones they have in Toronto, New York, London, and other barbarian capitals, but Tommy was able to persuade her that he would exercise rigorous control over the entire operation and that, at the first sign that anything was going wrong, he would, as he put it — unnecessarily, in my view — kick Carlton's butt out the door.

Mrs. Post took comfort in this. I did not. She gave the enterprise her blessing. So did I. I told Tommy that, in the circumstances, I would be happy to devote my full energies to the pursuit of this story, which would mean, of course, setting aside all other work. Billy Haldane, our junior reporter, could take up the torch, I said.

Tommy gave me one of his looks. "This is not a charitable organization," he said, one of his favourite lines, although I have never heard anyone, anywhere, make such an assumption. "You can do the other stuff in your spare time."

"By the way," he added, "we've hired a full-time photographer for a couple of weeks. Just to see how it works, since your pictures are always so lousy. Take her over to the Rotarians with you tonight."

I sighed and got up to leave. Tommy spoke again.

"Oh, this murder thing. I don't think you did it, Withers, and I expect you'll be found innocent. I certainly hope so."

I murmured a thank you.

"Because if you aren't, it wouldn't reflect well on the paper. I wonder," he was saying as I left, "if we could fire you retroactively, and wash our hands of the whole thing?"

SIX

THE ROTARIANS HOLD their bunfights in the Ye Olde England Room of the Dominion Hotel. There was a slight mix-up at the door, when I arrived with Hanna Klovack in tow at seven p.m.

"What is this?" Frank Oakley, the sergeant-at-arms, wanted to know, and I was thinking that if he didn't recognize a female human being, we were in for a lot of tedious explanations, but then Hanna held up her camera, and we were ushered to the press table. It was not so much a table, really, as a couple of places at one of the eight-person tables set up for the dinner.

The usual performance followed. There were club announcements, and a lot of fun stuff where they fine members and visitors for various things. Marvin Swack was fined fifty cents for having his picture in the *Lancer* last week (not that anyone recognized it; this was one of my efforts, so we very prudently put Marvin's name under it, so that people could see that it was not, as might be supposed, a photograph of streptococci dancing in the dark). Henry Roper was fined for sitting at the same table as his best friend, Colin Starnes, and I was fined for bringing a visitor, and Hanna was fined for being a visitor, and then she was fined again for being a girl (much whistling and laughter from the rubes). I paid this second fine, hastily, because I could see that Hanna was seething with rebellion, and I didn't want a scene.

"The money all goes to a good cause," I told her, "retarded children."

"I can see that," Hanna replied.

We ate dinner — rubber chicken, plastic peas, and fossilized mashed potatoes swimming in grey gravy — and then the president rose to introduce Orville Sacks, our MPP and a man who needed, the president said, no introduction. He then proceeded to give him one full of the ripest tripe you will find this side of an abattoir. This cleared the stage for Orville to lurch to his feet, wave grandly to his pals, burp twice, and then launch into about thirty minutes of oratory. He hammered the Liberal party which was, he wanted us to know, the most scandal-ridden bunch of slackers God ever strung guts in, a scurvy collection of knaves who would, unless we dismissed them at once and replaced them with the sterling, four-square, God-fearing representatives of the Conservative cause, undoubtedly drag this once-great province down the tubes within a twelve-month. All good stuff, if somewhat familiar; there was no need for me to make notes as he went along. It was the refrain as before.

Hanna got up and unlimbered her flash and fired off a few shots — Larry Beaminister, the high school prinicipal, sound asleep with his mouth open, Harvey Menzies picking his nose, Orville, in a pause from his labours, ostentatiously ogling Hanna. She also captured the great man waving his arms and thrashing the wicked Grits, and then she came back to the table and whispered in my ear.

"Hey, didn't you tell me that Sacks was the local MPP?"

"Certainly. He would never admit it if it couldn't be proved against him."

"But isn't this a Liberal riding?" The girl had obviously taken in something from those back issues of the *Lancer*.

"Yup."

"But then, isn't he attacking his own party? Holy cow, you've got a great story here, why aren't you making notes?"

I saw that a word of explanation was required. "For about the first forty years of his life as a politician, Orville was a Tory, and they re-elected him, regular as clockwork. Then he got into some sort of scandal too odiferous even for the Tories, so they dumped him, and he became a Liberal. By this time, people were so used to voting for Orville that they sent him back to Toronto as a Liberal. Tommy Macklin used to say that as long as we got him out of here, it didn't matter what they called him in Toronto."

"Then why is he attacking the Liberals?"

"I was just coming to that. Whenever he's had a few, and you will agree with me that Orville is in a somewhat liquid state of mind right now, he reverts to his old habits, so, when you shove a microphone in front of him, he attacks the Grits."

"Still, it makes a good story."

"Not bad, a few paras on page one, with a picture, and a modest turn."

"You mean the local MPP attacking his own party doesn't rate the black line?"

I raised the Withers eyebrow. "Oh, we don't put that part in. Wherever he says 'Liberal,' we change it to 'Conservative,' and vice-versa, until it comes out right. We always," I added, making it clear to the meanest intelligence, "support the party that hands out printing contracts."

"Dear God," Hanna muttered, "and I thought I was coming back to the simple virtues."

We were getting a few frowns from the head table by this time, so I very courteously asked Hanna to stuff a cork in it before the sergeant-at-arms came along and grasped her by the nape of the neck and the slack of the pants — not that there was much slack to her pants — and chucked her out the door. The chairman's thank-you to Orville for what had certainly been an insightful and thought-provoking discourse concluded the festivities, and we headed for the door.

Lying in wait for us just inside the exit was Harry Franklin, one of my neighbours from Bosky Dell, looking a bit sheepish. He is not a Rotarian, and I guess he felt a little out of place.

"Carlton," he hissed, "need a word with you."

He drew me to one side, while Hanna stood by, tapping her foot and registering impatience.

"That business with Ernie Struthers," said Harry.

"Yes, Harry?"

There was a pause.

"Well, Harry?"

"I, uh, understand he was found at your place."

"You understand correctly."

"And they think you did it."

"That is one of the opinions going around, yes."

"Do you think it's possible that somebody stabbed him up at the church, and then took the body down to your place?"

"We don't yet know where he was stabbed..."

"Well, listen to this," said Harry, and he went on to explain that, as one of our little group of church wardens, he had gone into the church this morning, to make sure everything was ready for Ladies' Choral Practice, one of the large entertainments held weekly at the church.

"I was just picking up some cigarette butts from one of the box pews — you know how the kids sneak in there and smoke, Carlton..."

Indeed I did; used to do it myself, matter of fact. Cigarettes seemed to taste better, somehow, in light of the knowledge that at any moment a lightning bolt from on high might bring the puffing to an abrupt halt.

"...and I was just going into the Flannery box to check for butts, when I noticed there was something dark on the bench."

He paused, to give it dramatic effect, "It was Ernie Struthers's hat. It had his name in it."

"But Ernie doesn't even go to church."

"Exactly. But he must have been there for some reason, and that might have been when he met the murderer and got himself killed."

"Was there any blood around?"

"Nope. I guess the killer could have cleaned it up."

"Cleaned up the blood and left behind the hat? That doesn't make any sense."

"Maybe he heard somebody coming. I don't know. Anyway, that hat definitely wasn't there yesterday morning, because I was in checking things out after the church committee meeting. But it was there this morning. So Ernie was there in the meantime."

"What did you do with the hat? Did you give it to the cops?"

"Be sensible, Carlton. I didn't know about the murder at that point. I took it around to Ephraim Wylie's this afternoon."

Ephraim Wylie, locally known as Ephraim of the Angels, was our permanent, Anglican minister. A gentle, broadminded soul, he always presided gracefully over his heterogeneous congregation.

"He told me about Ernie being killed, and he told me that Emma Golden had told him that Hanson Eberley was working on the case. I went straight over to Hanson's place, and gave him the hat. He said he would call the cops right away. He also said that I should tell you about it; he said it would cheer you up. So, when you weren't at home, I went to the newspaper after dinner, and they told me I could find you here."

I thanked Harry, but he said it was "no big deal. The wife and I were coming to town for the movie, anyway."

So Ernie had been at the church last night at some point, apparently; though it didn't follow that he had been killed there. But if he had been, and we could find the evidence to show it, that seemed to point away from me — I mean, why should I have gone to all that bother of lugging him home? But, on the other hand, the cops had no other suspect, and, knowing the cop mentality, that meant I was far from in the clear.

I said goodnight to Harry Franklin and joined Hanna.

"What was that all about?" she asked.

"Nothing."

"Well, nuts to you, too," she said, and banged out the door. Right into a teeming downpour. The local farmers, who had been crabbing about the lack of moisture for their crops, were about to get their just deserts. Hanna broke into a trot, then a run, shielding her camera with one hand. I passed her at the corner of Clarence and Lindsay, but she caught up to me again — younger legs — just as we arrived in front of the *Lancer* building. I very courteously started to open the door for her, when a large gentleman — when I say large, think of a bus, upended and walking on two feet —

emerged from a Cadillac Fleetwood Special parked at the curb, and squelched across the wet sidewalk, with one massive hand in the air in a halting motion. I halted.

"You Carlton Withers?" he asked.

One of my fans, no doubt. "That's me," I said.

"Then this is for you," he said, and balling up the massive fist, hit me between the eyes. Upon which, I decided, like Johnnie Armstrong in the poem, that I would lay me down for to bleed a while, then rise and fight again.

SEVEN

I AWOKE ON the couch in Tommy Macklin's office, with a headache and a general sense of grievance. There was light slanting in the window — Tommy gets a view — indicating that I must have spent the night here, and that the clouds, as well as a goodly number of hours, had rolled by. Hanna was hovering, and even Tommy looked a trifle worried. The man — I can read him like a book — was concerned that I was sleeping on company time. It was after nine a.m.

"You okay?" This from Hanna.

"As well as can be expected when I've had a mountain fall on me. That was a mountain, wasn't it?"

"If it was, it was one of the faster-moving mountains. I took a swing at him with my camera-bag" — she probably did, too, the girl has no sense — "but he jumped back in the car and they took off. I came and got Tommy, and he got a couple of the boys in the printshop to lug you up here. Tommy said there was no need to call a doctor..."

Tommy was no doubt terrified that this would get written down as a work-related incident, and thus require worker's compensation, and the filling out of forms.

"...so he said we should just let you sleep it off. When you started to snore, I decided he was right, so we left you for the night. Sure you're okay?"

I clutched my head and groaned. A little sympathy and soothing, I reckoned, would go well.

"Yeah, you're okay," Hanna pronounced heartlessly. "You'll feel even better when I tell you I got a picture of the car, with licence. Good thing I still had the flash on my camera. We can identify the buggers."

I looked at Tommy. Tommy looked at me. I looked at the ceiling. Tommy twiddled with his moustache, a growth which, popular rumour has it, supports an entire family of mice.

"That won't be necessary," Tommy said. "We already know who they are. Dominic Silvio's boys."

"How do you know that?"

I explained. "This is not Toronto. There is only one Cadillac Fleetwood Special in town. It belongs to Dominic Silvio."

"And who is Dominic Silvio?"

"Local developer. Pillar of the community and all that, but his aides are sometimes a touch impulsive."

"He is also," put in Tommy, "one of our major advertisers." He went on in an aggrieved tone, "What the hell have you been doing, Carlton, to upset a major advertiser?"

"Nothing, not a thing, I swear." Nor had I; upsetting major advertisers who control their own goon squads is foreign to my policy. I was just explaining this when Hanna, running her hands through her hair, said in scornful tones that if we were going to take up a collection on behalf of the thug's bruised hand, we could leave her out of it. She was going to print her stuff from the Rotary dinner. She left.

"Testy wench," said Tommy, and I had to agree with him. Actually, I always have to agree with him, but this time I really did.

"Great set of lungs, though," added Tommy. "Well, enough of this crap," he went on, ever the gracious host. "I'm not paying you to hold down a couch. Get the hell out of my office and file the Sacks story. Give me about eight inches, and none of your smart-ass stuff."

So I did that. Then, feeling in need of breakfast, I decided to forgo the roach poison that passes for coffee in the *Lancer* newsroom, and drive up the street to the O.K. Cafe. It would be nice to chew the fat with Silver Falls's premier tourist attraction, Belinda Huntingdon.

When I went down to the car, it wouldn't start, of course. I am the only man I know who, when he takes a girl out for a drive and tells her he has to pull over and park in a shady nook because the car suddenly won't go, is telling the truth. Alas, it costs so much to keep *Marchepas* on the road, even part of the time, that I can never afford to replace her. When she decides to sign off, I just hoof it until, as usually happens, she decides on her own, and without prompting, to go again.

Last night's downpour had presumably dampened her drive shaft, or something, and she was going to sulk. I walked the six blocks up Main Street to the O.K. Cafe, and fought my way to the counter, where panting hordes were hanging out and trying to peer down Belinda Huntingdon's blouse.

"Morning, Fathead."

"Morning, Scribbler."

"Poisoned any customers lately?"

"No more than usual. Written any lies lately?"

"No more than usual."

I hope you're impressed. By the crisp dialogue, I mean, the easy backchat with a girl who, as I have already indicated, ranks among the Top Ten in pulchritude. No, I lie. Make it the Top Five. Belinda is tall, with long, blonde hair and a curvesome body. S.J. Perelman, that exacting stylist, once described a girl emerging onto the boat deck of a cruise ship in a stiff wind: "Eyeballs popped like champagne corks, and strong men sobbed aloud." When I tell you that Belinda could produce the same effect on land, in a flat calm, you will see what I mean.

She is not brilliant and, indeed, she has about half an ounce more brains than a pop-up toaster. This is not a negative factor, locally. My recent inamorata, Mildred Tilbury, for example, would be hard put to hold her own in a battle of wits with a dustball, but that didn't prevent us from engaging in a friendly grapple on Friday nights in the back seat of *Marchepas*. When I had lost Mildred about three weeks earlier, it was not because of my demands on her intellect, but because she fell prey to the charms of Willie Tempest, an adenoidal clothhead whose magnetic qualities include slicked-back hair, an out-of-tune guitar, and a Can-Am sports car that starts every time. (So, to be fair about it, does Mildred.) In local terms, Belinda has it all, and displays quite a bit of it daily, in décolleté blouses

40

provided expressly for the purpose by the management, down at the O.K. Cafe. She is no teenager, our Belinda, but, perhaps because she has never known a moment's worry or a second's twinge of conscience, she looks as fresh and blooming as she did a decade ago. The O.K. does a roaring business, most of it among the male populace, even though Belinda, *comme chef*, is no great performer. It is not her hamburgers that draw the men and boys up to her counter; they come more to feast the eye than the body. Indeed, I have known Tommy Macklin to order four frosted malts in a row, just for the jiggling, and throw them all out.

Belinda and I grew up together. Not in the same house, but as near as makes no never mind. Her father, Foster Huntingdon, is a farmer, with a hundred acres of mixed farmland on the outskirts of Bosky Dell. In fact, the village was carved, back in the nineteenth century, out of the King's grant that became the Huntingdon farm. The first day I went to school, I shared a hard bench on the school bus with Belinda, and a skinny, sorry-looking little rat she was, in those days. We were the first picked up and the last dropped, every day. It forms a bond. From the very start, I could talk to Belinda and she could talk to me. That very first day at school, when we were sitting on the floor in a circle playing some idiotic game — Mrs. Smith Goes Shopping, I think it was — Millicent Bridges, the well-known loudmouth, suddenly began to bellow, in that joyous, accusatory voice of childhood, "Belinda wet her pa-ants, Belinda wet her pa-ants," and all the other little thugs shunned Belinda. Not me. Hers was not an unusual crime — not unusual to me, anyway — and I couldn't believe that one schoolroom accident indicated blackness of soul.

So we became fast friends, but not, you know, *friends*. We were, and remained, buddies, even when Belinda grew, and rounded, and all the other boys began to breathe heavily whenever she walked by. Oh, once, when we were about fourteen, I made a grab at Belinda, but she just smacked me and said, "Oh, Carlton, for heaven's sake, don't be silly." The flame went out. We are more like a brother and sister than most brothers and sisters — who seem to spend much of their time fighting. When, in Grade Nine, "Fingers" Gerlack, who taught geometry and also took the after-school detentions, began to hang around Belinda, radiating lust from every pore, I made sure that she never, ever was allowed to endure a detention alone with Mr. Gerlack. One time, it meant throwing out a term paper I had done, and drawing four detentions in a row. It was worth it. In return, on the notable occasion when Mary Farnsworth told a goggling gaggle of females at a slumber party that I had once attempted to thrust my hand up her sweater, Belinda socked her one, thus vindicating my good name, even though the charge was true as stated.

When she was fifteen, Belinda lost her virtue to Stephen Swackhammer, her father's hired hand. She gave it up without regret and indeed, I gathered from her telling, with enthusiasm, even though Stephen, she reported, had the coldest hands this side of Lapland. Three years later, she ran off to Toronto with a TV producer who came up to Bosky Dell to make a documentary on the joys of rural life and found most of them in the person of Belinda. That didn't last long. They lived in a swank Toronto apartment, but he wanted to talk about The Soul and Art, while Belinda's conversational specialities are Make-up and Clothes, so she came back to Bosky Dell, and pretty soon she landed the job at the O.K. in Silver Falls, where she has been ever since, burning toast and libidos. She was living, at this time, with an amiable gent from Thunder Bay, working in the area on a construction project, but I continued to be her — and she my — best friend, confidant, and ally. Nothing had happened, officially, in my life, until Belinda had been told about it.

So, as the morning coffee crowd thinned out, and the lads got their pulses back under control and wandered off, I told Belinda about Ernie Struthers's murder — much intaking of breath: she had known Ernie, and fought him off on a number of occasions — about the Rotary dinner and, of course, about the new employee over at the *Lancer*, Hanna Klovack.

Whether I was fair in describing Hanna as a "snot-nosed, tight-assed, stuck-up, big-city bimbo" is debatable. (Her nose, as a matter of fact, is rather attractive; it swoops down in a gentle curve and then suddenly takes a dive, giving her a faintly hawklike look — very regal.) But a man is entitled to his little exaggerations on these occasions and I was getting off a few good lines about Hanna's total inability to comprehend how a real, honest-to-God, by-the-people-for-the-people newspaper is run, when a slender hand slammed a bill down at the cash register by my side, and a familiar voice hissed, "Well, Mr. Withers, we meet again."

It was Hanna, of course, snorting like a steam engine and shooting flames out of the corners of her eyes. Not satisfied with the perfectly good coffee provided by management right on the *Lancer* premises, she had gone sneaking off to the O.K. Cafe, and had been sitting there, hidden behind a seething wall of men, I guess, all the while Belinda and I were exchanging views.

It is hard to know what to say on these occasions, but, after a brief, embarrassed pause, I thought of something. "Oh, Hanna," I said, "we were just talking about you. Hanna, Belinda, Belinda, Hanna. Say, Hanna, how about driving me out to Bosky Dell?"

The bold approach, you see. I was in the soup with this pestilential female anyway, so I thought I might rescue something from the wreck by hitching a lift home. The cab fare is six bucks each way, which would blow a monumental hole in my slender resources, and I knew I had to get back and check in with Hanson Eberley.

Hanna gave me a glance of the sort that peels paint, then jerked her thumb towards the street, where a newish Toyota Corolla lay in wait, and we left the cafe in solemn stillness and were on our way.

EIGHT

THE SILENCE DIDN'T last long, which was too bad; you can't get into trouble with your mouth shut. I directed Hanna onto the road to Bosky Dell — first right when you hit the end of Main Street, and keep going — and then she had to, or apparently felt she had to, comment on our recent contretemps. Where another, and more sensitive soul, might have let the matter rest, Hanna plunged right in.

"Tight-assed, big-city bimbo, eh?" is what she said.

Hard to know how to phrase a reply. "You said it, kiddo," seemed undiplomatic, while, "No, no, not at all" invited the question that if it was not the case, why had I felt compelled to say it was to Belinda? I hemmed and hawed.

"Don't mumble, speak up."

"What am I supposed to say?"

"Oh, I don't know. 'Sorry, Ms Klovack,' would go well, or 'Just kidding, Ms Klovack,' or, 'On further reflection, Ms Klovack, I can see I had you all wrong, and will hasten to make amends.' Any of the above."

"You don't give a guy much room to manoeuvre."

"No, I don't. That's the way it is with us big-city bimbos."

Conversation ceased momentarily as Hanna wheeled around a Ford Thunderbird, dove in between two Chevvies, popped out again to pass a panel truck on the wrong side, and, after an exchange of civilities with the driver of the last-named, suddenly caught sight of the sign that marks the county road into the Dell, slammed on the brakes, spun left across the nose of the panel-truck driver, and began to peel gravel off the surface of the road.

"And speaking of bimbos," Hanna resumed, "who was that bimbo in the coffee shop?"

"That was no bimbo, that was Belinda Huntingdon. One of the Bosky Dell Huntingdons," I added, "and a particular friend of mine."

"A particular friend, eh? Then how come you weren't trying to peer down her blouse, like the rest of that drooling mob in there?"

"I do not drool over women," I replied stiffly. This was not strictly true, but it seemed permissible to edit the facts a little. "And I do not go about peering down the front of their blouses." At least not, I amended to myself, Belinda's blouses.

"Above all that sort of thing, are we?"

"Not so much above as to one side," I replied.

Hanna's eyebrows shot up, but she said no more, for a mile or two, and then she started to ask about the murder of Ernie Struthers — everybody was talking about it at the O.K. Cafe, she said, "except those who were devoted to character assassination."

I told her as little as possible; Ernie had been found, dead, on my front stoop, and the cops thought I had done it, but I was going to be cleared, I hoped to God, by my old friend Hanson Eberley, formerly chief of the Toronto Homicide Squad. In fact, that's why I was so anxious to get back to Bosky Dell, to confer with Hanson.

"Wow!" said Hanna, "some doings!"

"You sound," I told her crushingly, "like Quarter to Three Winston."

As she had no idea who I was talking about, the insult was wasted, but at least it kept her quiet until we whisked past the hand-painted sign that marks the entrance to Bosky Dell, where, under my instructions — except that she ignored the one to "Slow down, for Pete's sake!" — Hanna veered right just in time to keep from plunging into Silver Lake, skittered along Lakeshore to the foot of Fifth Street, turned right again, and stopped in a small cloud of dust in front of Hanson's cottage.

He was sitting on the screened-in front porch with a notepad and a newspaper clipping — presumably the one discovered with Ernie Struthers. I got out and started to thank Hanna for the lift, but she got out too, so there was nothing for it but to take the pest in. Walked in as if she had a right to be there, she did, and when I introduced her to Hanson, she gave him a 500-watt smile and settled gracefully into a wicker armchair, obviously prepared to take root. This was going to make it a bit awkward for me to talk confidentially to Hanson, so I tried a tactful hint.

"Well, Hanna, it's been very kind of you to give me a lift, but I'm sure you have a million things to do . . ."

"No, I don't."

" . . . hang up the old toothbrush, fluff out the frilly dresses . . ."

Hanna gave me a look. "In the first place, I don't have my stuff unpacked yet; it just arrived from Toronto. And in the second place, I want to see how a real murder investigation is conducted."

Hanson appeared amused. "Well, Carlton," he said, "if Miss Klovack wants to sit in on our strategy session, I see no harm in it. We need all the help we can get."

Betrayed by my own friend. Hanna settled back to listen, obviously prepared to enjoy herself.

"Hanson, darling, please introduce me."

This was Mrs. Eberley speaking, as she hove onto the scene, dressed to the nines as usual, asparkle with gems and agleam with make-up as usual, and, as usual, slightly tanked. She is a slender woman, all joints and angles, although she retains the outlines of girlish good looks. She is a couple of decades younger than Hanson, and apparently she keeps her slenderness by substituting beverages for food. While I have never seen her falling-down drunk, I have seldom seen her entirely sober, either. She has a voice that normally perches somewhere between a shriek and a whine, and local opinion holds that when Hanson traded in his first wife for her, some years ago, he did not do a wise thing.

Nora Eberley lurched through the screen door from the living-room with one hand out to guard against obstacles, and the other clutching what looked like a glass of water, but was probably straight gin. I jumped to my feet, upsetting a small table in the process, and introduced Hanna.

46

"Such a pleasure," purred Mrs. Eberley. "We're not used to seeing Carlton with young ladies."

Which, just to set the record straight, is the case. Bosky Dell having the most sophisticated intelligence network outside the Super Powers, it has always been my policy to keep my dates miles away from the place; I do my gripping and groping elsewhere. Mildred Tilbury, for example, came from Silver Falls, where she was known as "Main Street Mildred, the Fun of the Falls."

"Not much for the girls, is he?" Hanna asked.

"No," replied Mrs. Eberley, "Carlton seems immune to female charms."

"Except yours, of course, Mrs. Eberley," I said gallantly. It seemed the thing to do.

Her eyes widened. "Why, Carlton," she trilled, "perhaps I've misjudged you. Well, ta-ta all."

Apparently, she had just come out to check on the voices, and see if it was anyone important. Since it wasn't, she stumbled back into the living-room, leaving one of those awkward silences.

Hanson brought out the clipping again, and handed it to me. "This mean anything to you yet, Carlton?"

It didn't. The truth is, I found it awakened memories of my parents so poignant that I couldn't bear to read the thing, much less pore over it for clues.

Hanna held out her hand, and I passed the clipping across.

"Oh," she said, "a newspaper clipping. What does it have to do with anything?"

Hanson explained, "It was found in an offertory envelope from the church just over on the next street. The envelope had Carlton's name typed on it, and it turned up quite close to the body of Ernie Struthers. What it means, if anything, we don't yet know."

"Well, then, I'd better check it for clues, hadn't I?" chirruped Hanna gaily, but then, as she read the article, the smile fled. She turned and touched me briefly on the back of the hand and said, "Oh, Carlton, I am so sorry."

I knew I had to change the subject, quickly. "Well," I said, "Ernie must have been been reading that thing over for some reason, when whoever it was snuck up and stuck him in the back."

Hanson said "Um."

Hanna, deciding, I guess, that she had been kindly long enough — twenty seconds or more — was more pointed in her response.

"I see," she said, "and then the murderer carefully folded up the clipping, put it into an envelope which he happened to have with him, hauled out a typewriter which he also happened to have about his person, typed your name on the envelope, and left it beside the body. He wanted to give the cops a fair chance."

"All right, all right," I said, "but people do things like that in murder mysteries."

"Only weak-minded ones," Hanna shot back.

Hanson noted, "Ernie was either bringing you this clipping for some unfathomable motive, or reading it, for some equally unfathomable motive, up at the church before he was killed. If he wanted you to have it, why wouldn't he just call round and hand it to you?"

"I can think of two reasons," I said. "The first is that we weren't on very good terms" — I didn't bother to spell this out for them — "the second is that the subject was not the sort of thing Ernie was ever likely to raise with me, or I with him, even if we were speaking. I mean, you don't go knocking on somebody's door to say, 'Oh, by the way, here's a little newspaper article I happened to come across when I was going through some back papers, about the time I wiped out your parents.'"

"I can't imagine him coming to your place with an article like that," said Hanna. "What reason could he possibly have?"

"No. Hold on a minute," said Hanson. "Let's go back to something you said a minute ago, young lady."

I could have told him you don't call young ladies young lady anymore, they are young women. Hanna started to bridle, but then shrugged and subsided as Hanson went on. "Suppose the whole thing was staged for the simplest of all possible reasons?"

"Which is?" I was completely at sea.

"Of course," said Hanna, and I could have kicked her. "Carlton was going to be made the fall guy. Even the cops — pardon me, Mr. Eberley — could see that he's the obvious suspect. What's more natural than that someone should put the envelope on Ernie, addressed to Carlton, to cinch the thing?"

"But the envelope *wasn't* on him," I pointed out. "It was under the bushes. If it hadn't been for Emma Golden, it might never have been found — it could easily have blown away."

"It's a point," said Hanson.

Pleased, I pursued it. "If you ask me, Ernie put the clipping in the envelope and was going to slip it in under my door." Hanna wanted to know why not in the mailbox, so I explained that we don't have such things. There is a bank of boxes at the top of each street. "Crikey," I added, "now you've made me forget where I was. Oh, yeah, Ernie didn't want to face me, although for some godawful reason of his own, he wanted me to have the clipping, but before he got to the door, somebody saw him, killed him, and the envelope fell out of his hand. The killer never saw it, because it was dark at the time."

Hanna looked thoughtful. "Well, the cops will test the envelope for fingerprints, and they can soon find out who handled it."

I gave her a pitying smile. "This is not the kind of community where everybody's prints are on file, and if the cops start rousting the populace for their prints, they will be able to hear the screams down in Toronto. What's more, nobody these days commits a crime without wearing gloves. Besides . . ."

Hanson held up his hand, like a traffic cop. "Hold it," he said. "I think we're going a little too fast, here. Before we speculate too much on the meaning of this newspaper clipping, we have to know a great deal more, such as, where and when, exactly, was Ernie killed? And, was the clipping a part of the killing, a motive for the killing or — and I have to tell you, this is my own view — did the clipping have nothing whatever to do with the killing, and does it have some other entirely logical explanation we know nothing of as yet?"

My heart sank. Here was a clue, a genuine clue, the kind of thing Perry Mason uses to tear the mask off the evil-doer just before the shampoo commercial, and it was turning into a red herring. Or not. Hanson gave me a kindly smile.

"Don't worry, Carlton, it's early days. In the end, most murders are solved by routine investigation, not dramatic clues. We'll get to the bottom of this yet."

So far, he was willing to admit, there was not much to go on. The OPP twosome had had a preliminary look at the church, and cordoned the place off. He had told them about Harry Franklin finding Ernie's hat, which was now in police possession. The hat, they agreed, might prove that Ernie had spent his last evening at the church, or, as Hanson pointed out, "That someone wanted us to think that was what happened."

"Has there been an autopsy?" Hanna asked.

"Not a full-scale one. There has been a preliminary medical report, not properly an autopsy. A much more thorough one will be done later. The police were kind enough to give me the result. Ernie's death was due to internal bleeding, undoubtedly caused by being stabbed with the pin punch. He died somewhere between six p.m. and midnight Monday night."

"Does the report suggest whether the body was moved?"

Hanson shot her a keen look. "That's a very astute question," he said. "No, it doesn't, not in so many words. But it does show something else."

"What's that?"

"There was extensive bruising on the back, and to one side, of Ernie's head."

"You mean he was knocked on the head and then stabbed?"

50

"It appears that way, yes."

The police had also done a cursory search of Ernie's home — he lived alone — which hadn't revealed anything astonishing, although no forensic analysis had been done there yet.

"Oh, yes, and the boys tell me they're getting some help," Hanson added. "Two officers from the homicide branch are coming up from the Toronto headquarters of the OPP. They'll do the real investigation, I imagine, while the local detachment do the routine work."

That was encouraging; the Toronto cops had to be better than Mutt and Jeff.

"How will they feel about you working on the case?" Hanna wanted to know.

"They won't object, I don't imagine, as long as I don't get in the way. If I do, they will very properly tell me to butt out."

"Well then, let's get it done before they get here," I said.

"We can but try," was Hanson's response. "What we must do," he continued, "is to work out who might have had a motive for killing Ernie, and then narrow it down to somebody who had the means, and the exclusive opportunity. When you have motive, means, and opportunity, you can usually see who did it quickly enough."

"As far as motive goes," I said, "there's... well, there's me."

"That's a fact," said Hanna, helpfully.

"As for means, well, there was my Dad's pin punch."

"And as for opportunity," Hanson chipped in cheerfully, "if Ernie was right there on your doorstep, you wouldn't even have to leave home to stab him."

This was not going well.

Hanna looked thoughtful. "Okay," she said, "Carlton did it. So what's the connection with the church?"

"Misdirection," Hanson explained. "To throw police off the scent."

"Certainly," said Hanna. "That's it. Shall I call the cops?"

"Yes, well, skipping all this delightful banter," I put in, "what we ought to be asking ourselves is, What in hell was Ernie doing in the church, supposing he really was there in the first place? The only time I ever saw Ernie cross the threshold of the church was the time he saw all the candles burning for evening service one night when he himself was lit up, thought somebody was holding a birthday party, staggered in, threw up, and passed out. The Rev. Wylie was not too pleased with Ernie, as I recall. He ticked him off properly, complete with some good stuff from the Book of Revelations."

"When was this?" asked Hanson.

"Oh, a couple of years ago. I doubt if the Rev. would have waited two years and then stabbed Ernie for messing up the pews."

Hanson agreed that it didn't seem likely, but Hanna wasn't so sure. "A lot of these clergymen are seething with suppressed passions," she said. "We once had a priest in the Ukrainian Orthodox Church, where my family belongs, who smiled and bowed and looked as gentle as a lamb, but if you got on the wrong side of him, he was as cruel as a cat."

"Caught you smoking in the vestry, did he?" said Hanson, "and smacked you one?"

Hanna looked impressed. "How did you know that?"

"He's a detective," I explained, "he detects. But, I can't see the Rev. Wylie in the role of killer. There is no way he would go about sticking things into people's backs — even if they weren't parishioners."

"Well, perhaps not," Hanna conceded, "but I still think we should drop in on him, maybe he can tell us what Ernie was doing in the church."

"Actually, I already have a pretty good idea about that," said Hanson, mysteriously, "but there are some points I'm not quite clear on, so why don't I give him a call, now, to see if he's free to drop by?"

Hanson went inside and reported back almost at once. "He's on his way."

So he was, and within a minute or so — Ephraim Wylie

lives on Sixth Street, right next to the church — we saw him turn the corner at the top of Fifth and lumber towards us, a large, dark, fat, unhappy-looking man in a clerical collar. He knocked timidly at the porch door, entered at Hanson's invitation, stood dithering through an introduction to Hanna, wiped a sweaty brow, and told Hanson he had something to tell him "of the Utmost Importance, you know, Touching the Matter we were Speaking of" — you could hear him putting the capitals on the letters.

He clearly wanted us to scram, and I began to get up, but Hanna grabbed my arm in a grip that will probably leave a mark that I can show my children, and stuck her nose in again.

"Does it have anything to do with Ernie Struthers's death?" she asked.

The Rev. looked startled, dithered some more, wiped his brow some more, and then blurted out, "It has everything to do with Ernie's death. I'm responsible for it."

NINE

"NOT PERSONALLY," HE added swiftly, in response to my startled yelp and yes, I admit it, the look of relief on my face. "I don't mean that I personally stabbed the poor man. No, no, of course not. What I mean to say, is that I believe I am responsible for Ernie being in the church last night."

"You're sure he was in the church?" Hanson asked.

"Quite sure. As you know, Hanson, he was doing me a bit of an, um, favour," the Rev. explained, looking slightly sheepish.

"Favour?" I couldn't imagine Ernie as a pal of the Rev. "What sort of favour?"

"Well, I had asked him to be there. For the meeting."

"Meeting? What meeting? A prayer meeting?" This from Hanna, missing another wonderful opportunity to keep her mouth shut. The Rev. immediately clammed up.

"Hanson . . . Mr. Eberley . . . Hanson . . ." He couldn't seem to make up his mind. "Could we not discuss this in, uh, more private circumstances?"

"Certainly, Ephraim, these folks were just leaving, anyway. We'll talk later," Hanson told me in an aside, and he whooshed us out the door like a householder giving an insurance salesman the bum's rush.

As we walked to the car, I told Hanna that if she hadn't insisted on butting in, we might have heard what the Rev. had had to say, and she said, no, we were going to be given the heave-ho no matter what. "So much for your inside story," she added.

"Hanson will fill me in later," I responded, "but we could have got it first-hand if you hadn't put the wind up the Rev."

She doubted it. "These clergy," she said, "tight-lipped bunch. You've got to pry it out of them."

Not in my experience; in my experience, the trick is to turn off the tap once the flow starts. In the Bosky Dell church, we have a system to curb the Rev. when he gets the oratorical bit between his teeth. When the sermon hits twelve minutes, the leading citizens begin to scrape their feet, and if he goes past twenty, Arthur Blenkins, a retired stockbroker and all-around imperious buzzard, gets up and stamps out, with Mrs. Blenkins whispering frantic asides as she wallows up the aisle in his wake. "Roast in the oven. Must go."

Hanna said that sort of thing didn't count, because it was official gab. "All clergymen are blabbers when you get them on Balak the son of Zippor, or what bums the Philistines were," she contended, "but on anything juicy, they're tighter than a bank vault."

Then, changing the subject abruptly, she asked, "Have you known the Eberleys long?"

"Quite a while." And I told her about Nora transmogrifying herself from Hanson's secretary to his wife when they were still on the police force, before the couple moved up here permanently.

"I'm not surprised," said Hanna, "he is a very sexy man. Don't you think so?"

Weird question. Why should I find Hanson sexy? I preserved a diplomatic silence.

Hanna got in, turned the key, and, just before I could slam the door and wish her Godspeed, asked, "What now? Can we rustle up a cup of coffee around here?"

We could. I could make one, and, after some hesitation, I agreed to do so. I wasn't keen on Hanna seeing my place, somehow, and I was even less keen on introducing her to the Widow Golden, who would be out the door with her eyes on stalks before Hanna had been on the premises for five minutes. Still, it couldn't be helped, so I directed Hanna around the two blocks over to Third Street. We entered by the kitchen door — at the side, and harder to see from the Golden spy-tower. Hanna looked about and rolled her eyes.

"The cleaning lady hasn't been in," I explained.

"Not since the turn of the century, I would guess. Tell me,

is this the result of conscious effort, or leftovers from the Great Bosky Dell Avalanche?"

I dug through the mound on the kitchen table until I located a couple of mugs and the coffee pot. Hanna held out her hand, took them from me, and cleared away a hollow in the kitchen-sink clutter, where she proceeded to scrub the things before handing them back. I ground fresh coffee — my only extravagance — boiled the kettle, and made a potful of the drip variety. The rich, dark smell of the brew filled the kitchen, covering some of the background dankness. I pushed the accumulated detritus off a couple of chairs onto the floor, poured out the coffee, and we were just sitting down to sip when there came a knock at the front door.

"The Welcome Wagon, no doubt," said Hanna.

"Our local version," I explained. "The Widow Golden. Lives across the street and likes to keep an eye on things."

In point of fact, it might not be so bad to see the Widow Golden, after all. The disadvantage of having her for a neighbour was that she was always popping over to spy on me; the advantage was that she usually hauled along some food, and it was lunchtime.

However, this was not the Widow Golden standing on the other side of the screen door, bent on charity, it was the same large plug-ugly who had busted me one outside the *Lancer* offices last night, bent on more mayhem, from the way he glowered at me. With a startled yelp, I slammed the inside door in his face. There came a blam, blam, blam on the screen door and a voice like the sound of tumbling coal.

"Open the door, Mr. Withers," this voice growled. "I wish to speak with you."

"Go away," I shouted through the door.

"Mr. Withers, I wish only to speak with you, is what."

"You wish only to hit me, is what." And I shouted back in the direction of the kitchen, "Hanna, call the cops, we've got an intruder."

Sheer bluff, of course. The phone is in my bedroom, not

the kitchen, and Hanna couldn't have found it without the aid of a tracker-dog. However, my bellow brought her into the living-room.

"Now, Carlton, we're not afraid of the Widow Golden, are we?"

"Yes, we are. But this isn't her. This is that galoot from before. The one who belted me."

"Is it, then?" said the fearless female, and she came marching across the room. "Let's by all means give him a Bosky Dell welcome."

Before she could get to the door, it was gone. There was a kind of rending sound — there goes the screen door, I thought — and then a crunching sound, and the inner door flew open, and there stood the plug-ugly, about six-foot six of him, and broad in proportion. He lowered his head, to avoid the door-frame, and peered in.

"Honest, Mr. Withers," he began, "I just . . . "

But that is as far as he got, when the Widow Golden's bell-like tones cut across his rumble.

"Out of the way, there," said Emma, "this thing is hot."

The galoot obediently shuffled to one side, and through the door came the Widow, wearing a pleased smile and a pair of oven-mitts and carrying a deep-dish pizza pan. While the galoot stood stunned, I slammed the inner door in his face and slid the bolt across.

"Mrs. Golden," I told her, "you'd have made a wonderful Italian St. Bernard."

"Oh, get out," the Widow replied. As she trundled through to the kitchen and hoisted the pizza-pan onto the stove, she asked, over her shoulder, "Say, Carlton, who is that man on the porch? Some sort of salesman?"

She re-emerged into the living-room, doffing her oven-mitts and giving Hanna a speculative glance. "And who might you be, young lady?"

Hanna smiled, demurely, a trick I wouldn't have thought she could pull off. "I'm a friend of Carlton's. Hanna Klovack. We work together."

"At the paper?" Maybe the Widow thought I was holding

down two jobs. Hanna nodded. "Then how come I've never met you?" She sounded accusing.

"Hanna is a new employee," I explained. "Just joined the saltmines today. She hails from Toronto."

"Aha," said the Widow, with a now-I've-got-you-pegged air. She looked both curious and satisfied. All those months of keeping the Withers residence under surveillance with nothing to show for it but paper boys and visions of the garbage going out, and now, in one day, a genuine corpse and an indisputable big-city bimbo.

"Shouldn't you do something about that fellow on the porch, Carlton?" she asked. "He's still there. Lurking."

So he was, peering forlornly through the little window in the inner door. He leered at me through the glass.

"Let him lurk," said Hanna. "He can't scare us."

"Speak for yourself."

Mrs. Golden went back to the kitchen, so we followed her out and sat down at the kitchen table while she dug out three plates, washed them, and began serving out the pizza. She suggested we give some to our lurking visitor.

"Who is he, anyway, Carlton? An angry subscriber?"

"He's one of Dominic Silvio's thugs. And I don't know why he de-frocked my front door."

"People are so rude these days," the Widow said, and, turning to Hanna, she added, "Carlton needs looking after."

Brief pause to give Hanna the old up-and-down, and then she closed in, purring, "So nice for Carlton to have a young lady come to call," she simpered. "We seldom see Carlton with ladies."

"Women," Hanna corrected. "I guess Carlton doesn't much care for them."

Emma begged to differ. "Carlton is a gentleman. Not like some I could mention." She went on, "And yourself, Miss, what is it, Klovack? Are you currently, ah, occupied?"

"Sure, I told you; I work at the paper."

"No, no, no, my dear. How foolish of me. What I meant was, is there a young gentleman in your life?"

No fooling around with the Widow. Goes straight for the facts.

"There was," Hanna replied shortly. "Although I don't know if you would call him a gentleman. A louse is what he was. The premier louse of western civilization, if you want to be accurate about it. That's why I left Toronto."

Aha, I said to myself, reasoning swiftly, the louse didn't do right by our Nell, which is why she downed tools at the centre of the journalistic universe and bobbed up here. What we had here was the classic case of a woman scorned, a notoriously tough proposition.

This was good. Two minutes into her acquaintanceship, and the Widow Golden knew more about Hanna than I'd gleaned all day. Shows what it means to be a trained reporter. While I had no reason to doubt the lousiness of this unnamed gent, I had to respect his raw courage. Doing wrong by Hanna is not the sort of task I, myself, would have taken on. I wondered what had become of the bold fellow, but I didn't want to seem nosy, and ask. Not to worry; leave it to Emma.

"And where is this louse now?" she asked.

"Toronto," snarled Hanna, "with his wife."

Wife, begad, here was something. Our Nell, it turned out, was nothing short of a home-wrecker. Or, as it turned out, a would-be home-wrecker.

"I see. Well, you'll find, my dear, that Carlton doesn't approve of carryings-on." Whatever that meant. The Widow nodded in a self-satisfied way.

"I'll bet," said Hanna. I was beginning to wish the Widow weren't quite so solicitous; she made me sound like the old boy on the Quaker Oats package.

The essay on morals was interrupted by a tapping, rather timid, this time, on the side door. The intruder had abandoned the front entrance, and was now peering in the kitchen window.

"My goodness, how rude!" exclaimed Emma. She jumped up, whisked open the door, and glowered at the thug.

"Well," she said, "what do you want?"

The galoot attempted a simper. "Say, I'll bet that's terrific pizza."

"It is," replied the Widow, grimly, "but not a sniff of it do you get until you explain what you're doing here. And why you tore Carlton's screen-door off its hinges."

"I knocked. Didn't I knock?" He addressed me in an aggrieved tone and I had to admit it to be the case.

"I see," said Emma. "Carlton, if he knocked, why didn't you let the man in?"

"I can answer that one," replied Hanna, "because the last time he did any knocking, it was on Carlton's face. With his fist. Isn't that right?"

The lout nodded. "That's why I'm here. To explain." He turned to me. "You see, we mistook our instructions."

"Who is 'we'?" I asked.

"Clarence and me."

"Ah, Clarence. He was the other thug. The smaller one who was driving the car."

"Clarence was driving the car. Thug, I don't accept. Clarence and me, we're businessmen."

"And," asked Hanna, "your business is?"

"This and that. Assignments for Mr. Silvio."

"Assignments such as beating people up?"

"Well, no, lady. I was just coming to that. But perhaps I'd better introduce myself."

"Well, then, come in." Mrs. Golden opened the door, and he slid past her into the kitchen. He had the nerve to raise his eyebrows at my housekeeping, and bobbed his head at Hanna. Then he fished in his jacket pocket, extracted a wallet the size of a suitcase, dug around in it, and came up with a handful of business cards. Solemnly, he handed one of them to each of us. The cards, heavily embossed, read "Silvio Developments" and, underneath, "Melville R. Firkin, Consultant."

He smiled. "Nice cards, aren't they?"

"Melville?" I asked, "you're a Melville?"

"Most of my friends call me Moose. Can I have some of that pizza now?"

This brought out the hostess in the Widow Golden. She drew up a chair for him, excavated another plate, scoured it, carved out about two-thirds of the remaining pizza, and deposited it on the plate in front of Moose. There was silence for a time, broken only by the champing of his jaws. The pizza lasted about ninety seconds, then Moose burped politely, rubbed his stomach, and smiled. "Great pizza."

Emma smirked. "You really liked it?"

"Terrific."

"You didn't think there was too much oregano? Sometimes I put in too much oregano."

"Just right," said the Moose.

I decided to intervene before they got down to swapping recipes. "Yes, well, I'm glad you approve, but why did you slosh me?"

Moose sighed. "It's like I was saying. Clarence and me, we made a little mistake. Just a slip-up. It could happen to anyone."

"Well, it happened to me. What was the nature of this mistake?"

"You see, Mr. Silvio, he's a developer. Man who develops."

"What does that have to do with you baffing me?"

"It's like this. Mr. Silvio, he has this plan to develop here and . . ."

"Here? In Bosky Dell?"

Moose nodded. "Right. Here in Bosky Dell." He paused. "Silly name for a place, isn't it?"

"Exactly where in Bosky Dell is this development to go?"

"Well, just about everywhere, I guess. Mr. Silvio's developments are kind of big. The last one, we built twenty-seven apartment buildings and condominiums over at Eel River. Took out the whole town. Fixed it up beautiful."

I remembered that the collection of concrete slabs, glass towers, and brick bunkers along Highway 501, where there used to be a quiet little village like our own, was one of Silvio's creations. So this was what he had in mind for Bosky Dell.

The Widow was agitated, too.

"Oh, Carlton," she asked, "can this be?"

"No." I was clear on that. "The village can't be touched. That's in the bylaws. In fact, you can't build a garden shed around here without going through about ten miles of red tape, and a hearing in front of the Ontario Municipal Board."

Bosky Dell is one of those leftovers from an earlier era, when the province was run by, for, and through the nobs, many of whom lived in the area in the summertime, and set up their own lines of defence. The village is directly incorporated to the province; it doesn't belong to any county or township. No outside planning board can give a permit to develop, only the local council. And the local council, elected in the reign of George III, haven't approved of anything since his demise.

"My good man," I told Moose, after explaining all this, "you're talking through your size seventeen hat. Bosky Dell cannot be developed. In fact, there is only one piece of property in the whole place that isn't tied up in about ten different directions, because it doesn't have to be, and that is . . . . oh, my God, the church!"

"Carlton, what is the matter?" The Widow put a plump hand to her cheek. "You look as if you'd seen a ghost."

"Not a ghost. A loophole. What could be a loophole. You see, the church was a gift to the village, decades ago, when there was almost nothing here. Old Sir John Flannery, the lumber baron, he donated the land and the money for the church, in hopes it would encourage settlement here. Very generous, everybody said. My Dad said the fact was that he'd made so much money robbing widows and orphans over the years that he needed to pile up points in heaven. Anyway, for whatever reasons, he gave the village the church."

"I knew that," said Emma.

"I'm sure you did, everybody does. But what everybody does not know is that the church was never properly surveyed. You know how these things were in the old days.

62

Even the official survey is pretty vague about where the church property begins and ends."

"Carlton." Hanna was getting impatient. "I'm sure we're all impressed with your grasp of local lore, but does it matter a hoot in hell?"

"Yes. It does. I was coming to that."

"Slowly."

I ignored this. "I once researched a piece on this whole business for the *Lancer*. We didn't run it, of course, because it might have upset people, but I still remember it. Anyway, it turned out that the church land deeded to the village was deeded from the village to the congregation, once it had been running for a while; apparently, that's normal in these arrangements. Quite recently, one of the lawyers on the church committee looked into this, and he wrote a letter saying that they'd better get a new survey done, because — mark this well — he said that, the way he read it, the church could own quite a lot of land to which the restrictions wouldn't apply."

"Why not?"

"Because the official survey wasn't conducted until 1920, and the land transfer took place in 1910. So you could argue — no one was very clear on this, but lawyers never are — that the rules don't apply to the church land. Which could be quite a large parcel of land."

Hanna said, "I don't understand that part. Didn't the deed say, from a point fifty feet southwest of the hitching-post to old Bill's fence, or something like that?"

"That was the problem, the wording was just like that. It said 'all that land situate in the Village of Bosky Dell from a point ten feet south of the village pump to the top of Sixth Street.' Something like that, anyway. And the trick is that nobody knows exactly where the old village pump was. It's been gone for years."

"Which means?" asked Hanna.

"Well, this gent said it meant that if the church wanted to develop, it could claim quite a chunk of land, and might be able to claim exemption from the building bylaws. He wanted the village to spend a lot of money to get it straightened out, but it was never done. Cost too much."

"So the minister could make a deal with this Silvio? Would it stand up?"

"I don't know. Who does? It would take about ten lawyers and a couple of judges to straighten out. But you know the way things work, these days; you just charge ahead and do it, and by the time somebody proves you can't, you already have."

"But it still doesn't explain," I added, "why I got plugged by Moose here."

Moose was looking sheepish. "Well, it turns out that Mr. Silvio knew about this piece that you'd written for the paper. The one that didn't run."

"How did he find out about that?"

"This we do not know. Mr. Silvio, he has connections. Anyway, he figured that, when the story came out that he was planning to uplift and upgrade the village of Bosky Dell, which is his sincere intention, the local people might have something to say."

"They would scream like stuck pigs."

"Then you would write another story for the paper, and this one would get in."

"A shrewd guess. So?"

"Well, he asked Clarence and me — this is going to hand you a laugh — he asked Clarence and me to be sure to treat you special. Those were his words, 'Treat Carlton Withers special.'"

"And by special, he meant . . ."

"It turns out — this is where the funny part comes — he meant, be nice to you."

"Whereas, you thought . . ."

"We thought, well, you know, *special*. Like a polite way of saying, push him around a little. Funny, isn't it?"

I wasn't laughing. Hanna was; she made a noise like a paper bag exploding, and even the Widow smiled, but I didn't find the situation amusing.

"So," said Hanna when she stopped snorting, "where does all this leave us?"

I replied, "It leaves us with the reason why there was a clandestine meeting at the church the other night. The Rev. was holding a little conference with Silvio, I'll bet, and for some reason, Ernie Struthers was on hand. Maybe as a witness."

I added, "I think it's time we got this information to a higher authority."

"You mean the cops?"

"I mean Hanson."

TEN

WE SAID GOODBYE to Moose and the Widow, who appeared to be settling down for a cosy chat, and walked back over to Hanson's. On the way, I asked Hanna if my surmise had been correct, and whether the aforementioned louse had, in fact, thrown her over. After inviting me to mind my own bloody business — a point she had refrained from making with the Golden Intelligence Service — she answered the question anyway.

"No, as a matter of fact, I threw him over. It came as quite a surprise."

"He wasn't expecting it?"

"It was quite a surprise when I found out he was married. It was the old story. His wife — are you ready for this? — didn't understand him. He worked it out that that was the same as not being married and so . . ."

"Why bring it up?"

"You got it."

"And how did it come up?"

"That's the rich part. I asked him, one day, quite casually, 'Hey, why don't we get married?' I mean we were, after all, you know . . ."

"Shacked up?"

This drew a glare.

" . . . not exactly strangers. It seemed logical that we might get married."

"But wasn't."

"Not with another wife in the picture."

Anything I said after this was bound to get me into trouble, so I shut up until we arrived back at Hanson's. He was still there, the Rev. Mr. Wylie having apparently told his tale and fled. Mrs. Eberley was also on hand, curled up on a wicker sofa with a drink clutched in one ring-laden fist.

When we came onto the porch, she hoisted her glass and told us, "Don't get up."

Hanna looked blank.

"I mean, pardon me if I don't get up."

This was easy, since there was a good chance that if she did get up, the alcohol sloshing around inside would list to one side and overbalance her. She leered at Hanna.

"I know you," she said accusingly. "You're a friend of Carlton's."

"When he isn't calling me names," said Hanna, "Carlton and I work together."

"He works at the Silver Falls *Lancer*," noted Mrs. Eberley. "Right."

"You work there, too?"

"That's it, Mrs. Eberley."

"Making two of you in all."

"Plus a supporting cast of thousands."

"Huh? Say," still clutching her drink, Mrs. Eberley leaned forward and lowered her voice to a conspiratorial croak, "Carlton's all right."

"Is that so?"

"Strange. Weird, even, but all right." She laid one finger alongside her nose, a trick I thought had been copyrighted by Jolly Old Saint Nick. "Carlton make a pass at you?"

The ghost of a smile flickered on Hanna's face. "No."

Mrs. Eberley shook her head in a wobbly way. "Here's a news bulletin for you, sweetie," she said, "he won't."

"Okay by me," said Hanna.

Hanson and I exchanged glances of mutual agony. It seemed wise to change the subject before Nora broke any more news bulletins, so I told Hanson about our run-in with Moose and what that large consultant had had to say about a Silvio development scheme for Bosky Dell. Hanson already knew most of this, as it turned out. In fact, that was what his earlier, mysterious hints about Ernie meant. The Rev. Wylie had dropped by a week earlier to see Hanson. He had had a phone call from Dominic Silvio and then a letter from a lawyer, setting out the ambiguous position of the church property, and suggesting a meeting between himself and Mr. Silvio, "at your earliest possible convenience," to discuss potential development on the site.

He hadn't known what to do, so he turned to Hanson for free legal advice. As a former policeman, he reckoned, Hanson must know something about the law. The lawyer on the church committee was totally incomprehensible to him and besides, he would probably charge for advice, once it became official. Hanson, he knew, would not. What Hanson knew about this kind of law would not fill an offertory envelope, but he glows with self-assurance, so he became the sturdy oak, as the Rev. put it, upon whom he would lean.

Hanson was intrigued — who wouldn't be? — by the ambiguities in the church's property deed, and he had advised the Rev. that he ought to go at least as far as having a meeting with Silvio, since he was going to have to lay the matter formally before the church committee. But it would be as well, Hanson suggested, to have a witness on hand at any meeting with a developer, perhaps an unseen witness. "Just in case," was the way Hanson put it.

So it was arranged. Hanson would go up to the church, conceal himself, and listen to whatever it was Dominic Silvio had to say. The meeting had been fixed for Monday evening, about nine p.m. However, about an hour before kickoff, Hanson discovered that he was not going to be able to make the meeting after all. Nora, he found, had "taken a turn for the worse." This, translated, means that Nora's system was lodging a protest and she was in the grip of what is technically known as the "heebie-jeebies."

The Rev., while full of Christian spirit, was not similarly strong on brains, and when Hanson phoned to say that he wasn't going to be able to make it, that trusting soul asked the first man he spotted to fill in for him. This turned out to be Ernie Struthers. Not an ideal selection, not even a church-goer, but when you're dealing with a village whose welcome sign reads, "Pop. 109," you don't get many choices when it comes to ringing in substitutes. The Rev. briefed Ernie, who was glad to sit in, figuring, no doubt, that he might hear something useful, even profitable. That's how he got to the church, and that's why, we now learned, the Rev. held himself at least partly to blame for what had happened to Ernie.

"He felt," Hanson explained, "that if there was a killer on the loose around the church, he unwittingly put Ernie in danger, but I think that Ernie's murder was probably deliberate and would have happened no matter where he went."

Hanna interrupted, "Did he talk to Ernie after the meeting?"

"No, he never saw Ernie, although he assumed he was in the church somewhere, because he'd said he would be. Apparently, Dominic Silvio insisted on taking Ephraim outside and walking him around, while they discussed what would go where in the development. He promised they'd leave the church itself alone, so he wanted to show Ephraim how they had it laid out, and . . ."

"In the dark?" Hanna butted in again.

"No, it wasn't really very dark yet; this was about nine o'clock, and at this time of year, it doesn't get really dark until nine-thirty or so."

"So they walked around, and talked outside?"

"Yes."

"Kind of blew the whole purpose of Ernie's being there, didn't it?"

"You're quite right, except that I gather the talk didn't come to anything. Rev. Wylie said that he had been thinking about it, and under no conditions could the church consider selling any property. Dominic Silvio asked him to think some more, or at least to take it to the church committee. But Ephraim said that although he would certainly tell the church committee, his mind was made up. So, he says, Silvio went over to his car and drove off, and he went back into the church."

I guessed, "But no Ernie?"

"But, as you say, no Ernie. Ephraim turned on the lights

and walked all around, but apparently Ernie had already left. So he went home and called Ernie's house, but got no answer."

"Well," I said, "it's perfectly clear what happened."

"Oh?" said Hanna. "What happened?"

"Ernie got to the church early and hid himself in one of the box pews."

I explained to Hanna, "We still have box pews in our church, where the grandees sit, avoiding contamination from the hoi-polloi."

Hanna said that was nice. In the Ukrainian Orthodox Church, apparently, God has to pick out the rich from the rabble by their clothes.

"Anyway," I went on, "Silvio came a bit ahead of time, too, and found Ernie spying, and killed him. Well, that's a relief."

"Here's a question for you, Lord Peter Wimsey," said Hanna. "Why?"

"Well, maybe it was later. Maybe Ernie overheard something Silvio said to the Rev., a threat or something, and when Silvio realized he had been overheard, then he killed him."

"He just told the minister, 'Pardon me a minute, there's somebody back here I've got to kill,' whipped out one of your father's pin punches, which he always carried in a pocket, just in case, stabbed Ernie, came back, sat down, and said, 'Now, where were we?'"

"Well, how about this? Silvio hears a noise while he's talking to the Rev., but he doesn't say anything, and then, when the Rev. sees him driving away, he really just goes around the block and he comes back and gets Ernie then."

"Think again," said Hanna. "Ernie had left the church when the Rev. went inside."

"Well, maybe he wasn't killed in the church. The only thing we have that points to the church is Ernie's hat and the fact that he was clutching an offertory envelope. Maybe they were planted."

Hanson nodded. "That's a good point. The police told me

they haven't, at least so far, found any traces of blood in the church, although that may be because any superficial stains were wiped away. We have no absolute proof, so far, that Ernie was attacked there. But we are left with Miss Klovack's earlier question, 'Why?' If Dominic Silvio had any motive to kill anyone, it might have been Ephraim Wylie, not Ernie Struthers."

"The first thing to determine," Hanna jumped in, "is where Ernie was attacked."

"The police will no doubt do a forensic check of the church in due course," said Hanson, "perhaps they'll turn something up."

"The police?" Hanna was scornful. "I think we should go and have a look ourselves."

"Not at all a bad idea," Hanson replied, "and if you'll wait a few minutes, I'll join you. First," he smiled ruefully, "I have to do the dishes."

Well, of course, we couldn't have that, so Hanna said she and I would do the dishes, and Hanson could get right up to the church and we'd join him there later. Which we did, in about five minutes, leaving behind a pile of dishes — washing by C. Withers, drying by H. Klovack — that were not, to put it mildly, exactly scoured.

The church is just one block from Hanson's; nip up to Forest Road and turn left. You can't miss it. When we got there, Hanson was outside, fooling around with his walking-stick, poking around the bushes under the windows.

There was a flatfoot on duty, sitting in a chair by the door, which was blocked off, if you could call it that, by one of those yellow tapes the cops string up to ward off the vulgar crowds, but Hanson had obviously been given the all-clear, and the flatfoot paid no attention to us whatever. He was engrossed in a well-thumbed copy of a paperback entitled, *Ravished by Love*.

"Find anything?" Hanna asked Hanson, in a stage whisper.

He replied in his normal voice, "Well, I haven't been

inside yet. One thing I learned on the force was to do things thoroughly, so I've been checking around out here."

"Gadzooks," I said, "looking for footprints."

"Footprints, or anything else that might prove useful. I've had a look at the door here to see if it was forced at any time."

"What would that prove?" Hanna wanted to know.

"I have no idea," Hanson replied, "but I think it is better to collect facts first, and form theories afterwards." He went methodically back to work.

That ought to have crushed the creature, but it didn't, of course. She sauntered right into the church and let out a low whistle. "Boy," she said, "snappy church. Are those the box pews?"

Indeed they were. The Bosky Dell church is an impressive edifice, not large, but impressive, a hexagon constructed entirely of wood, with large glass windows on all sides. The effect is that of a church which is part of its surroundings. Inside, there is the same simple design. The sanctuary is really nothing more than a raised platform on which sits the altar, one of those moveable affairs, made of pine. There is a font off to one side, which is where the infant C. Withers was dunked and christened. Most of the pews are simply long wooden benches, stretching in restful silence across the broad plank floor. The benches are hard and narrow, to keep the parishioners from dozing off during the sermons. There is nothing much in the way of art about the church, since so much of it is given over to windows; a couple of Crucifixes and one plaque memorializing the generosity of Sir John Flannery while hushing up all the dirty work he did to get to the point where he could afford to be generous, and that's about it.

The most unusual feature about this plain wooden structure is the clutch of old box pews, three on each side of the church. They are in the first row, each large enough to shield one upper-crust family from the jostling of the rude mob. These are made of basswood — the rabble gets pine — about three feet high and open only at the front, where there is a half-door through which you enter. This means that the occupants are on view from the waist up, more or less, but what old Mrs. Flannery used to refer to as "the nether limbs" are concealed from sight, thus preventing riots. Inside each box pew is a bench, just like the ones outside, except that this one is covered with a cushion. The general effect is that of the penalty box in one of the higher-toned hockey arenas, and when I was a kid I always wondered what the well-dressed folks inside had done to merit such punishment. It was from these box pews that the swells of Bosky Dell used to purge their sins every Sunday.

The boxes are shunned nowadays, except on those rare occasions when the church is jammed, because to enter one is to invite accusations of snobbery. Only Margot Flannery, the elderly granddaughter of Sir John, still uses the family box regularly. When Margot has a ticket-of-leave from Homewood Sanatorium and appears for religious duty, large sniffs of disapproval emanate from her box, along with the mixed fumes of camphor and rum.

When I was a kid, the trick was to get into a pew behind one of the box pews, where you could duck down far enough to escape detection from the altar, and, thus strategically situated, lob spitballs at your more exposed enemies on the naked benches.

By the time I had explained all this to Hanna, who didn't seem to care much, she was prowling around inside the boxes, and her triumphant "Aha!" which made me bite my tongue, came from the middle of the Flannery box itself.

"A clue, by golly," said Hanna, "or I'll eat my shirt."

Hanson had drifted inside the church by this time, and we both rushed over to the Flannery pew. Hanna was clutching a bit of torn cloth, and, attached to it, a Rotary pin.

"Was Ernie a Rotarian?" asked Hanna.

"Oh, Lord, yes," I replied, "you can't sell nails and light bulbs to the citizens without belonging to the Rotary. He was a vice-president."

"Well, then?"

"You may be right, Miss Klovack," said Hanson, "this

may indeed be an important clue, but more likely it will turn out to have no connection whatever to the case."

"Hey, wait a minute," Hanna protested, "how come the cops didn't spot this earlier?"

"Be fair," said Hanson, "they gave the place the most cursory look. A proper scene-of-the-crime crew will do all this later."

I raised another point, "Yeah, but then, how come Harry Franklin didn't see it?"

"Where exactly was this, Hanna?" asked Hanson.

"Right down in the corner, between the seat and the wall."

"Didn't you say Harry was looking for cigarette butts?"

I nodded.

"That explains it, then . . ."

"Sloppy police work," Hanna complained.

"What do you expect?" I asked. "This is not Toronto."

Hanson went out, bearing Hanna's find, to interrupt the cop on duty outside. He didn't like it much — I guess he'd hit the part in the book where the ravishing begins — but he agreed to get on the radio at once to the OPP in Silver Falls.

"Whatever can be done to check it out will be done," Hanson said, when he came back in. "However, the fact that Ernie was a Rotarian and that a Rotary pin turned up in the Flannery box may mean nothing. The police will have to do a cross-match with his jacket to see if that's where the material with the pin came from."

"Ernie was here, all right," I said. "Between the hat and the pin and the offertory envelope and the fact that he arranged with the Rev. to be here, what more do you want?"

"Yes, but it doesn't look as if he was killed here," Hanna pointed out.

Hanson agreed. "It rather looks as if he were not. The killer would hardly have cleaned up a pool of blood and left behind both the hat and the Rotary pin."

"Maybe he was knocked on the head here, and hauled away afterwards," I said.

"Perhaps. That is certainly what the autopsy report suggests. At least, it's something for the police to check on."

We pottered around some more, without finding any other clues. I wondered if there was any point in checking out the supply of offertory envelopes in the chancel in case there was some sort of clue there.

Hanson was sure that would be a waste of time, at least and until the police had compiled a full report on the one envelope they had.

"There is a great danger," Hanson explained, "in assuming that because some object is found near the victim of a crime, it is related to the crime. I think when all this is over, we'll discover that the envelope is only marginally connected with this case."

As we walked up the aisle to leave the church, I asked Hanson, "Why would somebody knock Ernie on the head here and then haul him over to my place to stab him?"

Hanna butted in again, one of her many failings. "Probably nobody did. He probably walked, or staggered, over to your place."

"You mean he was hit on the head here, taken outside, stabbed, and then left there?" Hanson sounded dubious.

"Yeah, and he woke up, realized that he was dying, and for some reason went over to Carlton's place."

"Nonsense," I said, "why should he do that?"

"To give you a warning, or a message. To pass over that clipping. To ask for help. Who knows?"

Klovack, as usual, was talking balderdash. Ernie and I were not chums, and if he wanted help, why stagger several blocks to get it when there were friendlier doors close at hand?

"Mr. Eberley . . ." Hanna interrupted my musing.

"Call me, Hanson, please, or you'll make me feel old."

"Well then, Hanson, if Ernie was hit on the head here and then, for some reason, taken over to Carlton's place . . ."

"We don't know that he was," Hanson interrupted mildly.

"Yes, but if he was, that means that, besides the pin

75

ELEVEN

WHEN WE REACHED Hanson's cottage and said goodbye to him, I noticed with surprise that it was getting on for three-thirty p.m. We strolled back towards my place, and I was pointing out some of the historic sights to Hanna (here is where I smoked my first cigarette, there where I lost my lunch as a result thereof, etc.) and the atmosphere was getting, if not matey, at least slightly less hostile than it had been between us, when up came the Widow Golden, scampering or as close to scampering as her figure would allow.

"Wait right there, Carlton," she said, and, as she heaved alongside, puffing, she added, "I don't think you want to go back to your cottage right now."

"Why not?"

"Well, after Melville left, I went back to my place and a few minutes later another car pulled up and a very large man got out. It was someone I've seen in town, but I don't know his name. Anyway, he began stamping around your house, banging on the doors. I got the feeling that he was very anxious to talk to you about something."

"Moose's friend, what was it, Clarence?"

"I don't think so. This man is quite as large as Moose, but he seemed to be in a much worse temper. I didn't like to speak to him."

I had never heard of the Widow going shy; this new visitor must be a brute indeed.

"Well, whoever he is, he's got a long wait," Hanna said, "Carlton's coming with me; I need someone to help me lug my stuff from the *Lancer* offices to my new apartment."

Hanna had had her worldly goods shipped to the newspaper, apparently, and now she imagined I was going to spend the rest of the day shifting it for her. In ordinary circumstances, I would have told off the peremptory female; the Witherses do not take orders from forward young women.

However, in this case it seemed shrewd to fall in with her plans. I told Hanna I would wait for her here, outside the village firehall, thus avoiding what might prove to be an embarrassing encounter, while she went back to my place to get the car. After all, I said, I didn't want to have to rough up this stranger, whoever he was. Hanna said Uh-huh, she understood perfectly, and she and Emma walked off. Minutes later, Hanna returned in the car — roared to a halt, actually, in her usual headlong way, looking pleased with herself.

I got in and as we streaked off for Silver Falls, Hanna remarked casually, "It was Dominic Silvio."

"Who was? The murderer?"

"No. Well, maybe. Anyway, it was Dominic Silvio waiting for you outside your house."

"How do you know?"

"How do you think? I asked him. I went up to him and asked who he was, and what was he doing stamping on your dandelions. I told him that, much as you didn't want to, you would probably have to rough him up if you found him on the premises when you got home, and for some reason he didn't take too kindly to that. Sort of swelled up, and said we would see about that in due course. Then he told me he was Mr. Dominic Silvio — big shot calls himself 'Mr.' — and that he needed to see you at once on a matter 'touching both our interests.' That's how he put it, which I thought was a pretty classy way to talk, for a hood."

I groaned. "He's not a hood, he's a developer."

"Same thing."

"And now he'll be even madder at me than he was before. Thanks a lot. Did he say anything more?"

"Nope. I asked him if he was the one who had stabbed Ernie Struthers, and he looked sort of startled, but he didn't say anything. Then I told him that if he hoped to see you, he was going to be hanging around for a long time, because I happened to know that you had gone to town. He let rip with a few ripe expressions, when Mrs. Golden, who was standing around drinking all this in, told him that she was a friend of yours, and that he could get his language in order or get out. He looked at her, obviously liked what he saw, and got all smarmy right away. Called her 'my dear lady' and apologized. They ended up chummy as sailors on shore leave, and before I left, Mrs. Golden had invited him over to her place to 'freshen up,' which I always think is a funny way of saying 'to take a leak.'"

The woman has no delicacy. No tact and no delicacy. She fell into a thoughtful silence which lasted until we arrived at the *Lancer* offices. Then I told her I couldn't help her until after I had written the Ramblin' John column for the week's issue, and she stomped away, muttering to herself.

Ramblin' John is a colourful, folksy, down-home character who drops a lot of his "g's" just to show how folksy he is, and who seems to think highly, as he rambles up and down the streets of Silver Falls, of anything he spots in one of the store windows of any of our major advertisers. Ramblin' John does not, of course, actually exist; he was breathed into life by our advertising department, and I keep him ramblin'.

By the time I had finished dropping g's, Hanna had been over to her new, furnished apartment and cleaned it up — the woman is a fanatic — so it was ready to receive the stack of suitcases, parcels, and boxes that had arrived earlier, and were now cluttering up the enlarged closet that constitutes our photo studio. However, I insisted on eating first, so we dropped into the O.K. Cafe — my request, Hanna wanted to take her chances at Wong's Chinese Deli — where Belinda Huntingdon gave us a couple of incinerated hamburgers and her synopsis of the movie playing at the Bijou. *The Thing That Stalks By Night*.

Of course, that ended with Hanna and I nipping over to the Bijou and taking in the show. All in all, a cultural evening, until we headed back for the *Lancer* to pick up Hanna's worldly goods.

I wanted to know why this couldn't wait until tomorrow.

"I need my stuff," said Hanna, shortly. "Anyway, I

checked out of the motel this morning. And besides, you may be in jail tomorrow."

"Oh."

The office was closed, of course, the time now being well after ten p.m., but I carry a key, so we dashed up the stairs and I started to grab boxes.

"Hold it a minute," Hanna ordered. "I have to check and make sure everything was delivered."

She started to fool around with her bundles, checking and repacking, unpacking some of her photography equipment to leave at the office and I wandered over to the city desk — pardon, work-station — and picked up a copy of the Toronto *Star*. I looked on Page 5, where the second-class and out-of-town murders generally appear, and there we were, under

Hardware merchant slain,
police expect arrest soon

The story had obviously been written from a phone interview and was about as accurate as the usual run of news story. That is, it had Ernie's age wrong (he was 57, not 59), spelled his last name wrong — "Stutters," instead of Struthers — described the murder weapon as a chisel and said the body had been found on the back porch — wrong — of the Second St. — wrong again — residence of a "local reporter" who worked, according to the *Star*, for something called the "Silver Falls *Dancer*." The piece made it clear that the fuzz were poised to make an arrest, and made it clear, too, that the arrestee was likely to be one "C. Lancelot Dithers, 27" — wrong once more on the name and age but not, I guessed, on the substance.

"Anything new?" Hanna asked, as she emerged from the studio.

"Um. Apparently, the cops have gotten around to checking the envelope against the typewriter in Ernie's store."

"And?"

"It was typed on Ernie's typewriter."

"That's interesting. Of course, it doesn't prove that Ernie typed it himself."

"There's more. They've got a paragraph on the fact that retired Staff Inspector Hanson Eberley is helping the OPP with their inquiries. They say a couple of leadheads from the OPP homicide division in Toronto have been sent up to conduct the case, making it clear that Hanson has no official role. And they've got Hanson's name spelled right, which is a miracle."

"Anything else?"

"Nope. Yes. Land-a-mercy!"

Hanna stalked over and grabbed me by the elbow. "Here," she said, "explain something to me. How come you talk that way?"

"What way?"

"You know what way. 'Land-a-mercy.' Calling the cops 'rozzers.' That way. In one of the columns I read, you used the word 'consarned.' And I heard you telling Tommy Macklin that something was 'codswallop.' Is this just a hick act you put on?"

"Not that it's any of your consarned business, Klovack," I replied warmly, "but I talk this way, and write this way, because my father did. Anything wrong with that?"

"Well, no, but . . ."

"But my father's dead, and people don't use that sort of language anymore, right? Well, fiddlesticks, is what I say."

"Fiddlesticks? You would say fiddlesticks?"

"Why not? Perfectly good word. Hasn't been used to death, like some other words beginning with the same letter. Now you've done it again."

"Done what?"

"You've gone and made me forget what I got so excited about."

There was a brief pause while I dipped back into the newspaper.

"Land-a-mercy," I said again.

"Land-a-mercy, what?"

"Well, according to this story, Ernie Struthers died 'leaving no near relatives.'"

"So?"

"Well, he always told us he had a brother and a sister. Made quite a point of it, in fact. He said his brother and sister were sick as mud when the rich aunt pegged out and left all her money to him, and nothing to them. Now it turns out, unless the paper has this wrong too, that there was no brother and sister. What do you suppose that means?"

"I suppose it means maybe there was no aunt, either."

"Then where did the money come from for Ernie to buy the hardware store?"

"The proceeds of crime, maybe."

"What sort of crime could Ernie commit around here and not get caught at?"

Hanna was scornful. "That one's easy. Blackmail."

"Codswallop," I said, automatically, but my heart wasn't in it. If Ernie was a blackmailer, was he killed by his victim? And what in tunket could there be worth blackmailing someone over in a quiet little backwater like Bosky Dell? It is not a place where you can keep secrets, at least not of the negotiable-for-blackmail variety, I wouldn't have thought.

"Well, here's another little surprise for you," said Hanna, "Emma Golden thinks you and I are an item."

"She does? What makes you say that?"

"Well, just before she headed off to her place with that guy Silvio, she said I wasn't to worry about you turning out to be a louse."

"She means well," I said.

"Yes, I know, but imagine, thinking you and I were a pair. Hilarious. Really hilarious."

I began to get just a bit peeved. One hilarious was okay but, for some reason, not two.

"What's so damn hilarious about it?"

Hanna was standing right next to me, now, and she looked up at me in what I can only call a supercilious fashion.

82

"Well, because . . . you know."

"No, I don't know. I mean, I know we don't get along, but Emma Golden didn't see that, and I don't have two heads, so I'm not entirely sure why it's so hilarious that she might think that you and I were . . ." This was a sentence I didn't want to finish.

Hanna snorted. "Well, I guess it's pretty obvious," she said, "that you're as queer as a three-dollar bill."

Once, when I was raking leaves around the old homestead, I put the rake down for a bit while I tried to wrestle the corpses into a garbage bag — failing utterly and getting very cheesed-off in the process — and I lost track of the rake, one of those old rakes, you understand, with square metal teeth and a long handle, and I was wandering around looking for it, buried beneath the leaves by now, and I stepped on the head and up came the handle and caught me a smart blow on the tip of the nose. It was the first time I ever understood the phrase, "Everything went black." Until Hanna got off her line I thought that had been the most unexpected jolt of my existence, but this feeling so far surpassed that one that I would have cheerfully gone on being bashed on the nose with rakes for hours and never a complaint made. I stood there for a moment, feeling numb. Then I reached across, grabbed Hanna by the shoulders, turned her towards me, and kissed the living hell out of her.

It was fine while it lasted. There was the smell of her hair, a hint of perfume, a pepperminty taste — toothpaste, I guess — and a nice feeling. Then I foolishly released her, and she uncorked a right cross that would have done credit to Sonny Liston in his heyday. She fetched me such a clout that, on cold days, I can feel the tingle yet. Then she turned on her heel and began grabbing boxes, and we packed her car, and drove off in companiable silence.

After about three blocks, with never a word spoken, she started in complaining.

"Well, then, what about Belinda Huntingdon?"

"What about Belinda Huntingdon?"

"You don't react."

"What do you mean, I don't react?"

"Every other man around here, as soon as Belinda Huntingdon heaves over the horizon, with those great . . . things of hers out in front, they fall over in a faint or something. You just pat her on the back. You don't even — migawd, you don't even peer down her front!"

"You mean, just because I don't lust after Belinda Huntingdon, and make a disgusting exhibition of myself, you think I'm . . ."

"Thought," amended Hanna, "thought you were queer." She added defensively, "It stands to reason."

"My dear young prune," I said, "if everybody who didn't fall over in a faint in the presence of Belinda Huntingdon were queer, the human race wouldn't last out the next generation. Human sexuality," I added, remembering a good line from Dear Abby, "is to be treasured, not plundered."

"What about what Nora Eberley said about you not making passes?"

"Well, that's just what she meant. I'm not crude, that's all."

"What it amounts to, practically, is false pretenses."

"False pre . . ." I couldn't continue. The woman was maddening. Men who leer and paw are disgusting, men who don't are queer, and if they aren't queer, they're sneaky. That's what she was saying. You couldn't win. But then, when can you? I decided to change the subject. It was either that or kiss her again and something told me this would not be a wise move. They did this sort of thing in old movies, and were well thought of in consequence. No more. In these modern, enlightened days, the girl you kiss without warning turns out to have a right cross like Sonny Liston.

By this time, we had arrived at Hanna's new apartment, which turned out to be, not an apartment, but two small, neat, furnished rooms in one of the town's outlying developments. We unloaded her boxes, and I asked Hanna if we could have a cup of coffee or something.

"No," she said, "especially not, or something."

"Ye gods, from the harmless, i.e., queer, Carlton, I have gone to Carlton the sex fiend in one leap. Could I then at least have a lift back to Bosky Dell?"

"No."

"Well, how am I supposed to get home?"

"Take a cab."

"A cab? It's close to midnight."

"So?"

"This is Silver Falls, not the metropolis. The cabs pack it in when the beerhall closes, at eleven p.m."

In the end, Hanna agreed to drive me back to Main St. and the motionless *Marchepas*. If the car wouldn't go, she'd take me back to Bosky Dell. But it did, first try, in that maddening way it has, so I bade Hanna a stony-faced farewell and drove off thoughtfully. I got almost home, as a matter of fact, before *Marchepas* conked out again and came to a halt in the middle of the road.

I coaxed and begged and pleaded, fooled around under the hood, kicked the wheels a few times, but nothing would persuade her to start again. Life, I told myself, was one damn thing after another. I pushed the brute over to the shoulder, and hiked the last mile or so to Bosky Dell. It was well after 2 a.m. by the time I got there, and I thanked the powers that be that the next day, or, rather, this day, was Thursday, one of our soft days at the *Lancer*, and I could sleep in. I felt as if I had been awake since about the eleventh century, and it was with a grateful sigh that, after creeping into the darkened cottage — no lights, in case Dominic Silvio was still on the prowl — I donned my bright green PJs with the orange clocks, and slid between the sheets.

Right up against a warm, unmistakably female, and mostly naked body that stirred, rustled, and whispered, "Darling, at last."

TWELVE

I HAVE OFTEN wondered since whether it was three feet straight up in the air that I leapt, or only two. Seemed like ten. I fetched up in the living-room, where I stood, trembling in every limb and waiting for my heart to stop hammering. There were sounds of whispering silk from the bedroom, the door creaked open, and Nora Eberley stumbled out into the living-room, partly in, but mostly out of, about half an ounce of some gossamer material that served rather to accentuate than to conceal her considerable charms.

I had to admit that, clad, or un, as she was, and softly lit by a moon that chose this ill-considered moment to shove its big fat face in through the living-room window, she was not unattractive. She looked a lot rounder, somehow, than she did in her street clothes. Rounder and softer. The sharp features were not so evident; it was the less sharp ones that drew the eye. I hastily looked away, only to find myself staring at a large beer tray, glowing in the moonlight on the wall, and bearing the proud slogan, "Property of the Leaside Hotel. Do Not Remove." One of my Dad's acquisitions. He held the view that stealing from hotels was not really stealing. What would my Dad have done in these circumstances?

Mrs. Eberley broke in on my reverie in a voice I can only describe as throaty. Throaty and throbbing.

"Why, Carlton," she throbbed, "aren't you glad to see me?"

No, actually, I wasn't. It would have been less upsetting, certainly less embarrassing, to have discovered a six-foot boa constrictor curled up on my pillow.

"Well, ah, Mrs. Eberley. Ah. Harumm. Such a pleasant ah, uh, surprise to find you here. Can I offer you anything? Coffee? Cigarette? Directions home?"

The woman paid no attention whatever to this babble. Twitching the gossamer garment, a thing I wished she wouldn't do, she undulated towards me.

"Carlton, darling," she murmured, "it's time we got to know each other better."

I was saved by my housekeeping. There are those — my mother led the list — who insist that the home should be kept always in a state of neatness, with a place for everything and everything in its place. Codswallop. If everything had been in its place, Nora Eberley would not have stumbled, after about the third step, into a half-full pot of mashed potatoes, which I had been eating while watching TV a few days earlier, and gone ass over teakettle onto the rug. Nor would she, striving to rise from that position, in a well-ordered home have put her hand into another saucepan, this one containing decaying spaghetti, which might have been placed there for that express purpose. I guess sloshing the foot into cold mashed potatoes and the pinkies into decaying spaghetti, in the dark, and in circumstances in which neither of these substances can be identified, unsettles the nerves. Mrs. Eberley gave a blood-curdling shriek and began to swear steadily, putting together verbs, nouns and adjectives, with hyphens, that I had never heard coupled before.

Still, you had to give Nora — I feel that once you have shared spaghetti with a woman in your night-garments, you can go to a first-name basis — full marks for effort. When I switched on a light, she started in on me again. Wiping her hands on the gossamer, which did not produce a pleasant effect, she sat down — after a wary check behind her — on the couch, and once more unlimbered the throaty tones.

"Carlton," she murmured, "this isn't exactly the way it looks."

I said not to worry, any time she was in the neighbourhood I was happy to see her. We keep open house on Third Street.

She ignored this, and went on murmuring. "We have to have a talk, and this. . ." a graceful gesture down the gossamer, somewhat marred by the fact that a blob of spaghetti chose that moment to plop to the rug, ". . . seemed the best way."

"Nothing would suit me better than a cosy chat," I replied, lying in my teeth. "Why don't we get together soon, you and I and Hanson, and . . ."

"Not Hanson," she interrupted, "he mustn't know anything about this."

I could see her point. I wasn't all that anxious for Hanson to join in the conversation right at the moment myself. But I was still a little perplexed.

"Mrs. Eberley . . ."

More throaty tones. "Call me Nora" — which, as we know, I was prepared to do.

"Well, then, Nora . . . does this, ah, little chat, does it have anything to do with the death of Ernie Struthers?"

"No. Yes. Well, it might."

This was not helping. "Perhaps it might be better, Mrs . . . Nora, if you just told me whatever it was you came to tell me."

"I can't, not right now."

This to-ing and fro-ing was beginning to get on my nerves. "Why not, for Pete's sake?"

"Because somebody just drove up and parked in front of the cottage. I think they're coming in."

It would have been wiser, I can see that now, to have risen quietly from my place, walked out the back door, and driven to Wyoming, leaving Nora to straighten things out with this new invader, but I panicked. I had been through a lot. I simply grabbed the poor woman — quickly shifting my grip when I realized where I had grabbed her — and stuffed her into the living-room closet, which I knew contained enough assorted junk to conceal the presence of the Red Army Choir. She didn't even protest, just rolled her eyes.

I made it to the front door just in time to keep Hanna from hammering it into smithereens — she is of the Blam, Blam rather than the tap, tap school of knockers. I turned on a light and bade her come in, state the purpose of her visit, and vamoose. Not the suave host, I admit, but I was not feeling at my best. She looked a trifle subdued. Not contrite; contrition is not in her repertoire, but not quite as belligerent as at our last meeting. I assumed she had come to apologize for her previous obnoxious behaviour, so I asked her, coolly, in what way I could serve her at this unholy hour?

"Well, to start with, you can put something on to cover up those godawful pyjamas."

See? Starting in on me already, and right in my own home. I retrieved the brown bathrobe from its customary spot on the living-room floor, and donned it.

"Better?"

"A little, not much. Say, where do you get your night things, anyway, Bargain Harold's?"

"Did you drive all the way out here in the middle of the night to discuss my shopping patterns?" The sarcastic note, you understand, to crush the creature, which, to my astonishment, it appeared to do. When she spoke again, it was in a subdued tone of voice.

"Well, no, Carlton. I've been thinking . . ."

A silence.

"Yes?"

"Carlton . . ."

Another silence.

"Standing by."

"I'm not exactly sure how to put this . . ."

"Take your time. Think it out. Dawn will soon be with us, another whole day in which to arrange your thoughts."

She shot me a look, then lapsed into humility, or something like it, again. "It's this way . . ."

Yet another silence.

"For God's sake, Hanna, spit it out!"

The eyebrows rose, and I could see the light of battle enter those flashing eyes. "We get a little testy without our sleep, don't we?"

I rose to the feet, gathered my robe about me — these PJs with ties at the waist are notoriously unreliable in times of stress — and pointed to the door.

"No, wait. I'm doing this all wrong. I don't know what it is about you, Carlton, but you make me do everything wrong."

You see? My fault again.

"I mean to say . . . The reason I'm here . . ."

"Why are you here, anyway? Why didn't you just phone?"

"I did. All I got was a message on your answering machine. So, I thought perhaps your car had broken down on the way out . . ."

"It did, just another wonderful moment in a perfect day."

"I know. I saw your car by the side of the road. And I came along to make sure you got home all right, and . . ."

"And what?"

"And . . ." The voice dropped to an almost demure note. " . . . to say I'm sorry."

"You're sorry?"

"Yes. Truly. Truly and humbly sorry." This was followed by a giggle, rather wrecking the effect, and a request to tuck in the flap of my PJs, which Hanna claimed was peeking at her. I ignored both, and Hanna seemed to realize that her apology was not complete.

"Truly," she said again. "And humbly."

"Do I get a hint?"

"How do you mean, a hint?"

"Am I to know why you are truly and humbly sorry, or is this one of those guessing games?"

"Oh, well, you know."

I did, of course. Her unspeakable, but spoken, suspicions. But I wasn't going to let her off the hook.

"No, I don't know. How should I know? You've done so many horrible things, I don't know which one you're apologizing for."

Hanna jumped up. Quick to anger, this girl.

"Well, that does it. I drive miles and miles and miles out here . . ."

"Pardon me, fourteen miles."

"At great expense . . ."

"Fifty cents, about."

"And no little inconvenience, to apologize, and..."

"Apologize for what?"

"For assuming you were a queer, and then assuming you were a lecher..."

"Thank you. Your apology is accepted."

"...when what you really are is a fathead."

"I see, well, now that you've made the grounds of your apology clear..."

"I haven't. I haven't made anything clear. Carlton, sit down."

I shuffled some debris, and sat. So did she. There we were, side by side, on the couch. Not cozy, though.

"Carlton, exactly how much do you know about Hanson Eberley?"

"I know that he is one of the finest men ever to don a policeman's uniform, and that's all I need to know."

"Is it? I mean, you're putting a lot of faith in him."

"No more than he deserves."

"Yes, but suppose he doesn't solve this murder? There is a case against you."

"Well, thank you at least for believing that I didn't do it."

"Of course you didn't do it. Anyone can see that."

"Thank you."

"You're utterly harmless."

"Thank you."

"Totally ineffective."

"Hmm."

"Cowardly, silly, incapable..."

"Look, this torrent of compliments is beginning to turn my head. Why don't we just call it a night, and you go home, and I'll go to bed?"

"Okay."

Hanna started to get up, stopped, let out a soft "Ah ha," fished down under the couch, and came up with Nora Eberley's brassiere, cast off, I imagine, in the disrobing process before I arrived. The almost-reasonable tone in Hanna's voice was gone in a micro-second, as she bellowed, "Who's the tootsie?"

Upon which the closet door opened and Nora staggered out, blinking against the light.

"Who are you calling a tootsie?" she demanded, and added, "Golly, Carlton, you shouldn't put anyone in that closet without a guide and a shovel."

Hanna gulped twice, like a bullfrog trying to swallow something that suddenly turns out to be two sizes too large, shot to her feet, and steamed to the door, while I bayed at her heels, trying, in vain, to explain that Things Weren't What They Seemed and You Remember How You Misjudged Me Before and other accurate but unheeded counsel.

At the door, Hanna turned and, fixing me with eyes that had assumed the aspect of a blowtorch, said, "There is no need to explain. I quite understand. It was wrong, foolish, and downright rude of me to intrude this way, Carlton." Well, it was, you couldn't get around that. "No, stop, don't apologize, don't explain. The fault is entirely my own. Your private life, perverse as it may be, is entirely your own affair. I will intrude no longer, so that you can get back to..." brief glance at Nora that would have ignited Kryptonite "...whatever it was you were doing with your valued friend's wife."

And she swept out, leaving me to wonder how words which, written down, made up the form of an apology, could leave me feeling as if I'd just been gone over by a triphammer in the hands of a careless operator.

In the ensuing silence, Nora gathered her other garments, which, now I looked around, pretty well festooned the place, and disappeared into the bedroom. She reappeared soon after, decently clad.

"We'll talk later," she said, and came over and kissed me, in a completely non-vamp manner, on the forehead. "Don't worry," she went on, "I'll explain things to Hanna."

"I wish you would," I replied. "It doesn't do to be at odds with a colleague."

"Colleague?" Nora's eyebrows rose. "Holy Christ, she's right. You are a fathead."

She took her leave, and not a moment too soon; I might

have said something really wounding. I was too stirred up to feel like sleeping, so I decided to clear away some of the debris, just in case there were other cast-off undergarments waiting to spring out at an inconvenient moment. I didn't find any, but I did find, behind the cushion on the couch, a battered old plastic case, quite a cheap-looking thing, and, inside, a pair of sunglasses, scratched and worn and with one lens cracked and one of the earpieces held together with a bit of masking tape.

It didn't look like anything that Nora would have dropped. Of course, anyone else could have plunked it there, today, or any time in the last six months. My first inclination was to simply chuck the whole thing in the garbage, where it obviously belonged, but something about it bothered me slightly, so I decided it might be better to talk to Hanson first. He could at least reassure me that there was nothing surprising about finding an extra bit of unaccounted-for junk in my cottage.

I finished the tidying job — well, stuffed the saving pots in the kitchen sink — and went to bed again. This time, there were no intruders. I was asleep in about ten seconds, and awake in another ten. Or so it seemed. It wasn't, though, because the sun was shining, again, birds were singing, breezes blowing, and all that rot. That is not what woke me, though. It was the repeated dull thud of someone whacking the front door.

Dominic Silvio, the demon developer. I'd forgotten all about him; presumably he was back. I crawled out of bed, dressed in seconds, slipped into the kitchen and out the side door, where I could get a peek at the front. It wasn't Silvio shaking the timbers with his fist at all, but the Widow Golden, who spotted me at once.

"Carlton, my, you sleep late," she beamed. "Say, did you know that you've got another body on your lawn?"

93

THIRTEEN

THIS WAS THE large, economy-size body, and it was lying on its face outside my bedroom window. At least it wasn't out front, where Ernie had been. Mrs. Golden gave a little yelp when she saw it.

"Why, it's Mr. Silvio!" she said.

Mr. Silvio. This was going to end in trouble. For starters, Tommy Macklin was going to be furious. Dominic's development firm was forever building projects that required large ads to entice the gullible to lay down their dollars for a roof, however leaky, over their heads, and to Tommy, advertisers were sacred.

"I thought he'd gone home."

"When? When, Mrs. G., did you think he'd gone home?"

"Oh, midnight, at the latest."

"Mrs. Golden!"

I was shocked. If Dominic Silvio had been at her place from the time we left yesterday afternoon until midnight, what were they doing? No doubt she had filled him with foodstuffs, her invariable habit, but they couldn't eat *all* the time.

"Oh, Carlton, don't be such a prissy-puss," said Mrs. Golden, using a phrase I had never heard before and hope never to hear again. And the son-of-a-gun looked pleased with herself. Pleased and proud. If there was going to be any blushing around here, it was going to have to come from me, so I blushed.

"Shall we see if he's dead or what?" asked Mrs. G.

What, as it turned out. When we loomed up alongside the corpse, it began to stir and twitch, uttered a massive, hollow groan. Silvio sat up, holding his head.

"Wha..." he croaked.

The Widow was at his side in a flash, murmuring, "Poor baby."

A twisted simper appeared on the Silvio phizz — a not unhandsome phizz, by the way, large, with fleshy lips and enough nose for several normal faces, but not unhandsome.

"Rosamund," he simpered, "it's you."

Rosamund, forsooth; I thought her second name was Myrtle; that's what it said on the Voters' List. When I taxed her with this, she said it was "Emma Rosamund Myrtle," but she only told "special people" about the Rosamund, a name that led, among the crass, to a certain amount of teasing. Dominic Silvio had apparently quickly qualified as a Special Person. She bent over and hooked a hand under his elbow and then, with a cheery, "Upsadaisy," heaved him to his feet, like a crane righting a railway car. The woman is a lot stronger than she looks.

"You just come along with me, honey," she said, "and we'll have a nice breakfast."

"Not so damn fast," I protested. "Explanations first, breakfast later. Mr. Silvio, what were you doing on my lawn?"

"You call this a lawn?"

"Never mind what I call it. What were you doing on it?"

"I dunno; I honestly dunno. I came over here after I left Rosamund's place last night to, you know, look around."

"Look around for what?"

"You. I was looking for you."

"Why?"

"Let's talk about it later."

"Yes, I should think so," interrupted the Widow Golden. "Here is this poor man lying out all night, catching his death and nothing to eat at all, and you want to keep him chatting away all day."

"But *why* was he lying out all night? That's what I want to know."

"Somebody must have slugged me. Look, I got a bump." And the big sissy lowered his giant noggin so the Widow could coo over an egg-sized lump just abaft his right ear.

"Poor baby," she murmured again, and I told her that if

95

she was going to kiss the place and make it better, I was going to be sick all over the lawn.

"And it's no good glowering at me," I said. "The man comes barging in here without a by-your-leave, using up space on my lawn that I require for other purposes, spying on me..."

"Hey," Dominic cut in, "who was the popsie in your bedroom?"

"Popsie?" It was the Widow Golden's turn to look shocked. "In Carlton's bedroom?"

This was not a popsie, as we know, but a tootsie. "I can explain that," I began, and then realized that, no, I couldn't.

"A real looker," leered Silvio. "She was asleep on the bed. I saw her there, in the moonlight. Sleeping. Who was she?"

"That is not germane to the issue," I replied coldly, uncorking a phrase I'd picked up covering the law courts. "The issue is, why were you prowling about my house at an ungodly hour?"

"Later, later," said Silvio, and the Widow Golden hissed, "Carlton, really. Not now."

She grabbed the stricken developer by the arm and marched him off across the street, no doubt to stoke him up again. It looked like the tug Rosamund shepherding a container ship. I followed to where the smell of cooked bacon and perked coffee produced a perfume that obviously spoke to the depths of Silvio's soul. He lowered himself onto a kitchen chair and proceeded to lay waste six eggs, eleven strips of bacon, and about sixteen slices of bread smothered in butter and preserves, under the sponsoring gaze of the Widow. If Silvio was our murderer, there was no need to bring him to justice; cholesterol would get him long before the courts could.

"This woman," Dominic said to me, with a heavy wink, "she's a marvel."

The Widow simpered.

"None of this diet crap," Dominic went on. "None of this soft-boiled egg and dry toast routine. None of this, 'Now,

Honey, are we sure we need another piece of toast?' and, 'Say, Sweetie, aren't we putting on just a teensie bit of weight?' Not like some wives I could mention."

When I refused to prod, he went on, "My ex-wife, to be exact."

"Oh, go on with you," gurgled the Widow, who was expanding under his praise like a balloon filling with helium.

"My ex-wife," Dominic continued, driving the point home, "spent her entire life, as far as I could tell, not eating. And not letting me eat. She didn't understand about food. Rosamund," he said, while the Widow Golden positively glowed, "Rosamund understands. Say, Withers, do you want to know what we did last night?"

"No thank you. The activities of consenting adults are none of my concern."

"No, not that." The silly simper died down, to be replaced by a slowly forming scowl. "Hey, are you insulting this good lady?"

"No, no."

"Are you suggesting that this good lady and I . . ."

I was, of course, and the good lady, for reasons of her own, had led me to the suggestion with a wink and a nod, but it seemed prudent, staring into Dominic's reddened face, noting the gathering of bulging muscles beneath the coat, and glancing swiftly at a fist bunching before me with an aspect so hamlike that it could have walked into a meat-packing plant and been stamped by a federal inspector, to lie.

"No, no, of course not. The thought never crossed my mind. What did you do last night, anyway?"

The hamlike fist unbunched. "Made lasagne. Two batches. We made one, ate it, then made another and ate some of that." He beamed across at the Widow. "Partly my mother's recipe, partly my own, with a few ideas from Rosamund. Delicious. You want some? Is there still some left, Rosie?"

"Why, certainly. I put it in the fridge. I'll just go and heat it up in the microwave."

So, while she buzzed off to fuss over the lasagne, I told Dominic, "Now is later."

"Huh? Oh, yeah. Listen," he said, "you work for the paper."

"I know that. And I know you knew that. Moose told me."

"Yeah, well, I'm sorry about Moose. He misunderstood. I guess he told you about how he mistook my meaning. Funny mistake to make, wasn't it, ha, ha?"

I said I didn't see what was so damn funny about it, and he said, no, he guessed I didn't.

"But anyway," he went on, "as you know, a group of my associates and I, we have a project we want to develop right here in Bosky Dell . . ."

"I know. I've heard about it. Not a chance."

"I wouldn't be so sure, kid. Stranger things have happened. What we have in mind is a condominium development, with special apartments for senior citizens."

"I repeat, not a chance."

"And what we thought was, that if you were to write a series of articles in the newspaper, you know, boosting the idea, it would get it off to a flying start. Tommy Macklin," he added, to forestall another protest he could see was coming, "is all for it."

"He is?"

"Yeah. We had a little chat the other day. The usual stuff. How many pages of advertising we'd need to get things under way, that kind of thing. And he seemed to be real enthusiastic. Said the *Lancer* would do a special advertising section."

It began to make a gloomy sort of sense. Tommy Macklin would promote condoms in St. Peter's Square if he saw an advertising special in the project.

"But why do you have to talk to me about this? I just take my orders from Tommy."

"Just wanted to fill you in. You know, get you on side. We know there's bound to be a certain element here that wouldn't like the idea. Some people are always opposed to progress. And we thought that you, with your roots in the community, if you came out for 'Adam and Eve's Little Acre' — that's what we're thinking of calling it, catchy, eh? — why, it would help things along."

"Well, you can forget about it. I'll do my job, but that's all."

There was a short pause. Silvio looked out the window.

"By the way, kid," I thought this was a change of subject, but it wasn't, "did you know there's a place called Bosky Dell in California?"

"There is?"

"There is. Spelled different. 'B-o-s-q-u-e D-e-l.' That's Spanish."

"I guessed that."

"They've got some very classy condominiums down there. So I thought, why not send young Carlton down there, first class, of course, to have a look around. You could write an article along the lines of 'California Comes to Canada,' you know, boosting Adam and Eve's Little Acre."

He had me, of course. By the tender parts. By the wallet. By the ego. A trip to California. On expenses. Not *Lancer* expenses, either (twenty-one dollars a day for motels and thirteen for meals and tips), but real, honest-to-god, advertising expenses.

"Sounds intriguing."

"Thought it might."

"I mean, after all, it is the duty of the fair-minded, objective journalist to examine all aspects of a story."

"Exactly."

"So if I were to go down and check out this Bosque Del in California, with your group picking up the expenses — your group would pick up the expenses?"

"Plus a bonus."

"Plus a bonus, it would really be a sort of service to the reader, wouldn't it?"

"It would."

An unpleasant notion entered my noggin unbidden, and would not go away. What would Hanna Klovack say to all this? Would she consider an all-expenses-paid trip from an advertiser who wanted his product boosted to be, well, a trifle compromising? Would she take it the wrong way? Do pigeons poop? She wouldn't see it for what it was, an opportunity to better myself, to broaden myself by travel and thus become a more effective journalist. Not a chance. She'd start in about selling out your own community for return airfare, and about sucking up to developers and abandoning journalistic principles, never realizing that the foremost journalistic principle in real life is to suck up to developers. Also, she would probably go on to point out that it could very well turn out that Dominic was a murderer. Which might well be the case, but which was entirely beside the main point, the main point being that Dominic represented first-class airfare and incidentals to California, a place I'd never been. If I played my cards right, I could get my trip in before they arrested Dominic and then, what harm could befall? The project would be dead, but I'd have broadened my outlook, anyway. Again, this was not an argument which, for some reason, I was anxious to lay before Hanna, and I had a feeling it was not a topic she would be willing to leave alone. Maybe it was just as well we were not — at least, I assumed we were not — on speaking terms right now.

Dominic could see I was cogitating, and misunderstood; he thought I needed another shove.

"This could lead to other things, you know."

"It could?"

"Sure. A big organization like the one I and my associates run, we are always on the lookout for talent. As, for instance, in our public relations department."

Public relations. A journalist's heaven. Expense accounts treated with flexibility and understanding. Buying drinks for former colleagues, and watching them snarl with envy. Beginning sentences with, "We here at Dominic Associates believe success comes in Cans, not Can'ts. . ."

The Widow Golden, who had walked out to the living-room so we could have our talk in private, broke into my reverie by suddenly singing out, "Boys, the police are here."

She added, "I forgot to tell you. I called them earlier, when I saw that extra body on Carlton's lawn."

FOURTEEN

IN THE END, it was the cops who got the lasagne. Mutt and Jeff, mostly. They were accompanied by two flinty-eyed gents from the homicide division of the Ontario Provincial Police. These, presumably, were the detectives sent up from Toronto to take over the case. Tall, rangy types they were, Sergeant Arthur Smollett and Detective Frank Thurston. Like most police investigating teams, they consisted of an experienced hand and younger man. I called them Smiley and Thuggy, to myself, of course. Smiley, the sergeant, was greying and gloomy; Thuggy was about my own age and had a craggy look.

Mutt and Jeff concentrated on scoffing the Widow Golden's edibles, while the imported talent, who had clearly been brought along in the first place to break down my foolish story and nail me for the murder of Ernie Struthers, got on with the investigation. Everyone's a specialist these days. They didn't say a whole lot, preferring to express themselves — this is often the case with flatfeet — with grunts and words of one syllable, "Huh," was one of their favourites, and if you don't think it is possible to convey a world of disbelief in the single syllable, "Huh," then you have not met Smiley and Thuggy. When they actually broke into speech, it was to work the old tough-cop-soft-cop routine.

Thuggy said, "All right, Withers, suppose you start telling us the truth for a change," and I stumbled, once more, through my tale, which even to my ears sounded like something you read on the front page of one of those supermarket tabloids that features Skydiving Grandma Gives Birth To Twins In Mid-Air, or I Worked In A UFO Slave Labor Camp, and Smiley beamed at me in a friendly way and said, "And then?"

What are you supposed to say when a cop smiles at you

and intones, "And then?" You feel obliged, somehow, to keep the conversational ball rolling, so you blurt out something you never intended to put on the public record. As when I explained that I had arrived home late at night, and there was no sign of anyone around the place, honest to God, officer, not that I was looking, you understand, I was tired, pooped, really, and just flopped into bed.

"And then?"

"And then Mrs. Er...whoops!" I stopped. Thuggy was on it like a duck on a June bug. "Who?"

"No one. Nothing. I made a mistake."

So, out it came. Mrs. Eberley had been passing by and had decided to pay a surprise visit and we had a little chat, and that's all, officer, cross my heart and spit. This was not received with that suspension of disbelief that the dramatist prefers to attend his story-telling. None of the cops actually shouted, "Liar, liar, pants on fire," but the phrase was implicit in the raised eyebrows and exchanged glances on the part of Smiley and Thuggy, while Mutt and Jeff broke off their chewing long enough to shake their heads, more in sorrow than in anger.

"You're forgetting about Hanna, dear," the Widow Golden put in. Just being helpful.

"Who's Hanna?" Thuggy wanted to know.

"Carlton's lady friend..."

"A colleague of mine, from work..."

These phrases chased each other out into the room, arriving in a dead heat. Thuggy chose to accept the Widow Golden's version.

"So, this bimbo came out for a little whatchamacallit and discovered you with the body, is that it?"

"Officer," barked the Widow, in a tone that snapped all the forces of justice in the room to attention, "you have it quite wrong."

So then she got into her version of the story. Heard a car screech to a halt over at Carlton's place, so she went to the window, saw Carlton's front door open, heard voices raised in anger, saw Hanna come bolting out of the house, jump into her car, and drive off.

"She seemed a little upset," Mrs. G. added.

Thuggy said, "That's probably because Withers told her he'd just murdered another man. You thought Mr. Silvio here was dead, didn't you, Withers?"

"No, of course not."

"Huh. You knew he was just unconscious, and you were planning to finish him off later, is that what you're telling us?"

"No, no, no. I didn't know he was out there. Honest. C'mon, fellows, be reasonable. If I'd known Dominic was out there, would I have calmly gone to bed?"

"And then?" put in Smiley, but I think it was just from habit, so I ignored him.

It was Dominic who persuaded the cops that it wasn't me who knocked him out. "Look at the fellow," he said. "Use your loaf."

I stand six feet one, but I am built along whippet lines, whereas Dominic is based on the bull mastiff model. Having nothing to go on, except, as Thuggy pointed out, the very real possibility that I had earlier terminated Ernie Struthers, they were forced to conclude that it was unlikely that I would attack someone like Dominic, even if he had dared to tread on my lawn.

They took me once more through the story of finding Ernie Struthers's remains on the doorstep, and then conceded that they did not have, as Thuggy put it in his comforting way, "enough direct evidence to make an arrest at this time."

They seemed to be intrigued by the fact that I claimed — claimed is the way they put it — that there had been a package of tools taken from my Dad's workshop.

"Wasn't that just somebody grabbing a souvenir?" I asked.

"Could be," replied Smiley.

"Or . . ." added Thuggy.

"Or . . . ? Or what?"

The rozzers all looked at each other. Mutt and Jeff looked at each other, then at Smiley and Thuggy. Eyebrows were raised. Superior smiles appeared. It reminded me of a meeting of senior bureaucrats. Dominic and the Widow looked out the window, checking for more bodies, no doubt.

Finally, Smiley unbent.

"The killer," he explained, "may be preparing to do it again."

"Oh my God!" I blurted.

"But I don't really think so," said Thuggy.

"Thank God!" I blurted.

"Because I think we already have the killer," said Thuggy, with a loaded glance at your obedient servant.

"Oh my God!" I blurted again.

Smiley broke what was becoming one of those silences pregnant with meaning to suggest that, at the earliest opportunity they should consult with Hanson Eberley, to bring him up to date on "this latest development." My heart sank.

"You're not going to tell Hanson about Mrs. Eberley, er, accidentally wandering into my place?"

"I don't see how we can avoid it," replied Thuggy, and positively wriggled in anticipation.

Smiley added, more kindly, "We have great respect for Staff Inspector Eberley. You can be sure this matter will be handled fairly."

Which, of course, is just what I didn't want. What I wanted was for it to be handled unfairly, viz., to be ignored, dropped, expunged from the record.

Finally, the cops left. Mutt and Jeff had to be pried away from the remains of the lasagne, which they were scraping out of the empty bowl. The Widow Golden and Dominic settled down in the kitchen.

"I'll just fix us a little snack," said the Widow, and Dominic smiled and reached for a fork, with which he was obviously intent on digging his grave. I wandered disconsolately across the street and back to my house. As I came in the front door, the phone was ringing.

It was Hanna.

"Where the hell have you been?" she demanded. "Seeing the tootsie home?"

I replied, frigidly, "Mrs. Eberley came to my place, apparently, under a misapprehension. Discovering that, she went home."

"Yes, well, strangely enough, I believe you. I've been talking to someone about you, and she said you were — she has a strange way of talking — 'without a stain on your character.'"

"You've met Tilda."

"I have."

Tilda is Tilda Handfield-Browning, our drama critic. Entertainment columnist they call it nowadays, but the entertainment stuff we just rip off the Canadian Press and Capital News Features wires — what's doing in Hollywood, some rock star's recipes for goulash and universal peace, that sort of thing. The local dramatic offerings are covered by Tilda. Not because she knows anything about drama; it's her pension.

Tilda began her working life back about the time of the Crimean War, when she was known as Gwen Funk, secretary to Sam Marston, founder of the Silver Falls *Lancer* and as pronounced a poop as ever drew breath, from what I've heard. He was one of those swaggering, puff-faced types; a lumber baron — that's where the early big money came from, in our county — who bought a newspaper late in life so that he could be sure to have swell things written about him in it. Sam and Gwen, a dainty, fawnlike thing in those days, became an Item, in due course. Her fawnlikeness got to him, and I guess she was attracted, as so many people are, by the stench of power and self-adulation he exuded like after-shave lotion. His wife didn't seem to mind — wives apparently didn't, back in the Golden Age of Fooling Around — and the affair went on for years and years until one day Sam keeled over at work and expired. Someone had just told him that the godless forces of socialism, in the name of the Co-operative Commonwealth Federation, were running second in the Ontario provincial elections, and Sam's affronted ticker couldn't take the strain.

Proving for all time what a poop he was, he left no provision for Gwen. Not a nickel. Sam's son-in-law and heir, Donald Post, the man who had had the good luck to hire me before going to the Great Newsroom in the sky, wasn't anxious to take Gwen on in either of her capacities — secretary or mistress. So he made her our drama critic. Why not? What skills are required to pen newspaper criticism? Eyes, ears, fingers. She had them all in working order, and the fact that she knew diddley-squat about the theatre meant that she could view productions as a consumer, without preconceived prejudice, in the same way that other newspapers hire relatives and intellectual cripples to review the arts. So she changed her name from Gwen Funk to Tilda Handfield-Browning, for byline purposes — it sounded like the kind of name a critic might have — and went into business. She was a howling success from the start, for the very good reason that she loved everything, and if there is one thing local dramatists like, it is to be loved. A sentimental soul, Tilda cried at musical comedies. She hated the villain in the melodramas and loved the worthy but dim-witted hero — just the opposite, you see, from most of our modern, frank, and fearless critics.

No play was so turgid, so lifeless, so appallingly performed that Tilda couldn't find something nice to say about it. When the backdrop of the main set in *Brigadoon*, the clunker we put on in my final year of high school, collapsed in Act II and damn near smothered the chorus, Tilda merely noted that "the sets, while they lasted, were splendid."

Anyway, that's Tilda, kindness on the hoof, and Hanna had met her, and been informed of my sterling character. I did not tell Hanna that Al Capone, Machine-Gun Kelly, and Attila the Hun all got rave notices from Tilda. Hanna went on to say, mysteriously, that Tilda had told her to tell me to go and see her. She had some information for me. And, even more mysteriously, that she, Hanna, was going to Toronto.

"Why?"

"To check on something."

"What?"

"All shall be revealed, my good man, in due course. In the meantime, have you worked out the clue of the newspaper clipping?"

"The what of the what?"

"The newspaper clipping, fathead."

"Well, no, not actually what you might call, worked it out."

"I'll bet you haven't even looked at it."

"Well, no, now that you come right down to it, I haven't. Why should I? Hanson says it probably has nothing to do with the murder."

"Yes, but what if he's wrong? What if Ernie was trying to tell you something with that clipping?"

"Then why didn't he just tell me? Why not leave a note that says, 'The butler did it,' or whatever? Why all this fuss?"

"That part's easy."

"It is?"

"It is. That is, to anyone with the brains God gave a graham cracker it is."

Silence.

"You aren't going to tell me, are you?"

"Can't you figure it out?"

"In a word, No."

"But you do have an explanation?"

"Not an explanation. Just a theory."

"I'll bet it's rotten."

"You'll never know if you don't listen."

"I'm listening."

"Okay. Ernie was in the church, waiting to spy on this meeting between the Rev. and the developer. He had this clipping with him . . . "

"Why?"

"We don't know, as yet. Don't interrupt. He had this clipping with him, for reasons unknown, while he sat in the box pew, waiting for the meeting between the developer and the minister to get under way. Maybe he was reading it, to pass the time. What did you say?"

"I said 'Fadoodle.' It's an old English expression conveying doubt."

"Well, fadoodle to you, too. Do you want to hear this or not?"

"Yes. I guess so."

"Where was I?"

"Reading old newspapers, in the dark, in the church."

"Oh, yeah. Anyway, Ernie was hidden in the box pew where he could see the killer, but the killer couldn't see him, and then he made a noise, or else he saw something that alarmed him, or made him think he might be in danger."

"Then, why didn't he just leave?"

"He couldn't, could he? He was trapped in the box pew. So he decided to leave a clue, just in case. He was worried that whoever he was afraid of would discover what he was up to, so he put the clipping in the envelope and sealed it."

"He already had the envelope typed out?"

"Well, yes. No, wait a minute. He was going to go to your place after the meeting, and that's why he had the envelope with him. But he made a noise, so he was discovered and killed."

"That's the dumbest thing I ever heard of. Suppose you had just stabbed somebody to death and he happened to be clutching an envelope at the time, addressed to somebody else. Would you just say, 'Oh, an envelope, eh? I'd better deliver this, we can't count on the mail these days,' pick up the body, with envelope, sling it over your shoulder, and carry it three blocks to my place, thus saving the deceased thirty-nine cents for a stamp?"

"I didn't say it was a perfect explanation, just a theory."

"Well, it's rotten, as predicted."

"It's a hell of a lot better than anything you've come up with."

"If you're so hot on theories, what's your theory as to why Nora Eberley inserted herself in my bed?"

109

"How should I know? Maybe Hanson isn't doing his husbandly duty. Maybe she finds you sexy."

"Me, sexy?"

"Well, you are, a little, you know."

"I am?"

"A little. I said, a little."

This was good. A little sexy, from the Klovack menace; it had to mean something.

"Hey, I've got a great idea," I said. "Why don't you drive over here and we can thrash this out?"

"Nice try, Withers. Now, where were we?"

"We were about to work out some plausible reason for Nora to come calling on me in night attire."

There was a long silence on the phone.

"Hey, you awake?"

"Certainly, I'm just thinking. Carlton, tell me again about Ernie Struthers."

So I told her again. Jerk. Drinker of Catawba. Grocery store clerk. Lecher. Beneficiary — or so everyone thought — of an aunt's estate. Hardware tycoon. Still a jerk...

"Hey, stop there. That could be it."

"What could be what?"

"If Ernie was as lecherous as you say and Nora is given to getting into other people's beds, perhaps at some point the two of them ... Nora may know more about Ernie than anyone."

"So you think she felt that the best place to explain that would be in my bed?"

"Maybe, especially if she was just looking for an excuse to crawl into your bed. No, that's out. You're not *that* sexy."

"Thanks, I needed that."

"I think you should go and confront Nora and ask her what was on her mind, besides lust."

"Not a chance. Hanson would be bound to find out about it."

"Well, if you won't, you won't. Maybe I'll tackle her. But all this does is to make one thing clear even to someone of your limited intelligence. Which is..."

" . . . that if there really is a clue anywhere in this mess that we can use, it's in that newspaper clipping."

"That's my boy."

"Well, if that's the case, I'm in deep trouble. Mysteries are beyond me."

"Along with most other things?"

"What?"

"Nothing. Don't worry about it. Look, I'll work out the clipping, nothing to it."

"I bet you don't."

"In the meantime, you go and see Tilda Handfield-Browning; she has something to tell you."

"Is it important? I mean, I've had a rather full day already, what with one thing and another."

"Well, I don't know. I guess it all depends on what you call important. She seems to think Tommy Macklin might be the killer. Well, I'm off to Toronto. See you."

FIFTEEN

AFTER THIS LITTLE bombshell, I decided to delay reporting for work — I was already late, anyway — until I had had a chance to talk to Hanson, so I walked quickly over to Fifth Street. Hanson and Nora were both on the porch, and Nora looked a little peaked, which was no surprise. She had had a busy evening, what with one thing and another, and it was only about eleven a.m., an hour she knows mostly by second-hand report. I shot her a quick glance — had she said anything to Hanson, I wondered? — and got back a tiny, almost imperceptible, shake of the head, which might have meant No, or might just have meant, Keep your big mouth shut.

I was a bit embarrassed, so I started right in with a cock-amamie story about deciding to clear up my cottage last night, just for something to take my mind off my troubles, when I came across this glasses case, complete with sunglasses, behind the cushion on the couch.

Hanson looked blank. "So?" he said.

"Well, I was going to throw it out, but then I wondered..."

"You wondered what?"

"I wondered if maybe it had been put there, for some reason. We were talking earlier about how the murderer might have planted clues to make me look like the murderer."

"You think these glasses belonged to Ernie, and somebody planted them on you?"

"Well, it's possible."

Hanson chuckled. "Carlton, I think you watch too much TV. Either that, or this business is getting to you. Chances are these things have been behind that cushion for the last year or so. They don't belong to Ernie. At least, I never saw them on him. Did you?"

"I don't know. I don't think so. They're broken, anyway, so he couldn't have worn them. But I thought they ought to

112

be turned over to the police, just in case. They could take fingerprints, and find out if they were Ernie's."

"Hmm. Well, give them to me. I'm sure it's a waste of time, but you're quite correct. Anything that seems to be out of order that might have the remotest connection with Ernie ought to be checked out. Have you got any other surprises for me?"

I told him about Hanna's call, and he seemed intrigued.

"This lady drama critic thinks Tommy Macklin might have done it?"

"That's Hanna's story."

"Why?"

"She didn't say."

"Hanna didn't say, or Tilda didn't say?"

"Tilda didn't say."

"Well, perhaps you'd better go ask her, and maybe, if you will be kind enough to drive me into town, I'll have a quiet word with Tommy Macklin. After all, we scarcely know each other, and now I'm practically working for him. It's time we got acquainted."

Marchepas worked, again, a miracle, so we drove to town at once, and I treated Hanson to lunch at the O.K. Cafe. He chewed his blackened hamburger thoughtfully, but didn't leer, not once, at Belinda, not even when she came and sat at our table for a while after the crowd thinned out. He addressed her throughout as "Miss Huntingdon"; she told me later that he didn't seem like any of the cops she'd ever met before. Then I drove Hanson down to the newspaper and took him up to Tommy's office. They had met before, I gathered, but really only knew each other to nod to. Tommy immediately put on his sucky expression, and invited Hanson to come in, sir, come in, it is such a pleasure to meet so distinguished a gentleman, while inviting me to get out, get out, and get some work done. As soon as they were settled, I charged off to see our drama critic.

Tilda Handfield-Browning, née Funk, works out of an

office on the ground floor of the *Lancer* building, a drafty, overstuffed room — not unlike Tilda, in this respect — containing a lot of old furniture, about a thousand theatre programs, and seventeen pictures of the late Sam Marston.

Tilda is a gentlewoman, in the old-fashioned sense. No longer fawnlike, she retains an air of poise and grace that even some of the wicked were able to capture in her generation, and which seems almost entirely missing in my own. She may have kicked up her heels in her time, but today, you can't even imagine her mentioning her heels in public, or offering Sam anything more personal than tea, crumpets, and cucumber sandwiches. As a matter of fact, she poured me a splash of Oolong as she waved me into a velvet-covered armchair festooned with antimacassars. I took a sip, burned my mouth, swallowed a curse, and smiled brightly at Tilda.

"Hanna told me you had some news for me."

"That is correct, Carlton." Pause. "She is quite a vivacious young lady."

"She is that."

"Perky. In my day, we would have called her forward, or even cheeky."

"In my day, we call her rude."

"And yet she possesses, shall we say, a certain gamine charm."

Tilda talks like that; it comes from reading old plays.

"I don't know about gamine charm. She has a dandy right cross, I can tell you that."

Tilda fluttered, positively fluttered, her eyelashes. "Why, Carlton, I believe you're smitten!"

Smitten. You see why I like living in the boondocks. Down in Toronto, when boy likes girl, he gets the hots for her. Here, he is smitten. Nicer, I think. I may have blushed; I've been doing that, lately.

"Why, you are, Carlton, you are smitten. Olga will be so pleased."

Olga Kratzmeyer, the Bratwurst Bombshell — she is of German extraction and ample charms — is the editorial secretary down at the *Lancer*, and a motor-mouth whose information service rivals the Widow Golden's.

"Tilda, if you say a word to Olga, you will, I swear to God, kill any chance I have with Hanna. She is not, as you say, smitten."

"I wouldn't be so sure, Carlton. She called you 'totally weird.'"

Well, it was better than "queer," maybe even a step up from "fathead." Weird implies exotic, doesn't it, and therefore interesting?

"Tilda, I beg of you, make this our little secret. Hanna has just been through a rough time . . ."

"A Tragic Affair?"

"A tragic, as you say, affair. This is not the time to put her through the old peer-and-leer routine they'll get up in the office if they think something is going on. Which, I hasten to add, it isn't."

"Very well, Carlton, you may count on my discretion. My lips are sealed." She delivered this line as if she had just invented it.

"Tilda, what's this about Tommy Macklin?"

"Carlton, you are very abrupt. All you young people nowadays are very abrupt."

"We are. Well?"

"As you know, Carlton, I am on the Silver Falls Amateur Dramatic Society Board. Honorary," she preened herself, "Patron."

"And?"

"And, after last week's meeting, Mrs. Macklin — she is on the board, too, Carlton . . ."

"Yes, yes."

"Not that she is really a patron of the thea-tuh. I remember the late Mr. Marston saying of her — this will amuse you, Carlton — saying of Bernice Macklin that she thought Sheridan was a hotel-chain."

"Very droll. And?"

"Don't bustle me, Carlton. You're bustling me."

115

"A thousand pardons, Tilda. You were mentioning about Mrs. Macklin."

"She said a very strange thing."

"What about?"

"About Tommy. She said that Tommy had come home from work the night before in a rage."

"Tommy's always in a rage, Tilda. You know that. So does Bernice Macklin."

"Quite. Quite. But this was different. He wasn't shouting, you know, the way he does. He was coldly furious. That was the phrase Bernice used, 'coldly furious.' I've never seen Tommy coldly furious, have you?"

No, I hadn't. Tommy is usually incandescent. He takes fire faster than an oil-soaked rag.

"At what was he coldly furious?"

"That's just the point. That's why I told Hanna, as soon as I heard about your little trouble, that I had to speak with you."

Long pause here, while Tilda peered over her glasses at me, a trick she had picked up from *Lady Windermere's Fan*, or some such place, and then said, "Ernie Struthers. Bernice Macklin told me — mark this well, Carlton — that Tommy had said he could just murder that Ernie Struthers."

"Oh. Well, thank you, Tilda, but I don't think that actually means a whole lot. Tommy offers to have my guts for garters about three times a week, but he's never actually hit me."

"But 'coldly furious,' Carlton?"

"Well, I'll pass it along, for what it's worth, to Hanson Eberley. Hanson," I added, "is helping me."

"I know. Such a distinguished man."

"Yes. I'll tell him. But the fact is, Tilda, Tommy was probably mad at Ernie over that three-part series we ran about his hardware store. I wrote the copy."

"Such a nice series, Carlton."

"Ernie bought four ads to go around the copy, and he didn't pay for them."

"That would make Tommy angry."

"It did. He sent me around to hound Ernie, and Ernie

116

called me names, and that's why I'm probably going to be slam-dunked into jail for his murder. No mystery there."

"I don't think it was that, Carlton. I really don't. That's the sort of thing that would make Tommy shout, but not go 'coldly furious.'"

"Hmm."

"I think you should go and talk to Tommy, Carlton. Confront him."

"Me? Confront Tommy Macklin? You can't be serious."

"You can do it, Carlton. You know you can. Be brave."

This one hurt. I would as soon tackle Tommy as ask a mother tiger if I could borrow her cubs.

"Think how impressed Hanna would be."

"Do you think she'd cry at my funeral?"

So we left it at that, that I would, perhaps, confront, ahem, Tommy Macklin and pummel the truth out of him. I pushed off upstairs to the newspaper, on the off-chance that Hanna might not have left for Toronto yet.

When I came into the newsroom, I could see that Hanson was still in Tommy's office. Then it occurred to me that the best way to try out Tilda's story might be to tackle Tommy with Hanson standing by. Tommy might not shout at me with a witness there. So I wandered down to the managing editor's office, knocked, and walked in. The two men were sitting with their feet up on the coffee table, sipping at the office scotch, which Tommy keeps in the bottom drawer of his desk, and which is known as the office scotch because it comes out of the editorial budget, not because anyone else in the office ever gets a sniff of it.

"Ah," said Tommy, "Carlton. We were just talking about our little project."

My courage is an evanescent thing. Gossamer, practically. It would look well on Nora Eberley. If I was going to do anything with it, I had to do it now, before it wafted away.

"Tommy," I said, sternly, "why did you say you'd like to murder Ernie Struthers?"

His feet crashed to the floor and his head jerked up. "Who said I did?"

"It's true, then?"

He gave me one of his looks. "None of your damned business, Withers."

"Now, now, now," Hanson interceded. "Everything is grist for the mill, Tommy. What's this all about, Carlton?"

"I have information" (the old police court formula again, you see) "that Tommy here was really teed off at Ernie Struthers, and now Ernie is dead, and I'm just curious, that's all."

"It's nothing that concerns you, Carlton."

"Now, I'm not sure that's quite fair, Tommy," Hanson put in, smoothly. "Everyone is undergoing some interrogation on this murder. The police even came to me and asked for an accounting of my movements on the evening of Ernie's murder. Quite proper, too."

"Oh, yeah, where were you?" Tommy obviously had decided that the best defence was a good offence.

"In the early part of the evening, I was, um, attending to my wife, and then about nine o'clock or so, an old friend of mine who happened to be in the area dropped in to see me." He paused.

Tommy, of course, wanted to know who the old friend was, and Hanson was delighted to accommodate him.

"Fred Burgess," he told Tommy, "the local OPP Inspector, and a very old friend of mine. He stayed until about 10:30, and then drove over to Kennedy Beach, where his kids have a cottage."

Trust Hanson to have a cop for an alibi. He looked across at Tommy. "Satisfied?"

"Well, of course, Hanson, I didn't mean to suggest . . ."

"No, of course not. Nor does Carlton mean to suggest anything, Tommy. It's just that when these matters come up, people like answers. Perhaps if you told us . . ."

"Well, I won't. By God," Tommy got to his feet now, towering to his full five feet four inches, "I certainly don't have to account for myself to Carlton. If I were to answer to every jumped-up reporter who comes barging in here . . . Get the hell out, Carlton."

It doesn't work this way on TV. On TV, the reporter just pops the question and the bad guy collapses with a sob of remorse. Tommy doesn't watch the right shows. He pointed his finger at the door, and I flowed back through it, like jelly slipping off a hot plate, and was gone.

I wandered back over to my work-station, and went to work on some of the routine stuff that always awaits me. "Nature Notes," I typed. "Mrs. Mary Brown of Bosky Dell reports seeing a Pileated Woodpecker in a pine tree outside her back porch," and I was just beginning to wring the drama out of that damn woodpecker when the phone rang. Not my phone, the one on the city desk. I walked over and barked into the instrument, "Silver Falls *Lancer.*" I got a patch of heavy breathing, and then a throaty voice rumbled, "I know who killed Ernie Struthers."

"That's nice. Who?" We get a lot of these calls, at the newspaper.

"Tonight. Ten o'clock. Under the north goalpost at the football field. Meet me there."

Click.

I chuckled to myself, and when Hanna turned up about 5:30 — she must have driven the eighty miles to Toronto, done whatever it was she was doing in about an hour, and come back again without let or pause — I told her about the crank call.

"Phone the cops," she said, shortly.

"I'm not going to phone the cops. It's a waste of time."

"Probably. Still, the cops like to know about such things; it keeps them busy."

"Maybe in Toronto. Here, the cops prefer not to be busy."

"Well then, tell Hanson."

"Why should I bother Hanson with this?"

"Because there just might be something to it; and, even if there isn't, you ought to tell somebody."

"But, suppose he tells me to go and meet this person at ten p.m.?"

"Well then, I guess you'll have to go."

"Yes, but, what if he turns out to be a lunatic?"

She brightened considerably. "Then I guess," she said, "there's a pretty good chance he'll cut your throat."

"I suppose I could ask for police protection."

"Look, as a matter of ordinary common sense, you ought to tell somebody about the call before you go off to meet some lunatic."

"That's easy. I won't go to meet the lunatic."

"But what if he isn't a lunatic? What if he has some important information?"

"Would you come with me?"

"No."

"Oh."

I should never have let Hanson wander off without telling him about this; I knew that. I had seen him get up, shake hands with Tommy, and leave the office about 4:30. He'd even given me a merry wave as he went, but I hadn't said anything. Crank calls are so common, why bother the man? Because it made sense, even as Hanna said. So I phoned him. He hadn't come home yet, Nora said. He had mentioned something about going around to the OPP office in Silver Falls after he finished at the paper and getting someone there to drive him home. Sure enough, I caught up to Hanson at the OPP detachment, in Fred Burgess's office. They had been talking over a new development in the case, Hanson told me.

"I'm glad you called," he added. "The new development is something that affects you."

"Yes, I know," I began, but he cut me off.

"The officers here have just had a chat with the lawyer who's handling Ernie Struthers's estate."

"Somebody called here at the *Lancer* . . ."

"And it appears you are a beneficiary."

"I am? Ernie left me money? How much?"

"Ten thousand dollars."

"Yikes! Now everyone's going to think I did it."

"Now, Carlton, no one is going to believe you would murder a man just for ten thousand dollars."

"Oh, no? They already think I did it for free."

SIXTEEN

IT WAS A thoughtful C. Withers who found himself that evening, in another teeming rainstorm, soaked to the skin, waiting under the goalposts at the old high school football field. I had much to think on. Ernie Struthers, while of sound mind, or as sound as it ever got, had left me ten thousand dollars in his will. Presumably, this was his peculiar way of saying that he was sorry he had killed my parents, something he never let on in life. That was good; it showed the man had some sense of guilt, after all, and if I ever got the $10,000, it would come in handy. A man can always find a use for $10,000. On the other hand — there is always another hand, isn't there? — this was bound to make the constabulary even more certain that I was the one who pin-punched Ernie to death. When I was eating dinner in the O.K. Cafe — burned ham, char-broiled eggs, torched toast à la Belinda — the two local OPP officers were sitting in the corner, drinking coffee. When I got up to leave, Smiley said, "We'll be seeing you."

"Soon," added Thuggy.

This did not sound like the cheerful exchange of courtesies between new-found friends; it sounded more like the rattle of a couple of rozzers who have applied for the warrant and are just polishing up their handcuffs for the arrest. It seemed to confirm my view that there was not a whole lot of point in asking for police protection for this evening's outing. I was thinking, as I tried, in vain, to shelter beneath the goalposts — very poor umbrellas, goalposts — that it would be nice if whoever made the phone call to the *Lancer* was not, after all, just another crank caller, but someone with genuine information. Hanson figured that the odds were against this, but he said it was just as well to check it out, anyway. You never know, he said. Which reminded me of a girl in our senior class in high school, the ever-popular

Melinda Murchison, who wrote in the yearbook, where you put your favourite motto, "I never No."

With the exception of a large, black dung beetle, which was, for reasons of its own, methodically crawling up the goalposts, falling off, then crawling up again, I had the place to myself. The loving couples who are usually to be found wriggling about the grounds and scaring the living hell out of the worm-pickers were snuggling indoors or doing without. I began to whistle. Might give new heart to the beetle.

We went on this way, me whistling, the beetle crawling and falling, for about ten minutes. I got through "Coming Through the Rye," "The Keel Row," "Here Comes the Forty-Second," and "Captain John MacPherson's Lament" — I used to play the bagpipes as a kid — and was just starting in on "The Campbells Are Coming," when, by golly, they did. Ern and Vern, the Campbell brothers. Woodcutters. Long, lean, and mean, very handy with axe, bucksaw, and chainsaw. Officially, they scratch out a living hacking up the woods for townees. Unofficially, they make a much better return flogging moonshine. I recognized their stake truck sliding down Morrissey Street towards the football field with the lights off and the engine barely ticking over. They stopped just opposite the goalposts, and there was a pause — big argument, I guess, about who was going to get out in the rain. Then a figure detached itself from the truck and came shambling through the downpour at a half run. It was Vern, the younger Campbell. He stopped when he got close enough to recognize me in the dim light from a far-away street lamp.

"Holy shit," he said. "You!"

"Who were you expecting?" I asked. "Tina Turner?"

"No. Matter of fact, Ern, he said Tommy Macklin was going to meet us here."

"Tommy Macklin?"

"Yeah. Ern, he talked to him down at the paper today. On the phone."

"That was me, Vern. I answered the phone."

"Oh, hell, Ern's gonna be cheesed. You don't have no money."

Too true. "Let me get this straight, Vern. You thought you were going to meet Tommy Macklin here tonight?"

"Yeah."

"And sell him some information for which he would pay you good money?"

"Yeah."

"Tell me. I'll tell Tommy, and he can send you the money."

He nearly went for it. Swift reasoning is not his forte; if it can't be hacked, or distilled, Vern can't deal with it. Then, "Naw, Ern said not to say anything till we got the money."

"See here, Vern, what kind of money are we talking about?"

Vern drew himself up proudly.

"Fifty bucks. Not a dollar less."

"I can give you fifty bucks, Vern. Well, by Thursday at the latest."

"Naw, I guess we'll just drive over and see if Tommy Macklin is still awake."

Desperate times call for desperate measures. Every seasoned reporter carries a little cache of emergency money, just in case he gets sent out of town and can't get to the office for an advance. I carry mine in a secret compartment in my wallet — right behind the picture of Gene Autry — and I had two twenties and a ten out under Vern's nose in a flash. They disappeared into a gnarled fist.

"Well?"

"About three weeks ago, Ern and me, we was delivering a face-cord of wood to Harry Franklin's place. Ash, it was. Good stuff."

"And then?"

"Mr. and Mrs. Franklin were having a fight. In the kitchen. We was stacking the wood in the woodshed at the back, and you could hear them arguing in the kitchen."

"And then?"

123

"Well, Mrs. Franklin, she was real upset. She kept saying, 'Harry, you've got to do something. Ernie Struthers will be the ruin of us all.'

"And Harry, he says, 'But what can I do? What can I do?' He kept saying that, and she kept saying, 'Something, Harry, you've got to do something,' and he finally says, 'Know what I'd like to do?' and she says, 'No, what?' and he says, 'Kill the sonofabitch, is what.' There, that's it," said Vern.

"Have you told the police?"

This drew a grunt. "Ern and me, we're not too close with the police. We figured to sell it to the paper. Say," he added, "you suppose Tommy Macklin would give us something if we didn't tell him we'd already told you?"

"Sure," I told him, and waved him on his way. Bless his larcenous heart. Tommy Macklin wouldn't give him money for a story, or anything else. I knew that, but Vern and Ern didn't, and I thought it might be a good thing for them to go over and bang on Tommy's door late on a rainy night. It would give them all a pleasant outing and I wished them well.

I shrugged a soggy shrug and wandered back over to where I had parked my car, got in, tried to start it, failed — *Marchepas* was having a fit of the vapours again — and then sat there, brooding. What the hell was all that about, anyway? Would Harry Franklin, a chubby, retired sales manager and a bit of an oaf, but not exactly the killer type, take a pin punch, supposing he knew what it was and where it was, to Ernie Struthers? And if so, why? Then there was Tommy Macklin. Tilda seemed to think he might have done it. Again, though, why? Finally, there was Dominic Silvio, the demon developer, and my own favourite candidate for murderer, though please, Lord, not to be arrested before my California trip.

It's a puzzlement, as the bald gent in *The King and I* used to sing. I tried the car again. It simply groaned, so I got out and was just starting to walk back downtown for a cab when a car came splashing down the street and pulled up into the

124

spot lately vacated by the Campbell truck. It was a Toyota. Hanna's.

She rolled down the window on the driver's side.

"Not murdered yet, I guess," she said. "Oh, well, maybe next time."

I jumped in on the passenger side. It had to mean something, didn't it, when she turned up like this? Better not press my luck, though.

"Evening, Hanna. Say, Hanna, guess what?"

"I don't have to guess, do I? You're going to tell me."

So I told her about the Campbell brothers and Harry Franklin and Tommy Macklin, and about my legacy from the late E. Struthers, and she couldn't make any more sense out of any of it than I could.

"Well, that maybe puts a crimp in my theory," said Hanna.

"You've got a theory?"

"I have."

"What is it?"

"You're not ready for it."

And, even though she very kindly drove me back to Bosky Dell, I couldn't get anything more out of her.

SEVENTEEN

WHEN WE PULLED up in front of my place, I started to slide across the seat towards Hanna, but she held up her hand, like a traffic cop.

"No, Carlton," she said, and then added, "not yet, anyway."

"You ought not to spurn my suit," I told her. "I'm a wealthy man."

"You mean the money Ernie Struthers left you? Are you going to keep it?"

"Sure? Why not?"

"It begins to look more and more as if Ernie got his money from a blackmailing racket. Doesn't that bother you?"

"Yes, it does." The damned female. "Maybe I should try to find out who the victims were and give it back."

"It's an idea. On the other hand, you'll probably need it for bail money, the way this case is going."

There was that. I wondered if there was any chance of getting the proceeds of the will before they started fitting me for leg-irons.

I sighed, got out of the car, slammed the door, waved a cheery goodnight to Mrs. Golden, who was no doubt at her station across the way, and headed for the cottage. Hanna drove off, but she was smiling, leaving me with a feeling, long held, that I will never understand the sex of which she is so interesting a member. Just as I went to sleep, about ten seconds after hitting the pillow, I remembered that, for the second time, I'd missed the chance to ask her what she'd been doing in Toronto.

The next morning, before heading for work, I walked around to the Eberleys, to report to Hanson. He was sitting in the living-room, staring into the fire. There was no sign of Nora, thank God, but then, there seldom is before noon.

This is a woman who thinks "a.m." stands for "after martinis."

"A bad business," Hanson said, as I sat down, "a very bad business indeed. I'm afraid those OPP fellows are making something of the ten thousand dollars Ernie left you in his will."

"But I didn't even know about it."

"You know that and I know that, but the OPP think you may have found out somehow. It does seem strange that Ernie would leave you money, after years of showing no sign of remorse."

I nodded. "Hanna thinks I'll have to use it for bail money."

"She may have a point."

My heart sank. Somehow, I thought Hanson would just clap hands, wave a wand, and, Hey, Presto! conjure up the killer.

"Well, it doesn't get any less complicated, that's for sure." And I told him about the Campbell brothers and their ersatz information-selling scheme. He perked up at once.

"Harry Franklin, eh?" he said. "Well, I suppose it's possible."

"No, it isn't. Harry just isn't the killer type."

Hanson gave me a glower. "There is no such thing as the killer type. In the right circumstances, anyone can commit murder. Even you."

"Yes, but what sort of circumstances would push a pudding like Harry Franklin over the line?"

"Oh, money. Money is a powerful motive. So is pride. So is jealousy."

"I can't see Harry Franklin, who didn't even know my father, as far as I'm aware, coming out here to swipe a pin punch from him and then puncturing Ernie Struthers because Ernie had been making out with tubby old Bernice Franklin. Was Ernie making out with tubby old Bernice Franklin?"

"I don't know, but" — and I got another glower — "don't assume that because Harry Franklin looks a little funny and

Bernice is no longer a beauty, if she ever was one, that Harry is incapable of feeling love for her. Or injured pride. Despite what you may read in the trashy novels, Carlton, love does not occur exclusively between shapely young women and tanned Greek godlings."

This I knew to be the case. My father usually looked like something that had been dropped from an airplane in a windstorm, and my mother, although comely, was nonetheless hardly the type to set pulses pounding in the supermarket. But she set Dad's pulse pounding, anyone could see that. Hanson went on; I'd never heard him talk like this.

"Then, there's pride. A man may do a lot; give up a lot; dare a lot — even kill, because of injured pride. I once worked on a murder case in which the victim was a young punk who'd broken into a lawyer's house in Rosedale. He had trashed the place, smashed a lot of fine china, including a superb porcelain collection, slashed the paintings, crapped on the living-room rug — created an ungodly mess. Well, the lawyer went to the legal aid authorities and offered to represent the punk who'd trashed his house, which everybody thought was noble as all get out. Then he drove his client out to Scarborough Bluffs to talk over the case and pushed him off. We got onto him at once, of course. He didn't care. He just kept saying he had to do it."

"So, you think Harry Franklin might have . . ."

"I don't know. Probably not. I merely point out that you mustn't assume that just because people are old or homely or both, they are immune to strong feelings. Murderous feelings."

"But I still don't see how Harry Franklin could have done in Ernie Struthers, or why he would have done so."

"Nor do I. But he might have been blackmailing Harry."

"That's what Hanna thinks."

"A shrewd young lady."

"Woman," I corrected him automatically, on Hanna's behalf. "So Hanna was right?"

"The police seem to to think so. Those two boys from Toronto, Thurston and Smollett, have pretty well taken over the case now. Smart chaps. So far, they've discovered that Ernie had about ninety thousand dollars in various bank accounts."

"And they think it came from blackmail?"

"It seems likely, especially in light of what the Campbell brothers told you."

"So Ernie set himself up in the stoves, bolts, and black-mailing business, got the goods on Harry — what sort of goods?"

"Oh, the silly old fool was probably fooling around with some young chippy."

"Got the goods on Harry and the chippy, was bleeding him, and Harry finally had enough and decided to bleed Ernie instead. Is that possible?"

"Barely. It doesn't explain, though, does it, why your Dad's pin punch was used for the killing, or why Ernie was found on your lawn."

"No, it doesn't."

"Nor does it explain the newspaper clipping. That girl of yours..." — I liked that — "...seems to put a lot of store in that clipping. Well, never mind, Carlton, at least we seem to be getting someplace, and at least we've got some evidence that points away from you — that's the main thing."

No argument about that.

So it was with light footsteps that I made my way home. Fairly light footsteps. I still had a murder rap, not exactly hanging over me, but hovering in the background. There was still the matter of making the Klovack menace succumb to my manly charms, if I could produce any, and I had to discover what, if anything, linked Tommy Macklin and Ernie Struthers — more blackmail? Still, the sun was shining, I could look forward to an all-expenses-paid trip to California, and there was a very good chance that, with any luck, I could be cleared of any connection with the murder, and some other poor sap indicted.

In the grip of this merry mood, I decided to go for a swim after breakfast. I wouldn't be needed at the office until about noon. I fell asleep on the dock in the sun, and it was after eleven by my watch before I got back to the cottage. That was the end of my merry mood; there was a little light blinking on the answering machine attached to my telephone.

The phone, you see, is safely buried in the debris, but the answering machine is in plain sight on the table in my office-cum-everything else. The newspaper provided the answering machine, which was not a stroke of unusual generosity on its part, but the result of the bankruptcy of Ray Furlinger's Office Supplies a couple of years back. Ray — "It's Our Good Deed to Meet Your Every Office Need" — did a lot of advertising in the *Lancer*, more, as it turned out, than he ever got around to paying for. By the time Ray had worked it out that the locals didn't need office supplies — doing most of their communication with quill pens on the backs of envelopes — and had gone belly-up, there was nothing left in his till. This meant that the *Lancer* had to take payment in kind, whatever kind there happened to be around the store. I got a lot of swell telephone memo pads, which I use in place of a regular notebook, a couple of boxes of ballpoint pens, imprinted with the Furlinger motto, "Our Good Deed, etc.," and one of the three telephone answering machines left in Ray's inventory. This last item allows Tommy Macklin to phone me up and, when I refuse to answer the phone — my usual policy — leave hectoring messages. One day he phoned up to tell me that the Miss Milkmaid contest, scheduled to kick off at the Silver Falls Fairgrounds at noon, had been moved back to eleven a.m. I missed his message because the phone answering machine was nowhere in sight, having been buried by the usual mound of odds and sods. When high noon discovered me at the fairgrounds, prepared to write an acre of prose about this year's bovine beauty, the ceremony was already concluded, and the crowd, such as it was, scattered to the four winds. Not one of the great moments in Canadian journalism, especially when you consider that the *Lancer* was the sponsor of this idiot contest. By the time I had run down the winner — one Prudence Wannamaker, eighteen, of Fairview Farm, R.R. 2, Wendover Cove, not that it matters a damn — I had made a firm resolve never ever to miss a message on the machine again.

Which explains the oasis of neatness in which it operates. When I come in the door, now, I generally register — there's a flicking light on the machine, nag, nag, nag — if there is a message. This morning, there was.

I prodded the machine a few times — I've never actually worked out how it functions, but I keep hitting buttons until it starts to spew out messages — and out came the reedy tones of the Rev. Wylie.

"Carlton," he said, "this is Ephraim Wylie. Please meet me at the church as soon as possible. There is something I must tell you. The time now is eleven a.m."

You note that "The time now, etc." This is what you're supposed to say when you get confronted by one of these machines, but nobody ever does. The Rev. had though, and I realized that he must have left the message on my machine about fifteen minutes ago. I ran up to the church. What the devil — pardon, heck — could he want? True, I had not weeded the gardens in front of the church this week — one of my duties — but he never summoned me into his presence for sins like that. Usually, he would just kind of press my hand as I came out of the church and murmur, "Too busy this week, were we, Carlton, to do our Christian duty?" leaving me feeling like a piece of cheese.

No, this had to be something a little more important, but what it could be, I couldn't imagine. I got to the church in about two minutes, and spotted the Rev. as soon as I came in the door at the top of the main aisle. He was sitting in the Flannery box pew, the very one the late Ernie Struthers had occupied, briefly. He had his head down, and appeared to be praying, so I tiptoed down the aisle, and slid into the pew immediately behind him.

We sat there. He kept praying, and I kept sitting. After a couple of minutes, I began to get fidgety. I mean, dammit, he had asked me to meet him here, so why did he choose to go into a marathon prayer-session? Could I interrupt him? I mean, what if he'd just established contact, so to speak, and along I came and broke the connection?

I picked up a copy of the Anglican Book of Common Prayer from the little shelf in front of me. Not the new prayer-book, you understand, the one where God is bit of a wimp, and full of forgiveness, but the old one, where — to cite but one instance of celestial tough-mindedness — "the wrath of God is upon him that removeth a neighbour's landmark." I wondered what they had replaced that with in the new version, and reflected that I would probably never know. We don't go for new versions in Bosky Dell.

This was getting ridiculous. I decided to draw the Rev.'s attention to my presence, even at the risk of a lightning bolt.

I coughed.

No response.

I whispered, "Psst . . . Rev. Wylie."

No response.

Finally, I reached out and touched the back of his shoulder, very gently.

"Psst . . . Rev. Wylie, it's. . . . Yikes!"

The "Yikes" was not a whisper, more of a blood-curdling shriek. When I touched his shoulder, the Rev. kind of slumped sideways, and then forward, and then, with a dull thump, toppled completely off the bench and onto the floor. To leap out of my pew, open the door to the box pew, and slide inside didn't take me a minute. Call it ten minutes. I knew what I was going to find, didn't I? Another corpse. I thought, briefly, of nipping quietly out the door, but something told me that leaving behind a note to explain that I'd decided to move to another country and take up another life would not establish my innocence. I sat there, trying to decide what to do.

I looked down, for inspiration, at the Book of Common Prayer in my hands, which informed me that "Predestination to Life is the everlasting purpose of God, whereby (before the foundations of the world were laid) he hath

132

constantly decreed by his counsel secret to us to deliver from curse and damnation those whom he hath chosen," a thing I hadn't known before. So, you see, the day wasn't entirely wasted. I picked up the leaflet from the previous Sunday and stared at that. I learned that life is abuzz with excitement these days in the Mother's Guild. Mary Miller, to name but one fascinating incident, recently reported on "Some Aspects of Christian Mothering" to an appreciative Wednesday evening audience.

Finally, I worked up the nerve to get up and go round to the front of the Flannery pew. Gingerly, I opened the door to the pew — it squeaked, causing me to shed about ten years' growth — quietly, I eased onto the seat and bent down to look at the body. Then I jumped about seven feet in the air as a voice in my ear said, "What the hell is this?"

It was Hanna, of course, large as life and twice as bumptious.

"Good God, Carlton," she said, "is that another body?"

I gurgled. I pointed.

"Well, well," said Hanna, "look at that. It's another one of those thingies, Carlton. Right in the middle of his breadbasket."

Whatever happened to the girls who fainted at the sight of blood? You remember them; they were wispy little things, and when anything went awry, they sank to the ground with a soft moan and the big, strong he-man had to step in and take over. I, for one, miss them.

"Hey," Hanna went on, "this must come from the same set of your Dad's that the other one came from, the one that did in what's his name . . . Carlton, what was his name?"

"Ernie," I gasped. "Ernie . . . Struthers."

"There, I knew you could talk. Looked for a while there as if the cat had got your tongue. Well?"

"Well, what?"

"Is that one of your Dad's punch pinners, or whatever?"

"Pin punch. It's called a pin punch."

"Is it called one of the Withers's pin punches?"

Naturally, what else? There were the condemning initials on the handle, staring up at me.

"Yes," I croaked.

"Well," said the young blight to civilization, "I certainly look forward to seeing how you talk yourself out of this one, Withers. It should be quite a treat."

"You mean, you don't think I did this one, either?"

The look was full of scorn.

"Carlton," she said, "I remembered this morning that your car was out of action, so I drove out to give you a lift.I was driving along the street here, heading for your place, when I saw you go into the church, which seemed funny to me, so I hung around and looked in the window. There you were, sitting in a pew, and there was the minister, in front of you. You sat there and sat there, and I didn't want to interrupt. I thought maybe you were having a little religious chat. Getting straight on supralapsarianism or something. So I waited. After a while, I saw you poke the Rev. on the shoulder and him fall over. And still you sat there, apparently deep in thought. So I decided to come in, and here you are, bending over the body."

"And?. . ."

"Well, heck, Carlton, you might just as well have a sign around your neck saying 'I Done It.' Which means, of course, that you didn't."

For once, her contrary nature was working on my behalf.

"Thank you for that vote of confidence."

"Think nothing of it. Whether the police will take the same view, of course, is another matter."

While she talked, Hanna was peering around the late Rev., not touching him, but looking as if she wanted to.

"What are you looking for?"

"I dunno. Clues."

"Well, you don't just find clues sort of strewn around the corpse like. . ."

"Aha!" Hanna suddenly leaned down and plucked something from the floor, which she immediately flourished under my nose. "What's this, know-it-all, if it isn't a clue?"

She held in her hand one of Ray Furlinger's mottoed pens, of the type used by C. Withers of the Silver Falls *Lancer*. I groaned.

"Why are you groaning?"

I explained.

"Well, it's a plant," said Hanna. "That's obvious. Anyone could get hold of one of these; you probably strew them all over the place, don't you?"

I nodded. There were fifty pens in a box, but only about half of them worked, so I tended to carry half a dozen or so in my pockets. I had pretty well broadcast them throughout the village by now, an ink-stained Johnny Appleseed.

"You're right, this pen being here doesn't mean a thing," I told Hanna. "I may have dropped it here myself, just now."

She replied, in her usual cheerful tones, "Of course, I doubt if that's what the cops will say when you give it to them."

"Am I going to give it to them?"

"Of course you are. This is evidence in a murder investigation. Two murder investigations, now. You didn't do either of the killings, we both know that. But if you start supressing evidence..."

"You don't think I could just kind of oil out the door and pretend nothing happened?"

"Nope."

"Wait for someone else to find the remains?"

"You blew that hope when you let out that shriek. Doors have been banging for the past five minutes and, unless I miss my guess, there will be a lynch mob here any second now."

"We do not lynch people at Bosky Dell."

"Tell them that." She gestured behind her.

I looked up and sure enough there was a gaggle — call it two gaggles — of people, one at each of the doors at the top of the aisles. There was a fair amount of stirring and muttering, as if they were trying to pick out a tree and calculate the length of rope required.

I waved. Not a cheery wave, kind of a floppy wrist-bend.

"It's the Reverend Wylie," I explained. "He's been stabbed."

Arthur Blenkins, the retired stockbroker, pushed through the mob. He was wearing a hat, which he took off.

"Stabbed, was he?" queried Arthur.

"Yes."

"That's terrible."

"Yes."

"Jesus in a jelly-jar," interrupted Hanna, to whom our slower-moving rural ways are obviously a trial, "don't stand here blabbing. Somebody go and call the police."

Arthur answered in an injured tone, "No need to be offensive. No need to call the police, either," he added, "there's a couple of them over at Carlton's place right now."

EIGHTEEN

HANNA AND I walked, quickly, but without vulgar rushing, along Forest Road, heading back for my cottage. Along the way, I told her — it had slipped my mind, earlier — about the sunglasses I had found on the couch the other night.

"Boy," she said, "this case has more plants in it than a greenhouse. Has Hanson given it to the cops yet?"

"I guess so, he was in the OPP office right after I spoke to him."

She nodded with satisfaction. "It'll keep those yo-yos busy, anyway," she said.

"Just give them one more reason to suspect me."

"Not this time. The fact that you turned the thing over to Hanson clears you. If it was anything genuine, all you had to do was ditch it."

That was true, and helpful; it gave me something positive to think about as I tottered off to meet the cops once more. Behind us came the gaggles from the church, muttering to each other and telling each other, no doubt, that they had always known that Carlton Withers was a wrong 'un. We made up the largest parade the village had seen since Cosmo Furlow, our radical chic lawyer, staged an anti-nuclear march a couple of years ago, and very prudently provided free drinks for all the marchers.

As soon as my cottage came into sight, I knew that something else had gone terribly wrong. All the lights were on, in broad daylight, which was wrong, but not terribly wrong. What was terribly wrong was that every-thing inside, to the extent that I could see inside the cot-tage, was neat, while the front lawn was bedecked with what looked like the midden pile from a medieval village. Or, to put it another way, all my most precious possessions were dumped on the grass, while the interior of the old homestead appeared almost nude. The Dutch break-front dresser, standing in the dining-room, and normally decently dressed in clothes, plates, tennis rackets, and the other debris of the busy life of a man about town, stood positively naked, except for a fringe of cake plates — my mother's collection — which had not seen the light of day for months. The curtains, which are normally hitched together with a large safety pin (to narrow Mrs. Golden's view inside), hung neatly on each side of the living-room window, and the living-room itself, instead of groaning under its proper load of blankets, old fruit, decaying dinners, books, newspapers, magazines, and other assorted oddments, contained instead nothing but the usual collection of furniture and an unusual collection of two upright bodies: Detectives Smiley and Thuggy.

The buggers had invaded my privacy.

I went through the front door, baying like a bassett-hound, but Smiley stopped me with a raised hand. It contained a search warrant. Apparently the lads had been through the place and decided — not that I could blame them — that the heave-and-scoop method was the best way to dig out my secrets. It hadn't taken them long.

"Well done, men," I told them. "I understand Maids Unlimited is looking for a few recruits. I'd be happy to recommend you."

Thurston grunted. "Read the warrant."

I sat down in an old armchair. It was green, a fact that I had forgotten — out of sight, out of mind — and read the warrant. It seemed to be in order — but how would I know if it weren't? I looked around the cottage, which also seemed to be in order, for a change.

"So, having nothing else to do with your time, you decided to come out and do my house-cleaning. Find anything?" I asked Smiley.

"Just this," Thuggy replied, "we found this, buried in the junk on the chair right where you're sitting." And he held up a black notebook, one of those little numbers you can pick up in any five-and-dime store for about a buck. (That's why they call them five-and-dime stores.) I'd never seen it before. I'm still working on my collection of telephone memo pads from Ray Furlinger's.

"Don't come the innocent with me," Thuggy rasped, "you know as well as I do what it is."

"But I don't. I've never seen it before; I swear it."

"It's Ernie Struthers's record book," explained Smiley.

"His record book? Records of what?"

But I knew, didn't I?

"His blackmailing racket," Thuggy replied, with grim satisfaction. "I guess you found it on him when you killed him, and decided you might take over the business, eh?"

There was a silence. Hanna looked at me. I looked at the floor. Hanna said, "Carlton . . ."

I looked at the floor some more.

"I think you'd better tell them about the minister," Hanna said.

Actually, the shock of having my home invaded had driven the late Rev. right out of my mind.

"What about him, then?" demanded Thuggy.

I gave him a winning smile. "Gosh, Detective Thurston, you're not going to believe this . . ."

"Try me."

'You know the, um, Rev. Mr. Ephraim Wylie?"

"The late," Hanna put in, "Rev. Mr. Ephraim Wylie."

"No," said Thuggy, "should I?"

"Oh, yes, yes indeed, Detective Thurston," I said. "He was a fine, fine man. One of my dearest friends."

"But now he's dead, right?" asked Smiley.

"Well, yes, in a manner of speaking, he is."

"Recently?" Thuggy wanted to know.

"Quite recently. As a matter of fact, today. About an hour ago."

"Oh ho," said Thuggy, and it was an "Oh ho" full of suspicion and menace. "And how did he come to die, this Rev. Whatshisname?"

"Wylie. Ephraim Wylie. He was, more or less, what you might call . . . stabbed."

"Oh *ho*," said Thuggy. "And I suppose there was a tool

139

just like the other tool from your Dad's set stuck into him?"

"More or less, well, yes."

"And I suppose you're going to tell us you didn't do this one, either?"

"Officers, I swear to you, I didn't."

I said it with the utmost sincerity, but my words were greeted with what I can only call a high degree of scepticism. Hanna put forward her view that things looked so black for me I must, perforce, be innocent, but the policemen, as she had foreseen, were not convinced. She also introduced the ballpoint pen clue.

"It probably fell out of the killer's pocket during the struggle," said Thuggy nastily.

"But Carlton had no reason to want Rev. Wylie dead," Hanna pleaded, and then rather wrecked the thing by asking me, "Did you, Carlton?"

"No, of course not," I said. "He was a friend of mine, and a friend of my father's."

"So was Ernie Struthers," grumbled Thuggy as he whipped out the handcuffs and did his duty.

NINETEEN

THE LONE CELL in the OPP headquarters at Silver Falls is cold, small, cramped, and damp, with two tiny metal cots, a sink, and one overhead light constituting the combined amenities. It possessed an even crummier ambience than the interrogation room upstairs. It smelled of old urine, stale socks, and Saturday night drunks, who are the usual guests. I was a celebrity. The last time the Silver Falls rozzers had made a really big arrest was back in 1967, when a local woman carelessly spiced up her husband's hot chocolate with a dash of arsenic. Molly, this lady's name was, and a cruel fate had condemned her to marry a man named Jolly. He called her, "My dolly, Molly Jolly," which may have been why she slipped the poison into his bedtime drink. She got off. This was in the days when Canada still hanged people, and no jury was going to hang a woman just because she wasn't such a hot cook; but she did spend several nights in the hoosegow, which was probably the last time it got a good cleaning. My cell, not to dwell on the matter, was a playground for cockroaches and other multi-legged beasts, and the walls were inscribed with slogans not fit for Sunday school. I bore up bravely. My own cottage, when you came right down to it, had kind of eased me into this sort of living.

I was hauled out of my cell for a couple of hours of True Confessions in the interrogation room by Thuggy and Smiley, with Mutt and Jeff glowering on the sidelines — they had clearly been hoping to work me over themselves — and I was allowed one telephone call. I naturally decided to call my favourite local law firm, which rejoices in the name Wright and Wong, Barristers and Solicitors, etc. (They are my favourite local firm, but not my favourite law firm in all the world; that one is to be found in a village in Suffolk, England, according to a piece I read in the *Globe and Mail*, and is called Delay and Fibb.) However, I didn't get either Mr. Wright or Mr. Wong; instead, I found myself connected to an answering machine, which invited me, in a cheery voice, to leave a message at the sound of the beep. The message I left may have given offence; in any event, I never heard from them.

By the time the Prisoner Withers had been properly processed, with fingerprints and all, and a new statement taken — superseding the one collected during my last visit to this home away from home — the dinner hour had come and gone, but not a morsel of food did I get.

So I lay on the flat metal strips which a munificent constabulary kids itself constitute springs and a mattress, hauled up the two woollen blankets that make up the bed linen — scratchy, but serviceable — and settled down for a cozy, if hungry, spell of sorting things out in my own mind. One new and puzzling piece of information had come to me, via Sgt. Smiley, before I was ushered into the slammer. The police had taken the bit of cloth attached to the Rotary pin Hanna had found in the Flannery pew over to the morgue, to see if it came from Ernie's jacket. It did not. Then where in the hell did it come from?

I would no doubt have worked this out if I hadn't fallen asleep in the midst of my contemplations.

I woke up several hours later, when Charlie Passenden, one of our town employees, came clomping down the hall. Charlie combines the task of looking after the police cell, when it has customers, with janitorial work at the municipal building, and is known, in consequence, as Jail-Pail Passenden. He it was who had told me that I was a celebrity, when he ushered me to my cell in the first place. Not in so many words, but he called me "Mr. Withers," when he has never called me anything but Carlton down at the O.K. Cafe, and he murmured shyly, as he clanged the door to behind me, "You're my second killer," in a proud sort of way. I guess Charlie had stood on guard over Molly Jolly, and he knew that he was due to be a hit down at the O.K., describing to the crowd how the guilty man looked.

On his reappearance after my nap, he had another customer in tow, who smelled like a distillery and looked like the wrath of God, and turned out to be Vern Campbell.

"Company for you, Mr. Withers," Charlie explained. "Come on, Vern, and for Pete's sake, this time, if you're going to be sick, do it in the sink." Vern shuffled in, looked up at me, slyly, staggered over to the other cot, and slumped down on it.

Just what I needed, someone to talk to. And then it occurred to me — have I been watching too much television lately? — it occurred to me that there was something strange about Vern's presence here, right at this moment. It was barely eleven p.m., for one thing, and Vern doesn't usually reach a state of bliss until about midnight. Besides, it was Friday night, when everyone knows the proper time to get so tiddled they have to arrest you is Saturday night. Vern would not be careless in such a matter of etiquette. And, why throw him in jail, anyway, merely for getting drunk? Just falling down on the street won't get you into the slammer in Silver Falls; a single-cell town has to be particular in these matters. You have to smash up furniture in the beverage room, or make a lewd suggestion to the wrong kind of female walking down the main street, i.e., anyone with the rank of member of the Rebekah Lodge or the Junior League, or a relative of someone on the town council. Generally, Vern was just laid to rest down by the canal when he got too sozzled, and allowed to sleep it off. Could it be that he had been sloshed with rye on the outside, and inserted in my cell as a police stool-pigeon? It could.

"What are you in for, Carlton?" mumbled Vern.

"Socage in fief," I replied, speaking loudly, so his tape-recorder, if he had one, could pick it up.

"Huh?"

Silence.

"I'm in," Vern decided to try again, "for drunk 'n' disorderly."

"What did you do, Vern, make a pass at Mrs. Wembley?"

Vern chuckled, then suddenly grew serious. He also leaned forward, getting the tape-recorder out front, I guess.

" 'Course not," he said, "wunnerful woman."

This clinched it. Mrs. Wembley, known to all as Wombat Wembley, is the mayor's wife, and if Vern, in a bad imitation-drunk accent, was saying nice things about her, he was talking for the record.

"C'mon, Carlton," he wheedled, "whaddidyado?"

"Nothing." I leaned forward to speak directly into Vern's chest, where the tape-recorder seemed to be. "The police seem to think I had some connection with the deaths of Ernie Struthers and the Rev. Wylie, but I didn't."

Vern was looking, if anything, even slyer than before. "Oh," he said, "they think you did it?"

"They think I did it, but of course I didn't."

"Too bad."

"How do you mean, too bad? Too bad I don't go around pin-punching people? Or, too bad they think — quite wrongly, Vern — they think I go around committing mayhem?"

"I forget," said Vern.

The swift give-and-take was obviously too for much him, and he lapsed into silence for a bit. Then, glancing with a cunning grin at me out of one corner of his eye, and giving a passable imitation of a man from whom no one, ever, would buy a used car, he said, "Did you do it, Carlton? You can tell me."

"I can tell you, and I do tell you, Vern, that I was," and here I paused to add emphasis, "NOT," another big pause, "in any way responsible for these deaths. And," I added, "that's the truth."

Silence ensued, broken, shortly thereafter, by the wall-trembling snores of a Campbell without a conscience.

The next morning, about seven a.m., Jail-Pail reappeared, and told Vern the judge was ready to see him now — which could not be the case because, as we know, no judge in the nation rises before nine a.m. I smiled a secret smile as Vern was led off, no doubt, to report to the cops that he had failed in his mission to worm a confession out of me. Foiled by the superior cunning of a seasoned reporter.

A couple of hours later, I woke again, feeling flea-bitten and hungry but in good spirits, and when Mutt and Jeff, the local Ontario Provincial Police's notion of a dynamic duo, rolled around, I greeted them cheerily.

"Come to apologize, have you, boys?" I chirruped, but Mutt — the long one, remember? — gave me a sour look and Jeff extracted one of those tiny tape-recorders you can buy, these days, in any electronics store, from his jacket pocket.

"Want you to listen to something," he said.

"Fine," I replied. "Always happy to help the police with their inquiries."

This proved what I had so cannily suspected; the cops, who know no shame, had sicked Vern onto me, probably in return for turning a blind eye to the Campbell brothers' free-enterprise liquor operation out in the woods. They were undoubtedly ticked off because Thuggy and Smiley had been called in from Toronto to solve the murders, and hoped to pull a swifty, before I baffled them by refusing to cough up a confession. I smiled, complacently.

Jeff punched a button on the tape-recorder, and out came the unmistakable tones of Michael Jackson telling somebody, with the accompaniment of a lot of drums and horns, that he was bad, bad, bad. Jeff cursed, stopped the tape, flipped over the cassette, and punched the button again. This time he got it right, and we heard the throaty tones of Vern Campbell asking what I was in for, and self telling him for socage in fief. Then came our little exchange about Mrs. Wembley, and I was smiling and thinking what saps these leadheads were, wasting the public's funds on tape, when we suddenly came to a change in the program.

Vern asked me, once again, "Whaddidyado?" and I replied, "Ernie Struthers's death. . . . I did it."

Jeff gave me a big smile, and the tape rolled on. There was Vern, once more, assuring me I could tell him, and self replying, "I was responsible for these deaths. . . . And that's the truth."

The swine had doctored Vern's recording. Hell, I'd even made it easier for them, by my dramatic pauses. All it took was a razor blade, quick fingers, and a little scotch tape to rejoin the splices; then they just re-recorded it onto a new tape, and it came out as the Withers's confession.

I was stunned. "You rigged the tape," I told Jeff. "But it won't do any good; it's not admissible in court." I hadn't learned much in my days on the court beat, but I had learned that much.

"No," Jeff admitted, "it's not; but it will keep you in jail until we can make the case against you air-tight. Oh, by the way," he added, "we've had a little chat with Ephraim Wylie's widow. She said that her husband was very agitated about something just before he made that telephone call to you. He'd been out for a walk past your place, according to Mrs. Wylie, and seen something that disturbed him. At first he didn't know whether he should talk to you about it, she said, but then he decided that he must. Which is why he called you."

"He didn't tell her what it was about?"

"No, you're lucky there. All he said was something like — Mrs. Wylie isn't sure of the exact words — 'Carlton must have some explanation.' Interesting, eh?"

And with that, the two cops drifted out, leaving me to my thoughts, which were considerably darker than they had been before. They couldn't use the tape, that much was clear, but the fact that they went to the trouble to get it showed that they thought, they really thought, by God, that I had done in Ernie Struthers and then, presumably because he had found out about it, spiked the Rev., into the bargain. Who could blame them? Well, I could. Silly flatfeet, why didn't they go out and catch the real murderer, and leave me alone?

Why were they so anxious to nail me, anyway? Well, I knew the answer to that, didn't I? I was the obvious suspect; ergo, I did it; ergo, any little tricks they could pull that might result in a confession were okay. When I remembered the cops who had machine-gunned a travelling salesman in a Sherbrooke motel because they thought, on very little evidence, that he might be an escaping robber, I realized that Mutt and Jeff were, if anything, models of decorum.

Jail-Pail appeared a few minutes later, with my breakfast — an egg-in-a-bun concoction from the O.K. Cafe, burned to a crisp and containing, as I discovered too late, when I had already bitten into it, a note from Belinda Huntingdon. It said, "Hi, Carlton, don't g---" I had bitten off whatever came after this, presumably, "give up hope." Then there was a crude drawing of a file, suitable for zipping through jail bars, and a scrawled, "Love, Belinda." The note cheered me up again; not only was it a sign that somebody out there still cared, it tasted just about as good as the rest of breakfast. I was still chewing on it, both physically and metaphorically, when Jail-Pail returned.

"Time for court," he told me, as he opened the cell door and fastened handcuffs on my wrists.

"Who's the judge?"

"Carlton, it's Saturday morning. There's only one judge on Saturday morning."

"Tinkerbell?"

"Yep," said Jail-Pail, and I tottered off to meet my doom.

TWENTY

THE CANADIAN SYSTEM of justice is acknowledged by all the best legal minds to be one of the finest in the world. This ought to give us some concern about the legal systems of the world, because one of the minor drawbacks of the Canadian system is that it tends to throw up onto the benches of the land the flotsam and jetsam of the political system. It has been said, correctly, that in the United States, they elect their judges, while in Canada, we defeat them. The prime requisite for high legal office is to make a run for politics at the behest of one of the party bigshots and flunk the test. Next time there is a vacancy on a court somewhere, you will reap your reward. This would not be so bad except that, once installed, a judge cannot be removed, except for heinous crimes and misdemeanours. Mere incompetence doesn't count. Thus, Herman Fotheringham Tinker, back in the dim and distant past, ran, and failed, for the Conservative cause in Bellingham County and was, in due course, elevated to the bench, where he remained, dumber than a doorpost, and now, to add a dash of piquancy to the proceedings, deaf as a doorpost, with it. He won't wear a hearing aid, and can't hear most of what goes on in court. So they try to confine the damage by giving him the Saturday morning drunk court to handle, where all that is required of him is to bang his gavel at a signal from Cyril Filmore, the court clerk, who actually runs the proceedings, and bellow, "Guilty; fifty dollars or ten days."

He would take my bail hearing, and it did not look good. When I came into the musty old courtroom, with Jail-Pail hovering at my side, fearful, once he had de-cuffed me, that I would make a break for it with consequent ruin to his reputation down at the O.K. Cafe, I discovered that I was the only person in the prisoner's dock. No sign of Vern, or any other drunks. Hanna was in the body of the courtroom, and so was Hanson. There were no other spectators. Hanson nodded and smiled. Hanna called out, "Hi, Carlton," and got a glare from the sheriff's officer in charge.

"Who's the girl?" Jail-Pail wanted to know, nodding over towards where Hanna sat wearing, if you can believe it, a skirt and blouse.

"My moll," I told him. He looked gratified.

Mutt and Jeff were on hand, but not the Toronto cops, Smiley and Thuggy. (Hanna told me later that they had heard about the doctored tapes and wanted no part of that operation; indeed, they had already filed a complaint with their superiors.) Also on hand was the Crown Attorney, Stanley "The Slammer" Spencer, who was widely known to be much-bullied at home by his wife, and who got his own back by taking it out on the dregs of humanity who passed through his hands in court.

In due course, we went through the All-Rise, and Tinker-bell entered stage left, swishing his robes and hefting his gavel. He wore a befuddled expression, but that didn't mean much; he always wears a befuddled expression.

He nodded at Cyril and then looked down to the lawyer's bench, just beneath his own. There was, to the astonishment of all, a defence lawyer there. Drunk charges, the normal Saturday fare, don't usually draw defence counsel, since the fee is bound to exceed Tinkerbell's usual fifty-dollar fine, but this morning, we had Parker Whitney, a member, as I knew from my newspaper work, of the local bar. All the local bars, come to that, but the one that concerns us here is the bar of Queen's Bench. Parker is the counsel for the Silver Falls *Lancer*. He is not very expensive, which is why the *Lancer* hires him, and not very good. I guess he hadn't been to see me in jail because that might have cost extra. When the judge nodded at him, Parker rose in his place.

"I represent the accused, Your Honour," he explained, and added, "at the request of the Silver Falls *Lancer*." Tinkerbell banged his gavel.

"Fifty dollars or ten days," he said.

"Take it, Carlton," shouted Hanna, "you'll never get a better offer."

Fortunately, Tinkerbell didn't hear this, and merely muttered "What, what, what, what?" And then, for good measure, "What?"

Cyril turned around and whispered in his ear. Waste of time, of course. So he bellowed, "Not drunk, Your Honour. Murder."

"Murder? Bless my soul!" Tinkerbell whipped out a pair of glasses, from somewhere in his robes, and gave me the once over. "Why," he said, astounded, "it's Carlton Withers! Isn't it? Is that you, Carlton?"

"Yessir, Your Honour, it's me all right."

"Carlton," and he wagged a judicial finger at me, "who have you gone and murdered? Not your poor father, I hope?"

"No, sir."

"That's good. Carlton's father," Tinkerbell explained to Cyril, "splendid fellow. We play golf together."

They had, too, at one time. My father was no snob, and would even play golf with a judge. Tinkerbell was almost as bad at the game as Dad, and cheated just as blatantly, so they got along splendidly.

"He's dead, Your Honour," I explained.

"He is? Carlton, you should be ashamed of yourself."

Stanley Spencer, representing the awful majesty of the Crown, leapt up and came up to the bench and between Cyril and Stanley, they managed to get the judge on track. I hadn't killed my father, hadn't killed anybody, come to that, according to my story — Stanley conveyed, with this information, a strong sniff of disbelief — but the police had charged me with the death of Ernest Charleston Struthers and Ephraim Elias Wylie, D.D., the names on the charge sheet in front of His Honour.

Tinkerbell turned to me. "Well, I am relieved to hear that, Carlton. You didn't kill your father."

"No, sir."

"Just these other chaps. One of them is D.D.; what does that mean?"

"Doctor of Divinity."

"Eh?"

Once more, the Crown Attorney intervened, poor sap.

"Doctor," he bellowed.

The judge frowned. "You want a doctor, Mr. Spencer? Are you ill?"

"No, Your Honour."

"Then why do you want a doctor?"

"I DON'T," yammered The Slammer.

"Then why ask for one?" snapped Tinkerbell, with the air of one who has pinned a witness in cross-examination. "Silly fellow," he explained to me, "asks for a doctor in court. Then says he doesn't want one after all."

The clerk got up and wrote something for the judge.

"Ah, I see," he said, "this fellow you killed, Carlton, the second one, he was a minister."

"Sir, I didn't kill anyone." I was looking straight at him, so I guess he could read my lips.

A look of real cunning came over the old buzzard's face. "But one of the ones you didn't kill, Carlton, was a minister."

"Yes, sir."

"Well, I'm glad we've got that straight. All this talk of doctors, just a waste of the court's time. So, your position, Carlton, is that you didn't kill anyone?"

"Yes, sir."

He was puzzled. "But it says here that you did."

"No, sir, I didn't."

"But these chaps are dead?"

"Yes, sir, they're dead all right."

"Well, that's that, then. Carlton, you be sure to give your father my best."

There was no suitable reply to that one.

At this point, Spencer decided to try, once more, to take charge. He explained, in outraged bellows, that this was a bail hearing, and that the Crown's position was that the Accused — he glared at me — was charged with a Most Serious Crime, to wit, murder, and it was the Crown's view that he should be held in jail, without bail, until his trial.

"We have no objection to that," said Parker Whitney. Thank you, Tommy Macklin, I told myself, and added, aloud, "Well, I have an objection, Your Honour."

"Well, in that case, accused will remain in custody until. . . . You do?"

Apparently, he had heard me.

Tinkerbell looked down at the lawyers. "He doesn't want to stay in jail," he told them.

"They seldom do, Your Honour," The Slammer explained.

There was a bit of a hubbub at the lawyers' bench, as the two cops huddled with The Slammer. Filling him in, no doubt, on the incriminating tape-recording.

So it proved; Jeff produced his little tape-player from his pocket, and there was much whispering to and fro. Tinkerbell didn't seem to mind, just sat in his throne and picked his nose for a bit, until The Slammer got up and announced that he had a bit of tape he thought His Honour might wish to hear in the privacy of His Chambers.

This brought a raised eyebrow from Tinkerbell. "Tape, what sort of tape? Nothing salacious, I hope?"

"No, sir, but the Crown takes the position that this tape, while not admissible in court, might be heard by Your Honour, off the record, as to the question of bail."

Well, you couldn't do that, even I knew that, so I looked down at Parker Whitney, who smiled and said, "We have no objection, Your Honour."

Of course, it didn't work. They all went to the judge's office and came back about five minutes later. Tinkerbell looked more befuddled than ever.

"Played some music, Carlton," he told me in a loud whisper that bounced off the back wall of the courtroom, when we got settled down again. "Michael Jackson, of all things." The judge was obviously more up-to-date than I thought. Then he peered over his glasses and laid down the law.

"The Crown's position in this matter is that the accused, Carlton Withers, ought to be bound over without bail until his trial on a charge of the murder of . . . what were those fellows' names, Clerk? One of them was a doctor, I remember. Say, this other one, Ernest Charleston Struthers. . . that isn't Ernie Struthers, down at the hardware store, is it? It is? Well, I guess it was bound to happen one day. You know what he charged me for three nails the other week? However, that is neither here nor there. In any event, the Crown believes this is a case for the utmost caution, and Defence Counsel does not object.

"However, the prisoner does object, and I must say, I see his point. Filthy jail, you know, gentlemen. The Court is personally acquainted with the accused, who is a friend of my daughter Amelia."

By golly, I'd forgotten about that. Amelia Tinker, as homely a bird as roams uncaged, used to help me with my algebra, and I took her to the Junior Prom one year, when it was clear that it was me or nobody, and I took a lot of kidding for it, at the time. The truth is, we both had a nice evening, and here I was, years later, receiving a second benison for that night.

"It is the Court's view," Tinkerbell went on, "that the accused is not likely to leave the jurisdiction, and is not a public danger, and I am accordingly binding him over on a recognizance of twenty-five thousand dollars, to await his trial."

And he glared down at the lawyers, and banged his gavel.

It was a show of faith, I guess, but not much use. Where was I going to find twenty-five thousand dollars? I waved a sad farewell to Hanna and Hanson, and Jail-Pail slapped the handcuffs back on my wrists, and led me back to the jail.

TWENTY-ONE

I OWED MY freedom, when it came, and it was only tempo-
rary and on sufferance, to Loophole DeLeonardis, who rep-
resents Silvio Developments. He arrived on Monday
morning with a bond for twenty-five thousand dollars. He
came not a moment too soon for my liking. I had been
playing cribbage with Jail-Pail Passenden for most of the
weekend, and I was holding his IOUs for $1.65, which he
was beginning to resent, with frequent references to the
criminal element in games of chance. I had eaten seven of
Belinda's burnt offerings — I think some of them were
hamburgers, it was hard to tell, and the rest fried-egg sandwiches, complete with cheering notes — and my stomach,
even hardened as it was by own cooking, was sending complaints up to head office.

Loophole suddenly appeared at my jail-cell door, right in
the middle of a crib-game, with Hanna Klovack frisking
about him like a damn lamb.

"Here we are, Carlton," she carolled. "The U.S. Marines
have arrived. This is Mr. DeLeonardis."

"We know each other," said Loophole and, "Morning,
Loophole," I said.

"Your name is Loophole?" Hanna asked.

A steely smile from the lawyer. "It's by way of a sobri-
quet, Miss Klovack," he explained. "Actually, I take it as a
compliment. My proper name is Anthony."

"Well, be that as it may," said Hanna, "Carlton, this nice
man has just posted your bail, courtesy of Dominic Silvio.
Which is too bad, in a way, since we both had Silvio marked
down as a possibility for the murders, but I guess it wouldn't
make much sense to frame someone and then put up his
bail money, would it?"

I said I didn't think so.

"Actually, just between us," and Hanna leaned up close to

the cell bars, "I went to see Silvio when I realized what a hash that other mouthpiece was making of things, and told him that it would be a smart idea to raise your bail. I told him you might help him out later, by writing some nice things about his crummy development. We all know you won't, don't we, Carlton? But no need to blab that around right now. So," she straightened up and resumed her normal voice, "here we all are. Isn't this the place where they strike the leg-irons off?"

Jail-Pail, once he had read the bits of paper Loophole showed him, drew out his key and opened the cell door, and I stepped out into the hall, my debt to society paid, or, at least, translated into a mortgage. Hanna stuck her hand out.

"Congratulations, prisoner," she said. "Decided to go straight, have you?"

I stepped inside the proffered hand and clasped her, as the saying goes, to my bosom. Which is not nearly as nice a bosom as her bosom.

"Phew, you stink," she said, which is not one of the great love-lines of all time, but she didn't baff me, as she had on the last occasion when I grabbed her.

Outside, we were accosted by Smiley and Thuggy. Smiley smiled; Thuggy told me all the unpleasant things he'd do to me if I tried to scarper. Furthest thing from my mind.

We went down to the *Lancer*, where I conferred, briefly, with Harry Hibbs, who had put together the week's issue — most of which I had written long since — in my absence. Tommy Macklin was lurking in the background, and, the moment he was sure all the real work was done, he came stomping by the desk and, without stopping, or even looking up, grunted out of the corner of his mouth, "Oh, Withers, I'm glad to see you're out of jail. I was just about to send down a messenger. You're fired."

Well, I guess I should have seen it coming. The staff of the *Lancer* does not get itself arrested, however blamelessly, and remain the staff. You get dumped. It makes the advertisers feel safe. Hanna went to bat for me, following Tommy back to his office to hector him — not noisily, but with a kind of quiet determination. When he remained unmoved, she handed in her own portfolio. She came back and told me what she had done, and I told her she was an idiot and she told me to mind my own damn business. Then she told me to move out of the way, sat down at my computer and typed in, all in capital letters, TOMMY MACKLIN IS A GOLD-PLATED ASSHOLE, and sent that as an internal memo to everyone on staff, even though, as I pointed out, everybody already knew.

When we came out of the office, *Marchepas*, which was still sitting beside the football field, started, the filthy thing, so there went my chance to get Hanna to drive me out to Bosky Dell, to take up the matter of where we went from here with her at — how shall I put it? — close quarters. I got out of the car, leaving it running — there was always the chance that it would stall and quit again — and I went around to where Hanna was waiting on the sidewalk, with her arms crossed — no trespassing, I recognized the sign. I put out one hand onto her arm and tugged it, gently, but it remained in place.

"I suppose you'll be going back to the city," I said.

"I suppose so."

"Nothing to keep you here."

"No. Nothing."

"I should tell you that Tommy Macklin has fired me about twenty times in the last nine years. He usually gets over it and hires me back again."

"He probably can't find anybody else dumb enough to keep working for him."

"There is that."

"Just the same, I wouldn't go back to work for him, even if you would. He's a treacherous little creep."

"Aren't all managing editors?"

"Not all. Some of them are treacherous big creeps."

"Wouldn't you like to stay around and see how all this comes out?"

"Oh, I shall follow your future career with interest, Mr.

Withers. If they get you on a double murder, no doubt I'll read about it in the papers."

"Not in the Silver Falls *Lancer*, you won't."

"I guess not."

"Say," I said, "why don't you come out to Bosky Dell, and I'll fix us some lunch? I'll bet you've never tasted Bean-a-ghetti."

"What's that?"

"An old Bosky Dell recipe. One can of beans, one can of spaghetti, mix, heat, and serve."

"Sounds lethal."

"It is."

"I think not. Carlton?"

"Uh-huh?"

"I can't get involved again, you know. Not for quite a while."

"I know."

"You want to get involved, don't you?"

"Well, I thought it might help to pass the time, before they put me back in the slammer."

"Yes, well, I'm sorry."

"So am I." I smiled, my best Ronald Colman bitter smile. "Now, who's going to help me with the mystery of the newspaper clipping?"

"Oh, that. That's solved."

"It is? You did it?"

"That's what I was doing down in Toronto. I thought it might be useful to check out the rest of the newspaper that clipping came from, so I went down and did a quick search in the Toronto *Star* library."

"You did? Did you find out anything new?"

"Well, I did and I didn't."

"Hanna, you're driving me crazy."

"Yes, I can see that. Sorry. What happened is that I thought I would learn something new about the clipping by looking in that day's newspaper. I thought, you know, that maybe something had been cut off the bottom or some-thing. But it wasn't."

"So, the whole thing was a waste of time?"

"No, not exactly."

"You found out something else that wasn't in the clipping?"

"Uh-huh."

"Well, what was it?"

"I can't tell you."

"You can't? Why not?"

"State secret. Hey, don't look so glum. I told the cops. It will all come out in the end, I promise."

"Say," I went on, "I've got a great idea. Why don't you bring your notes out to the cottage, and we can go over the whole thing together?"

She smiled. "I don't think that would be such a wise idea, Carlton."

And she turned and walked away.

I got into *Marchepas*, slammed it into gear — it just purred — and drove out to the Dell.

I knew I had to go and see Helen Wylie, Ephraim's widow, to pay my condolences. It also occurred to me, I admit, that she might clear up the matter of her conversation with the police about Ephraim's anxiety to see me, the morning of his death.

When I knocked on the cottage door, a pleasant voice sang out, "It's open," and I went in. I found Helen sitting in the living-room of their cottage, with a photo album in her lap. A pleasant, handsome woman, she held her grief close. I could see she had been crying, but there were no tears now.

"Oh, Carlton, it's you. How nice of you to come. Can I fix you a cup of tea?"

I looked around — the place was awash with tea-cups, recently used. Obviously, the neighbours had been in.

"No, no thanks. I just wanted to tell you how sorry...Ehpraim was such a decent man...How very sorry..."

If I didn't watch it, I was going to be blubbering too.

"Thank you, Carlton. Yes, he was a decent man, wasn't he? Some people thought him not very forceful, and no one ever called him brilliant, but he was kind and tolerant and, as you say, decent."

"Well, I won't trouble you further . . ."

"No, Carlton, don't go." She paused, and gave me a stern look. "There is something I must say to you."

"There is?"

"Carlton, when the police came to see me about Ephraim, I told them this, and I think you ought to know, too."

"Know what?"

"The reason Ephraim called and left a message for you to go and see him at the church, Carlton, is that he was very disturbed by something he saw at your place the other day and he was hoping you could explain it."

"Something he saw at my place? What sort of something?"

"I hardly know how to put this, Carlton. When he came back here, he was most upset."

"Upset? Why?"

"Friday morning, about ten o'clock, Carlton, Ephraim was out for a walk."

"Thinking out a sermon, no doubt."

"I daresay. Anyway, he told me that, instead of going straight down Fourth Street to the public dock, the way he usually does, he took a shortcut, through the path between Third and Fourth. And that's when he saw it."

I didn't want to rush the woman, but I was beginning to get impatient, and perhaps it showed in my voice. "Saw what?"

"Carlton, this is very embarrassing for me."

"Mrs. Wylie, it's maddening for me. What did he see?"

"He saw Nora Eberley, Carlton, sneaking — he said there was no mistaking the furtive way she was moving — sneaking out of your back door."

"I see."

"She looked around, he said, in a very furtive fashion, and just sort of scooted over to Fifth Street."

"Mrs. Wylie, I can explain . . ."

"In the normal course of events, Carlton, this would not be anyone's concern except yours and Nora Eberley's." Pause. "And, just possibly, Hanson Eberley's."

It was cool there, in the darkened cottage, with the curtains drawn. Why then was I sweating?

"Mrs. Wylie, I assure you, it was not what you must be thinking."

"I'm sure that is the case, Carlton. And, in any event, it is not my concern, except as something that may throw a light on Ephraim's death. That is my concern."

"Mrs. Wylie, I give you my oath that I was not even in my place at ten a.m. last Friday."

"You weren't?"

"I was not. I was down on the Third Street dock, swimming and sleeping."

"Well, Carlton, I must say, that is a great relief to me. Then, what do you suppose Nora was doing at your place?"

"Perhaps she came to borrow a cup of sugar?"

Another small smile. "Now, Carlton, she would not go to your place for that, would she?"

"Mrs. Wylie, you say you have already told the police about this?"

"Yes, they came to see me, Friday morning, right after . . ."

She stopped.

"Have you mentioned it to Hanson?"

"No, should I?"

"I think you should. I have far more faith in Hanson than I do in the police, and this is something that not only involves his wife, but is bound to come out anyway."

"I see."

I had, I admit, another and ulterior motive in putting forth this suggestion. The police may or may not have told Hanson about this, but if they hadn't, it would have a different and better sound to it, coming from Helen Wylie. Besides which, I wouldn't have to tell Hanson myself.

She sat there a moment, thinking. "Perhaps you're right," she said. "I'll call him right away."

So, we left it at that, and I drove home, feeling sorry for myself. Had I overlooked one of Nora's flimsy garments in my cleanup the other night? Was that why she had come calling again? If so, she must have found it, or the cops would certainly have been waving it under my nose long before this.

The cottage seemed emptier than it had ever felt to me, except for the dreadful few weeks after my parents' death. With its superficial neatness, thanks to the police search, it no longer even seemed like my own place. Oh, hell, I thought, in for a penny, in for a pound, and I went to work and scrubbed the place from top to bottom, piling out for pickup some of the accumulated garbage of the last two years. Harry Burns, the local collector, was going to get a kick — if not a hernia — out of this.

The Widow Golden turned up at about seven o'clock, with a pot of stew and an apple pie. So we ate that and gabbed a little, and I told her that Hanna Klovack was a pie-faced little fathead, and that it was no doubt a matter of the greatest good fortune that our relationship — what relationship? — had come to an end with no harm done.

"There, there," she said. I had a feeling she didn't believe me.

I went back to work and by about eleven-thirty, the cottage was clean for the first time in two years, and I was all mimsy, and physically pooped. I decided to take a shower. What with the spell in jail and the house-cleaning, I had accumulated an outer layer of grime about four inches thick. I went to work on that with a bar of soap, and, after a while, scrubbing away, I began to feel a trifle better. Crushed, you understand, a veritable toad beneath the harrow, but not a completely mournful toad. In fact, a singing toad. I sang "When Cockle Shells Turn Silver Bells" and "The Water Is Wide," and I was just starting in on "The First Time Ever I Saw Your Face," when I thought I heard, over the sound of the shower, the slamming of the kitchen door.

I switched off the vocal. It was now somewhere close to midnight in a village where lights out is normally about ten o'clock. Johnny Carson doesn't live here. The water — I had been in the shower for quite a time by now — was beginning to cool off a bit. That must have been why my teeth were suddenly chattering together. The kitchen door didn't slam itself; it is one of those old-fashioned jobs, with a heavy spring on it, not likely to get frisky because of a passing breeze. There flashed through my mind that scene from *Psycho* — you know the one — where the killer comes creeping up on the girl in the shower with a knife in his hand and murder in his heart. Well, this was it, all over again.

"Anybody there?" I called out. Let the killer know I'm onto him, see, maybe he'll slink away. No response. I started to sing again, although no one could call it robust, "When roses, gro-o-o-ow, in winter sno-o-o-ow, Then will my love re-tu-ur-ur-urn to me," and then I heard something go Thump! in the bedroom. Which is to say, the room next to the bathroom. That was when I remembered — who can think of everything? — that I had not even bothered to close, much less lock, the bathroom door.

What was really getting me down was that I felt so silly. I mean, there I was, naked. What was I going to say when the killer came through the curtain, "Take one more step and I'll soap you"? I wondered, briefly, if I could get out the tiny bathroom window behind me — yep, right in the middle of the shower, one of my Dad's inventions — before the psychopath came through the door, and I had just decided that I couldn't, when the lights went out.

No fooling around, now. That slamming door I heard, that could have been someone else's door, that thump on the bedroom floor, that could have been my overwrought imagination, but the lights going out, that was real. I was going to be carved up in my own bathroom, probably with one of my Dad's own tools, and the only comforting thought I had to cling to was that, this time, they couldn't blame it on me.

I moved to the back of the shower. The fiend was going to have to come in after me, by God, I wasn't going to stand

there and take it. I heard the bathroom door squeak back —
it was now fully open. The killer was inside. There was a
soft footstep on the mat. I reached up onto the shelf of the
small window at the back of the shower, looking for something, a razor, anything, with which to defend myself. I
came up with a sponge. That was nice. I'd give the bugger a
rub-down. I turned the shower-head towards the curtain-
opening. Not much, but it might surprise the foul fiend if
he caught about a quart of water in his face. Another footstep, closer, this time, just outside the shower. I ducked
down. When the killer came in, he'd probably have a
weapon of some sort thrust out in front of him. A knife, a
gun, whatever. No, not a gun. If he had a gun, he'd just stand
back and let me have it through the curtain. Hell, if he had a
gun, he would never have turned out the lights.

I thought, briefly, of calling for help. Who would hear me?
If anybody could hear me, there'd have been complaints
about my singing before now. I was going to die, but before I
did, I was going to crouch down here and when the killer
came through the curtain, I was going to jump him. He was
going to be as blind as I in this dark. I'd grab the weapon, and
then we'd see.

The curtain — I couldn't see it, but I could feel it stir —
was moving aside, and a figure — blacker, even, than the
surrounding blackness, stepped into the shower-stall. This
was it. I pounced.

"Ye gods and little fishes, Carlton, is that any way to greet
a guest?"

What I clutched, it appeared, was Miss Klovack, formerly
of Toronto, currently residing in Silver Falls, Ont. Miss
Klovack, starkers. That, she told me later, was why she had
turned out the light. Shy little thing. Never reckoning what
she was going to do to my nerves by creeping up on me like
this — or, not giving a tinker's dam — she had decided to
announce the fact that, on due reflection, she had concluded that maybe it wouldn't hurt too much to get just a
little involved, and jumped into her car to bring the glad
tidings out to Bosky Dell. I nearly killed her in that first

TWENTY-TWO

THE NEXT MORNING, we walked, hand in hand, over to Hanson's place. I was a bit embarrassed, not about what we had been doing — hell, I was proud of that — but over the fact that I knew that Hanson knew that his wife had been seen sneaking out of my cottage last Friday morning, for some mysterious reason, which, I hoped, had all been made clear by now. I, for one, was not going to bring the subject up. I gave a guilty start when I recognized the two homicide cops, Thuggy and Smiley, emerging from the Eberley porch. Smiley gave me a curt nod; Thuggy stared straight ahead.

"Keep up the good work, officers," I told them, as we walked to where Hanson was holding the door open. He was smiling broadly.

"Well," he said, "I see you two are getting quite friendly. Come in, come in. There have been," he went on as we sat, together, on the couch facing his big tub chair, "some developments."

"Yes, well, Hanson, before we get into that, I should tell you that the *Lancer* has fired me. Again," I added. "So I guess the project is off."

"Never mind that." He waved a generous hand. "Nobody's going to shut me out of the investigation at this point. Heavens, I'd almost forgotten what fun it is, working on a murder case."

Fun? Well, look at the man; he was beaming. "Now I'm in, and that's all that matters. As a matter of fact, I'm beginning to get a glimmer about this case . . ." he held up his hand as I started to yammer " . . . just the beginnings of a glimmer, nothing to get excited about, but I may have something for you pretty soon. In the meantime, those two from Toronto keep telling me that they're keeping me informed as a courtesy only — it's their show — but I gather the

165

Inspector has made it clear that I am to get whatever information I want, provided I don't interfere."

"And what information have you got?"

"Well sir, the boys have been through Ernie Struthers's little black book, the one that, er, turned up at your place the other day, Carlton. There were initials, a series of numbers that probably referred to dates, and another series of numbers, probably payments."

"And the initials?"

"They didn't mean anything to the Toronto cops, but they did to me. Actually, that's why they brought it to me."

Hanna asked, "How many were there?"

"There were three sets of initials, or, at least, three pages with initials at the top, and what appear to be records of payment underneath."

"Whose initials?" asked Hanna.

"I'll bet one of them was HF," I said. "Harry Franklin."

"It was."

"And TM?"

"Right again. Tommy Macklin. Well, we'd had hints about those two, but there was another one that'll interest you. DS."

"DS? Dominic Silvio?"

He nodded. "Looks like it."

"So one of those three might be the murderer, rather than yours truly? Boy, I hope it's Tommy."

"We'll soon know. The homicide boys are off to interview him now. They've already talked to Harry Franklin, and I gather the local OPP spoke to Silvio."

"They have? What was Harry Franklin being blackmailed about?"

"Harry Franklin was having an affair," Hanson said, "with Lillian Wentworth."

"Lillian the librarian?"

"Uh-huh." Wonders never cease. Lillian Wentworth is a cheerful, outgoing, helpful soul but not exactly a sex kitten. Actually, when you come to think of it, Lillian looks quite a lot like Bernice Franklin, and I couldn't help wondering why, if this was the type that lit Harry's fire, he didn't just check around his own bedroom one night, and see what turned up. We are probably not meant to understand these things. Anyway, it cleared up one mystery for me. Every time I went into the library in Silver Falls, Harry was there. I thought he was thirsting for knowledge, and here all the time, he was thirsting for Lillian. Hanna seemed to find all this amusing, when I explained it to her. She said, "I thought the boondocks were boring, and it turns out they're a cesspit of simmering sexuality."

"Silently simmering sexuality," I pointed out, and that was the issue. "If Lillian Wentworth was even mentioned in connection with a divorce suit, she'd be paraded in front of the Library Board and defrocked, or whatever it is you do to librarians."

"I think you cancel their cards," said Hanna, "but you aren't serious?"

"Darn right," I said. "Librarians may live a hell of a life down in torrid Toronto, but up here, by golly, they're classed with Sunday school teachers, and if word gets around that they're having fun on Saturday nights, the moral fibre of the whole community is seen to be under attack."

"Which means..."

"... which means that if Ernie was onto the romance, which I guess was no great accomplishment, there would be hell to pay."

Hanna was dubious. "Surely even in a place like this, extra-marital affairs are not unheard of?"

"Oh, they happen, all right. But yes, they're unheard of. Or, at least, the trouble doesn't start until they're heard of."

"Why?"

"A little hanky-panky is okay, but if the affair came up at, say, the Daughters of Rebekah, or the Women's Institute, or one of the other pillars of rectitude, and was spoken about out loud, as opposed to mere behind-the-hand whispering, why, then, Bernice would have to kick Harry out, maybe even sue him for divorce, whether she wanted to or not."

"And they call it 'the simple life,'" said Hanna. "Why would Bernice have to dump Harry if she didn't want to?"

"Face," I said, and Hanson nodded agreement. "Ubangi tribesmen," I went on, "Chinese diplomats, and small-town citizens everywhere put great value on face. It doesn't matter so much what you've done that counts, as what you can no longer ignore admitting has been done to you."

"My sainted aunt," commented Hanna, "you do live. But this suggests that Harry did have a motive, bizarre though it seems to me, for killing Ernie, and..."

"Yes, well," Hanson interjected, "that's where it breaks down. When the police spoke to Harry, he told them that he wasn't in Bosky Dell last Monday night. Couldn't have been. He was in Silver Falls."

"That's what he says," Hanna snorted. "Have the cops checked his alibi?"

"I'm afraid they have."

"And?"

"It was Chugalug and Chowder Evening at the Dominion Hotel, and Harry stayed the night," Hanson explained.

"He stayed the night?" Hanna sounded doubtful. "Again, that's what he says. He probably dropped a rope out the window, slid down out of sight of the desk clerk, drove over to Bosky Dell, stabbed Ernie, and was back in bed before anybody knew he'd gone."

"No," I said sadly, and Hanson chimed in, "No."

"How come?"

"Stayed the night. That's local talk," I explained. "Unless I've got it wrong..." Hanson shook his head; I didn't have it wrong, "...it means, translated, that Harry got himself so zonked on Chugalugs and Chowder that he couldn't go home. Not wouldn't, but couldn't. Right?"

"Right," Hanson confirmed. "Apparently, Harry drank several rum and cokes, tried to pick a fight with Quarter to Three Winston, threw up in a lobster pot, and passed out in the Hearts of Oak Lounge. They put him to bed, and he didn't come back here until early Tuesday morning."

"You mean he went up and cleaned up the church with a hangover? What devotion to duty!"

"Strong drink, my mother says," Hanna commented, "is the curse of mankind."

I added, "It is also the alibi of Harry Franklin. He may have trifled with Lillian Wentworth, he may even have been blackmailed by Ernie Struthers, but he was too paralysed to kill him. Well, never mind, we've still got Dominic."

"Couldn't have been Dominic," Hanna said. "He put up your bail."

I'd been thinking about that. "Maybe that was just to put people off the scent. Maybe Ernie found out something about Dominic that was going to queer his development plans. So he killed Ernie, and then, because the Rev. was opposed to the development, he decided to kill him, too."

"Doesn't sound likely," said Hanson. "Men like Silvio don't go around stabbing people any more. They hire lawyers."

"Lawyers go around stabbing people?" This was new to me. "Does the Upper Canada Law Society approve?"

"No, silly," Hanna said. "Mr. Eberley is quite right. They hire lawyers to tie everything up in court and then they go ahead and do whatever it is they want to do while all the lawyers scream at each other. And then it's too late."

I was beginning to get discouraged. "It'll probably turn out that Tommy and Dominic Silvio were attending evening mass together on the night in question, in full view of thousands. The way this thing keeps pointing to me," I added, "I'm starting to think I must have committed the murders in a fit of absent-mindedness, and forgotten all about it."

"Never mind, love," said Hanna, "I've got a little surprise for you."

"Something you picked up in Toronto, that surprise?"

She nodded.

"Well?"

"Not yet. Soon. Not yet."

"Oh, Hanna — Criminy!"

169

Hanna turned to Hanson, who was fingering his ascot and looking thoughtful. "Criminy. Do they really say that around here?"

"Um. Carlton does."

Hanna said, "Well, enough of this idle chitchat; we've got to get to town and check up on those alibis."

"I think you can safely leave that to the police," said Hanson, mildly.

"Nuts to that," Hanna responded. "The police are sure Carlton did it. They're just going through the motions. We've already picked up a few things they don't know, haven't we, Carlton?"

This was accompanied by an arch look. Hanson looked a bit surprised, but he didn't say anything, and Hanna went on, "Well, Carlton, let's get the show on the road. Is your car working yet?"

"That I can't say. With *Marchepas*, it's a matter of mood."

"Okay. My car doesn't have moods. We'll take it."

I ought, properly, to have insisted on staying behind for another chat with Hanson about the case, but a certain constraint seemed to have sprung up between us, and I was glad enough to get out of there without having to discuss the matter of his wife's visitations with him. So we drove off to clear the sacred Withers name by destroying the alibis of the three suspects in Ernie's blackmail book.

Waste of time, of course.

We tackled Dominic Silvio first, in his office, which is in the back of a warehouse. The warehouse looks tacky, and is tacky, but at the end is a suite of offices that looks like something out of a movie. The picture window feasts the eye on a comely stretch of the Silver Falls River. We passed through two batteries of secretaries, but Dominic agreed to see us at once. Probably he hadn't heard about my being fired from the *Lancer*, and was keeping on friendly terms, just in case. He offered us espresso, which was delicious, but not much else. He had already been through an interview with the cops, so he was pretty well primed on what to say. He told us that he denied that Ernie Struthers had been blackmailing him, and if we told anybody anything to the contrary, he'd sue us for libel.

"Slander," I said, and Dominic said, "Huh?"

"When the publication is by word of mouth, that's slander," I explained. "It's libel when you print it."

"Well, whatever it is, I'll do it. Say, look, Carlton" — he gave me the broad smile — "I don't blame you one bit for trying to find out whatever you can about this case. Stands to reason. But," and the smile vanished, "I am a reputable businessman. I'm also one of about fifteen people in this town alone who have the initials DS, and I've already told the cops where I was the night Ernie was killed. Which was bowling, in front of about half a dozen witnesses who know me. So, my advice to you is to go find some other sucker, okay?"

Well, nothing could be fairer than that. And we exited, with his instructions to give his best to the Widow Golden ringing in our ears.

After lunch at the O.K. Cafe — "Why don't they call it the O.K. Corral?" Hanna complained. "It's just as deadly" — we drove back to Bosky Dell to speak to Harry Franklin. Hanna pointed out that it made more sense to tackle Tommy Macklin first, since we were already in town, but I demurred. I was leaving Tommy Macklin until last.

Harry told us to get lost; he had said what he had to say to the police, and it would be a frosty Friday in the middle of July before he would discuss his personal affairs with the press. I told him we were no longer of the press, having been canned. That cheered him up a little, but did not make him any more forthcoming.

Harry refused to discuss what Ernie had been blackmailing him over — even when we told him we already knew — and stuck to his story about driving over to Bosky Dell on the Monday night and, as he put it, "letting off steam with the boys." He gave us the names of three other merrymakers, all of whom I knew, who could testify that he was, as he put it, "incommoded" from about seven p.m. onwards on the night in question. I thought we ought to clear this up right away, but Hanna insisted that the time had come to confront Tommy.

On the way back to Silver Falls, I noted, bitterly, how differently things seemed to work in Bosky Dell than on, say, "Murder, She Wrote." In any well-constructed television show, I noted, when the amateur sleuths start sniffing around, the bad guys throw off confessions like a Catherine wheel. All we'd picked up was one threat of a libel — pardon, slander — suit, and an invitation to drop dead and turn blue. It didn't seem fair.

Hanna said, "Uh-huh."

I was talking, in point of fact, more to keep up my morale than anything else. I was not looking forward to the coming conversation with Tommy Macklin, a man with the temper of a Brazilian killer-bee. Thus it was with feelings of inexpressible joy that I noted, as we pulled up in front of the *Lancer* building, that Tommy was emerging from the premises in the company of that well-known OPP officer, Mutt, who ushered him into a waiting police cruiser. Jeff held the door for him. Then Mutt got into the driver's seat, and they drove off.

I jumped out of Hanna's car. "Hey, Tommy," I shouted, "decided to confess, have you?"

Tommy jerked his head up, but didn't say anything; just sat there in the back of the cop car, looking guilty. Then a voice spoke in my ear, making me start like a frightened hare.

"Ah, Mr. Withers," said Det. Frank "Thuggy" Thurston, "you're just in time to join the party. Get in."

He gestured towards what we used to call "a plain brown wrapper" when I was on the police beat. An unmarked cruiser. He put one hand under my elbow and kind of moved me along, so I decided to do the courteous thing and accompany the officer. Hanna, I saw, was being invited to get in the back seat with me, by Det. Arthur "Smiley" Smollett. The two cops sat in front, with Thuggy at the wheel, so we weren't under arrest.

"Hey, where are we going?" I asked Smiley, but it was Thuggy who replied.

"On a wild goose chase, if you want my opinion," he said.

TWENTY-THREE

THIS HAD OBVIOUSLY been pre-arranged.

"This has obviously been pre-arranged," I told Hanna. She looked thoughtful.

"Naturally."

"Hey," I prodded Thuggy in the back and asked again, "Where are we going?"

He glanced back. "Don't do that," he said, and I decided not to do that.

"Well, where are you taking us? You can't just pull people off the streets, you know. This is a free country. More or less."

"We're going to church," said Smiley.

"To church?"

"We're going to your church in Bosky Dell. Staff Inspector Eberley asked us to assemble all the principals in this case at the church. He has a theory he wants to try out."

"Holy mackerel," I said, "Just like television. Did you hear that, Hanna? Hanson's cracked the case. That is what you do with cases, officers, isn't it? Crack them? Why crack them, I wonder? Why not break, or smash, or, more simply, solve? Why not . . ."

A soft hand, firm but soft, clamped suddenly over my mouth. Hanna thought I was babbling. Well, I was. But this was babble-worthy news. Hanson, I knew he could do it. He would confront the bad guy, demolish his arguments with ridiculous ease, and wring a confession out of the rascal. I was still unemployed, broke, and a criminal suspect, but things were looking up. I kissed the hand that shushed me — which was hastily withdrawn.

I reached out and took Hanna's left hand in my right. She looked startled, but didn't withdraw, and when I squeezed her hand, squeezed back. We rode to the church in what was, for me at least, perfect contentment.

Whether the officers were perfectly contented was another matter. Probably not, is my guess. As we pulled up in front of the church, Thuggy grumbled, "This is an asshole idea."

"What harm can it do?" asked Smiley, and Thuggy shrugged. We went into the church.

Hanson was up on the raised platform at the front. The pine pulpit had been moved off to one side, and Hanson had set up a table in its place, with a couple of kitchen chairs drawn up to it. There were a few documents on the table — "Clues, I'll bet," I told Hanna, who murmured, "The boy's a genius" — and a pin punch, just like the ones from the missing set. Unless three decades of television had led me entirely astray, we were about to get a re-enactment of the crime.

Hot diggety dog. I fished a notebook out of my jacket pocket and a ballpoint pen out of the lining of my jacket, where the buggers always migrate. The ballpoint didn't work — they seldom do — but I was able to borrow one from Mrs. Golden, who was there in her capacity of official observer or neighbourhood snitch, and dressed formally. That is, she was carrying a purse. In the Dell, that's formal. She produced a pen from its cavernous depths when I told her I needed one to write my story, and she said, "What story, Carlton? You've been fired."

How in tunket did she know that?

"I can sell this one in Toronto," I replied, "freelance."

Tout le gang was there, ranged along the benches, though not, of course, in the box pews: the Widow, now sitting next to Dominic Silvio; Moose, and another beefy gent who was, I presume, Clarence, his business colleague and fellow heavy-hitter; Harry and Bernice Franklin; the Campbell brothers, looking truculent; Tommy Macklin, sitting by himself and looking pale and wan, a great improvement over his normal, red-faced rage; Nora Eberley, wearing a demure shirtdress and an expression of injured innocence; and Lillian Wentworth, the librarian. Add in Hanna, self, and two more cops and you had a better crowd than turns up most Sundays. It was a pity that the Rev. couldn't be here — he might have counted the crowd and decided to take up a collection.

Lillian the Librarian was sitting right next to Bernice Franklin, and they were whispering together, boding no good whatever for poor Harry. Comparing notes, no doubt. They looked so much alike that I was moved to wonder, once more, why Harry bothered to range afield for that same flower that bloomed so close at hand.

Hanson gave a tiny tug on one end of the immaculate cravat which, as ever, topped his customary costume — blue blazer and grey flannels. Then he cleared his throat and rapped once, sharply, on the table. The four cops, who had been murmuring together about halfway down the centre aisle, immediately spread out. Mutt took the left aisle, Jeff the right, Smiley stayed in the centre, and Thuggy moved up to the front, just behind where Hanson now seated himself at the table.

"Well, ladies and gentlemen," he said, "suppose we get started. I have asked you all to come here, and I may say I am grateful to you all for coming, and for the cooperation of the police, because it is my hope that together we will be able to clear up the mystery surrounding the murders of Ernie Struthers and Ephraim Wylie."

Under-the-breath muttering at this, in the crowd. The murderer, I guessed, was writhing.

"The facts," Hanson went on, "are not complicated. Ernie was discovered, deceased, on the front stoop of Carlton's Withers's place on Third Street last Tuesday morning. The Rev. Wylie was discovered, deceased, in this church, last Friday morning in the Flannery pew.

"Preliminary autopsies suggest the time of death in the case of Ernie Struthers was somewhere between six p.m. and midnight, give or take an hour, on Monday night. Rev. Wylie's slaying is rather easier to pinpoint. He was still alive at approximately 11 a.m. last Friday morning, and was discovered, dead, by Carlton Withers, at approximately 11:30.

"Death in each case was caused by stabbing with a pin

punch, very much like the one you see here on the table before me. These tools, commonly employed in woodworking, came from a set which belonged to Carlton's father, and were kept in the workshop behind the Withers home on Third Street. Since they were readily available to anyone, we cannot yet attach any particular significance to their ownership."

I nodded. Damn right.

"There were no fingerprints discernible on either instrument belonging to anyone in police files" — this was new to me — "but these days, when even the most elementary student of crime knows about using gloves, that doesn't mean much, either.

"The rest of the set, incidentally," he added, "was discovered this morning, in the lake, down by the public dock."

Mild sensation in the audience.

"Ordinary police routine," Hanson went on, "led to this discovery. Sergeant Moffitt and Constable Jeffrey, in the course of a normal search, checked the waterfront, and some boys who had been swimming there told them of finding a set of tools in a plastic case. It is one of these that now sits on the table in front of me."

He smiled, briefly. "It may become useful, as we go along.

"There were a number of puzzling aspects to the case," Hanson resumed, when we had all finished gawking and stirring, "at least at first. One was this: a number of clues suggested that Ernie had been hiding here, in one of the box pews, and that this had something to do with his murder. A Rotary pin was found, attached to a torn piece of cloth, which might have indicated a struggle. However, the pin did not belong to Ernie, though it might, of course, belong to his killer. His hat was also found in the pew. But when the Rev. Mr. Wylie returned to the church after his meeting with Dominic Silvio, Ernie was not in the pew. Why not?"

"I know why not," I ejaculated. I had just figured it out.

"Then perhaps you would be good enough to explain to the rest." Hanson smiled benignly, as on a favourite pupil.

"It was the wrong pew."

"Merciful Moses, the man has flipped," said Hanna, and for the non-Bosky Dellers present, the statement did seem strange, but Hanson soon explained it.

"Precisely," he said, "the wrong pew. For outsiders, I should explain that the box pews here are, symbolically, quite important, almost" — a fleeting smile — "sacred. Oh, not so much sacred, as privileged. They have from the first been occupied only by the social leaders of Bosky Dell. Now, Ernie Struthers was a snob to his fingertips, like most villagers, and there is no way on earth that he would have inserted himself into Miss Flannery's box pew in order to eavesdrop on a conversation between Reverend Wylie and Dominic Silvio, which was the ostensible reason for his presence in the church."

"Where else could he hide?" asked Silvio.

"In the vestry, right behind me. It isn't as close, but with the acoustics in this fine old building, it is quite close enough. If he wanted to conceal himself here — and mark that 'if' — he would simply have gone into the vestry and left the door open. He could see, because he was looking from the darkness into the lighter body of the church, whereas, in the box pew, he'd have to duck down below the front wall, and hope that nobody looked directly in, for fear of being spotted. If he moved, he'd be heard, and if he was heard — or spotted — he would have had no way to escape, whereas, from the vestry, he could simply duck out the back door.

"No, ladies and gentlemen, the one fact that was clear from very early on was that Ernie did not hide in the Flannery pew."

"Then how about the hat I found?" asked Harry Franklin.

"Misdirection," Hanson replied promptly. "Easily planted clues designed merely to confuse the investigation, or at least slow it down. The church is important only in pin-pointing the probable time of the meeting between Ernie Struthers and his killer. Rev. Wylie's statements, combined with the rough estimate of the time of death, put that time at somewhere around nine p.m."

"Well, what about the newspaper clipping?" Hanna asked.

There was a brief, but perceptible, pause.

"Probably part of the same misdirection," Hanson replied. "We haven't yet worked that part out. Presumably, the killer put the envelope into Ernie's hand to direct us to the church, and it fell out."

Hanson went on, "We now come to the matter of suspects."

Hanna stirred discontently at my side. "What about the clipping?" she complained. "He brushed that off."

I made a firm resolve to speak to the pipsqueak later; this niggling was likely to break Hanson's concentration. I needn't have worried; after a brief, wintry smile in our direction, he went on.

"At first, it seemed possible that Dominic Silvio, for reasons that were not quite clear, might have been responsible. He may well have believed that, with the Rev. Mr. Wylie out of the way, a new minister might have seen things differently in connection with the proposed development he had in mind here. That is an argument that works only if the Rev. Mr. Wylie had been the first victim. However, it is hard to see why Ernie Struthers would have been killed, and then the minister. Ernie had nothing whatever to do with the development, or the church. The attack on Carlton outside the *Lancer* offices also pointed to Mr. Dominic — or, at least to his helpers."

Rich blush from Moose at this.

"However, as it turned out, this was a simple error. Mr. Silvio, it has been established, was bowling on the night of Ernie's murder, in front of witnesses who have been interviewed by the police. Nor would he have arranged for someone else to do the killing for him, because Ernie's death could not have benefited Mr. Silvio. The question of the possible development of a condominium complex on church property, which the Reverend Wylie opposed, did

178

not depend on anything Ernie Struthers did. It, literally, did not matter to Mr. Silvio whether Ernie lived or died."

Hanson shuffled his notes, cleared his throat, was obviously starting to go on, when Hanna butted in.

"Hey," she said, "what about blackmail for a motive?"

"It did not apply to this individual," said Hanson, shortly.

"Why not? Didn't the cops find the initials DS at the top of one of the pages in Ernie's handy-dandy little notebook?"

"They did indeed."

"Well, then?"

"The initials, police investigation determined, were those of someone else."

"Oh, yeah, who?"

"It doesn't matter." Pause. "A resident of another community."

The Widow Golden put up her hand, the bright kid in school who has the answer.

"Dorothy Sternblossom, I'll bet," she said, and added in a loud aside, "you know, that woman from Panny Point who got caught cheating in the Daughters of Rebekah Bridge Tournament last winter. They had the dickens of a time hushing it up."

"Was Dorothy Sternblossom the one referred to in Ernie's notebook?" Hanna asked.

Hanson looked very stern. "That information is not relevant to this inquiry," he said. "What is relevant is that the police were able to satisfy themselves that the initials were not those of Dominic Silvio."

The Widow babbled right through this in a loud stage whisper, "Though why Dorothy would pay to keep something like that hushed up, I can't understand. Everybody who is anybody knew about it."

"I didn't," I said.

"Oh, Carlton," she responded, "you never know anything."

"That's why they call me a reporter."

"If we can get back to the point at issue," said Hanson,

giving us both a dirty look, "we can say that ordinary police procedures showed that Dominic Silvio had an alibi for the relevant time, and had no motive for wanting Ernie Silvio dead."

"One down," I said.

"Next, it seemed possible that someone who was being blackmailed by Ernie had, in desperation, killed him, and planted a number of confusing clues, in such a way that the blame would, in the end, fall on Carlton."

"I don't follow," said Tommy.

"I do," I said. "The killer wanted to point to me, so he planted the body at my place and then set up the other clues to point to the church. It was pretty likely that the police would soon work out that the murder didn't take place there, so the trail would lead back to me, again, without seeming obvious."

Hanson took up the thread again. "Miss Klovack has already referred to the fact that a book containing code numbers, dates — presumably of payments — and amounts, in Ernie's handwriting, was discovered." He did not say where. "This apparently detailed the payoffs from a number of blackmail schemes. There were no names, merely initials and numbers which presumably represented regular payments."

"How many sets of initials?" Harry Franklin wanted to know.

"There were three."

"Jesus," said Harry, "up until today, I thought I was the only one."

"You were indeed one of the victims," Hanson said. "Because of an incident" — flicker of eyebrows — "that does not concern us here, you were paying Ernie $200 a month. However, the police have checked the statement of your, uh, whereabouts on the night of the murder, and it is obvious that you could not have committed the crime."

Harry relaxed, just a trifle. He was still in trouble, but not headed for durance vile.

"Two down," I said.

"We now come to Tommy Macklin," continued Hanson, and Tommy was on his feet at once, protesting, "Hanson, that's got nothing to do with this case."

"Mr. Macklin," Hanson rolled on over his protest, "was another victim of Ernie's blackmail schemes, for reasons which, again, do not concern us here."

"Oh, my," sang out Lillian Wentworth, "now everybody's going to know that Tommy was a draft dodger."

Stop the presses. Tommy Macklin, one of the brayingest, breast-beatingest patriots in the land, a draft dodger? Yessir, Lillian explained in a swift whisper, despite Tommy's repeated remonstrations, he had sat out World War II on a farm-help exemption. This is the man who writes the only white-hot editorial that ever appears in the *Lancer* — once a year on Remembrance Day, saluting the bold heroes who fought for our freedom in two world wars and Korea, let us not forget Korea, and lambasting the sunshine patriots, Commie pinkos, and other ne'er-do-wells who stand around refusing to shed their blood for the causes of righteousness. Something like that, anyway. Turns out that Tommy got himself an exemption back in 1942, when Canada was going in for conscription, on the grounds that he was needed on the family farm. While he never exactly said it in so many words, he always managed to leave the impression, whenever the talk around the office turned to matters military, that he had been the first man ashore on the beaches of Normandy, and had ravaged the Nazi hordes with an occasional assist from his pals Bernie Montgomery and George Patton.

Tommy didn't come from our area; he was an outsider, from Stirling, forty miles away, so he could get away with this line, but Ernie must have picked it up somewhere, and pried hush-money out of Tommy. Nobody else really cared any more about who was or was not up in arms four decades ago, but there was the matter of face, and Tommy, like the previously mentioned Ubangi tribesmen, was strong on face. He was no longer pale and wan, in fact, back to his normal enraged purple, and would no doubt make life difficult for Lillian in the future. But, for the moment, she was merely smiling demurely. The damage was done.

Hanson called the meeting back to order. This damn gaggle was not following form. "Yes, well, for whatever reasons, Tommy Macklin was paying Ernie Struthers blackmail money. Again, however, the potential suspect was able to give the police an account of his whereabouts on the night of the murder, and, again, it held up."

"I was at a golf tournament in Toronto," said Tommy. Golf tournaments, like Chugalug and Chowder nights, run to the liquid. Tommy, too, was paralysed at the relevant time.

"Three down," I said. This was getting good. This was where, when all the obvious suspects had been eliminated, Hanson would suddenly confront the killer. And so he did.

"But what if," he said, "the blackmail clue was, like the church clue, merely misdirection?

"Most murders, in my experience, are simple. They arise from simple causes, and, outside the pages of Agatha Christie, are simply solved. A moment of passion, an outburst of greed, or the long culmination of a series of small brutalities, will produce an explosion. Most murders, in my experience, can be solved if we concentrate on the essentials. Which are, as every reader of crime fiction knows, motive, method, and opportunity. We can assume, because the same weapon was used, that the two murders were connected, that, in all likelihood, Ephraim Wylie was slain because he had information about the first killing. So we must apply our three tests of motive, method, and opportunity to the slaying of Ernie Struthers, and when we do this, when we clear away the misdirection, we find that the answers are glaringly obvious. They point in one, and only one, direction."

He paused dramatically, and looked around the room, checking, no doubt, on the presence of the cops before he unloaded his bombshell.

"Carlton Withers."

TWENTY-FOUR

YES, WELL, I said to myself, that makes sense. I was even, for God's sake, writing down my own name on my memo pad and nodding as I wrote when it suddenly occurred to me that, hey, this was not the way it was supposed to go. There was a great deal in this case that confused me, but I knew one thing for sure, and that was that I had not stuck a pin punch into Ernie Struthers, much as he deserved it. Nor would I ever have murdered Ephraim Wylie, as harmless a bird as ever broke bread, and a minister to boot. Wore his collar backwards, and everything. So I was a bit taken aback when Hanson Eberley suddenly shoved the whole thing off onto me. I wondered if I could get out the door before the cops reacted, but realized I couldn't. And then, just when I was reeling — if you can reel when you are still seated — and trying to get my tongue untangled from the roof of my mouth to murmur a protest, a single word ripped out into the stunned silence that hung within the church.

"Bullshit!" shouted Hanna Klovack, bless her irreverent soul. "Bull-bloody-shit!"

And she ran up onto the dais, over to the table where Hanson was sitting, dug into the back pocket of her blue-jeans, and pulled out a piece of paper. This was it, I guessed, the big surprise she had been hugging to herself all this while. I hoped it was good.

"I've listened to this farce because I wanted to see where it was going," she said. "Hanson Eberley sits up here, look-ing cool and composed in his goddam cravat, as calm as a codfish on ice, but let me tell you, everybody, the perform-ance you just witnessed was an act of desperation."

"Desperation?" Hanson smiled, a tolerant smile. "My dear young lady..."

"I am not your dear young lady, jerkface. You may have

Carlton dazzled, because of the poor sort of trusting simp he is, but I'm onto you."

I wasn't crazy about "poor sort of trusting simp," and I wondered if I shouldn't interfere and, in a manly way, take over things at this point from Hanna, except that, when you come right down to it, it seemed to be more dignified, somehow, to preserve a restrained silence. I could assert myself later. Or not.

"Did you notice?" Hanna turned away from Hanson now, faced the gang in the front row, and began waving her arms about as she talked, "did you notice how he strung all that stuff together as if it made sense? Hell, he even had us nodding at it. But what was it? Pure fabrication.

"'The church is important only in pin-pointing the probable time of the meeting between Ernie Struthers and his killer.'" She had dropped her voice to imitate Hanson, and it went up an octave when she returned to her own voice. "Bunny baubles. The only reason we're told that Ernie must have been in the church about nine p.m. is that Mr. Sherlock Holmes Eberley is covered for that time, because his old police buddy was at his place. The whole argument was worked backwards. Hanson wanted us to think about the church and about nine p.m. or thereabouts. That's why he planted the Rotary pin in the Flannery pew when he went up to the church just ahead of Carlton and myself the other day."

"I don't get it," I said.

Hanna gave an exasperated sigh. "Think about what happened that day. We had just worked it out that probably the killing didn't have anything to do with the church at all, and the offertory envelope was a false lead. Remember? Then suddenly there were you and I doing the dishes, and a few minutes later we go up to the church and there is Hanson, fooling around outside, and we go inside, and voilà! we find the Rotary pin in the Flannery pew. It doesn't really mean anything, as we have just learned, but it gets us all thinking that Ernie must have been there at about nine o'clock or so. Not a perfect alibi for Hanson, by any means, but good enough, as long as nobody really thought about it.

"But what if the killing took place much later? What if, as seems most likely, Ernie just wandered off when the meeting moved outside, and went to drink Catawba, or whatever he does for recreation, and then, much later that evening, he went over to your place, Carlton? And what if he was seen going there, and knocked on the head and stabbed with that horrible thing there, and just left? Leaves our hero without an alibi, doesn't it?"

Hanson smiled indulgently. "An impressive line of reasoning. Unfortunately, it raises more questions than it answers, and it is not supported by the slightest shred of evidence. Moreover, I can give you my solemn word, not that I expect it to weigh much with you in your present, ah, excited state of mind, that I did not have anything to do with putting a Rotary pin in the pew at the church. It was bound to be discovered to be a false lead; surely you accept that a man with my experience would see that?"

"Well, I may have the pin wrong, but I'm right about the desperation, by God." Hanna was spitting out the words, now, you could practically see the blood of her Cossack ancestors surging through her veins. "There was one bit of evidence you have been blipping over since this whole thing started. The newspaper clipping that was found with Ernie Struthers. Here it is."

So that was what she had in her hip pocket. Scarcely seemed room for it. She waved the bit of newspaper about in the air.

"Take a good look at it, Hanson," she went on, "because it's what sank you."

Hanson seemed more amused than anything. "You mean there is something in that clipping that somehow proves I killed Ernie Struthers? I should be delighted to hear what it is."

"I didn't say that. What I said was that it was the clipping that sank you, not that it said anything about you. Your name isn't even in it."

Tommy Macklin was getting impatient. "What in hell are you talking about?" he demanded.

"Hello, Tommy," Hanna gave him a broad grin. "Fought any good wars lately?"

Tommy subsided.

"What I was about to explain," Hanna went on, "is that the newspaper clipping had to have some relevance, didn't it? The most likely thing is that Ernie was taking it around to Carlton's place, to slip it under his door, when he ran into the killer, just as he got to the porch. They quarrelled, struggled, he was hit on the head, and knocked unconscious. The envelope fell out of his hand, and the killer didn't see it in the dark. That part's easy enough. But why was he bringing Carlton a newspaper clipping about an event that must already have been engraved on the poor darling's mind?"

You got that "poor darling"? It took the sting off "poor sort of trusting simp."

"Well, okay, I'll bite," said Dominic Silvio, "why?"

"It was to answer that question," said Hanna, beginning to stride up and down the platform — my, she was enjoying this — "that I went to Toronto."

"Huh?" said Harry Franklin.

"You see, I figured that if I had a look at the newspaper, the whole newspaper, from that day, I might find out something else about the accident, or, at the very least, some reason why Ernie would have been bringing the clipping around to Carlton, a man he obviously didn't like. So I went down to the *Toronto Star* — I used to work there, you know — and got a friend of mine who works in the library to get out the microfilm of that day's paper."

I asked, "And what did you learn?"

"Absolutely nothing. I was sitting there, going over and over the paper and getting nowhere, and chatting, off and on, with my librarian friend, and she wanted to know what I was doing since I'd left the *Star*, so I told her I was up here, working on a jerky little paper..."

"Hey, hey..." Tommy had come back to life.

"...a jerky little paper called the Silver Falls *Lancer*, and she said that was funny, she had just filed some stuff about a murder that the *Lancer* was trying to help solve. A famous detective, she said, was working on it. A man named Eberley, who used to be on the Toronto force.

"I said, sure, sure, yeah, yeah, not really paying any attention, and she said, 'Why don't we pull his file?' Librarians," she explained, "are always pulling files; it's their recreation. So we did. And guess what? Bingo!"

"How do you mean, Bingo?" I asked.

Hanna then hauled out another piece of paper, not a clipping, this time, but a computer printout, just a short one, which she proceeded to read.

"This is a readout from a story that appeared eight and a half years ago," she told us just before she launched herself, "and was back on about page 88, among the truss ads. The heading is very small, and all it says is 'Police Officer Suspended.' Obviously, the fix was in on the coverage of this one:

Staff Inspector Hanson Eberley has been temporarily suspended by the Metropolitan Toronto Police while a disciplinary panel checks into a citizen's complaint that the chief of the city's homicide squad was caught driving while under the influence of alcohol.

The citizen, a lawyer, Russell S. Miller, of Chaplin Cres., charged in a letter to the police complaints bureau that he saw Eberley, whom he recognized from court, stopped in the same safety check that he had been stopped in last January.

Eberley, according to Miller's letter, was obviously drunk at the time, but no action was taken against him. In fact, a police officer got in his car and drove him away, presumably to his home.

The next day, Miller checked the arrest dockets, and, discovering that no charge had been laid against the homicide detective, filed his complaint, which resulted in the suspension announced today.

Staff Inspector Eberley was not available for comment.

Hanna lowered the piece of paper and looked up, for applause, I guess.

"Pardon me, dear," piped up the Widow Golden, "but I'm not sure this gets us anywhere. I mean, it probably explains why Hanson retired so suddenly — presumably he was allowed to get out of the force in return for dropping the charges and then the whole thing was hushed up. But that doesn't explain why Hanson should have killed Ernie. And it especially doesn't explain why Ernie, if he thought his life was in danger, would go around to Carlton's place with a newspaper clipping about the crash. If he wanted to leave a note, why not just something that said, 'If I'm killed, Hanson did it'?"

"Because," said Hanna triumphantly, "Ernie didn't know his life was in danger. That's not what the clipping was about at all."

I was totally fogged. "Then what in blazes *was* it about?"

"I believe I can answer that." Suddenly, we heard from Smiley again. He had moved directly behind Hanson Eberley now, and the other cops were edging down, and, all in all, things seemed to be coming under control at last. "Ernie wasn't indicating his killer. Miss Klovack is quite right in stating that he didn't even know he was in danger. What he was hinting at was that he knew who had killed Mr. and Mrs. Withers, Carlton's parents."

"Hanson killed my parents?"

"No, we don't think so," Smiley responded. "We think Mrs. Eberley did."

There was a stunned silence in the room, as everybody turned to stare at Nora Eberley. She didn't move a muscle, didn't say a word, just stared straight ahead.

"It's our belief," Smiley went on, "that Nora Eberley was driving the truck that killed Carlton's parents. From what we've been able to put together since we began to reinvestigate after Ernie Struthers's death, the Eberleys persuaded Ernie to take the rap for Mrs. Eberley. We have located a witness who says that the Eberleys drove home from town that day with Struthers in his truck, and that all of them had been drinking. As most of you know, Hanson Eberley does not often drive a car, much less a truck. Since the, uh, incident in Toronto, he usually finds someone else to drive him. It seems likely, given the blackmail which we knew was taking place, that Nora Eberley took over the wheel from Ernie somewhere on the trip home, and that she was driving when the accident occurred."

Nora twitched, and looked as if she were about to say something, but Hanson said, firmly, "Not a word, my dear. This is all nonsense."

Smiley went on, "We believe that, after the crash, the Eberleys persuaded Ernie to get into the driver's seat again, and they just got out and walked home through the woods. There was no one on the road, and by the time the police arrived, all they found was Ernie behind the wheel, drunk, and Mr. and Mrs. Withers, dying."

"But why?" I wondered. "Why would Ernie agree to take the blame?"

"Money. Quite a lot of money. Staff Inspector Eberley had retired from the Toronto police, with quite a comfortable pension fund. Ernie got most of it."

"So that's where the money came from for the hardware store?"

"It appears that way. We haven't finished checking out the bank transfers yet, but from what we have already dis-covered, in Eberley's bank" — the title had suddenly disap-peared, I noticed — "a good deal of money changed hands within a year of your parents' death. For Ernie, because he only got three months in jail, it was pretty good pay."

I turned to Nora. "Mrs. Eberley, is this true?"

Hanson spoke a single warning word, "Nora" — and again, she stared straight ahead. The police were moving down the aisles now, cutting off escape, but I still couldn't take in what Smiley was saying.

"But why did Ernie suddenly decide to tell me about it, and why was he killed?"

"The two are probably connected," said Smiley. "When Eberley said earlier that there were three sets of initials in

189

the blackmail book we found at Carlton's place — planted there, no doubt, by Eberley himself — he was quite correct. But there had been at least four names, originally. One of the pages had been torn out. It was very carefully done, but, just as part of our routine, we counted the number of pages in the notebook. It came to 31; the same kind of notebook we picked up in the stationery store in town had 32 pages in it."

"Pretty smart, these leadheads," I told Hanna.

"Shut up," she said. "He's still talking." And so he was.

"It's pretty clear from Struthers's bank records that Ernie was bleeding Eberley, more often and for more money than his other blackmail victims, and Hanson was running out of resources. Ernie made the same mistake most black-mailers make; he got too greedy."

I looked back at Hanson, to see how he was taking this. He was craning his head around, checking to see if there was any way out, no doubt. Obviously, he'd had no idea that the fuzz had been so busy on his behalf. He caught me watching him, shrugged, and half-smiled. He had been down this road too often not to know that the jig — what-ever that is — was up. Why up?, I wondered. I wondered about a lot of things. I decided to see if I could clear some of them up.

"But why would Ernie be bringing the clipping around to me? We weren't exactly chums."

This time, it was Thuggy, moving ever so slowly closer to where Hanson sat, who replied.

"Just as Miss Klovack says. It was a clue, a pointer. It didn't even matter if you worked out what it meant, we believe. Ernie was going to leave it for you to find, at your front door. It might mean something to you, or it might not, but, whatever happened, you would take it to your friend, your very clever friend, Hanson Eberley. Ernie could count on that. Eberley would get the message. Or, even if he didn't, he would know that any dealings between you and Ernie, under the circumstances, had to be a threat to him. The whole thing was aimed at pressuring Eberley to come across with more money. Ernie apparently thought Eberley was holding out on him."

"But if Hanson killed Ernie, why at my place? And why didn't he just remove the envelope?"

Smiley took over again. "Our guess is that he ran into Ernie, quite by accident, while he was out for a stroll late that evening, after the meeting at the church. Miss Klovack is quite correct, again, when she points out that the whole purpose of trying to draw attention to the church was to establish an alibi for Eberley. He was covered for the time between about nine o'clock and about 10:30. It is clear now that Ernie Struthers spent most of that time drinking, probably down at the federal dock, which was his favourite hangout; there is seldom anyone there."

These gents had being doing some local research. The federal dock at Bosky Dell is normally deserted because it is one of those government boondoggles, built in entirely the wrong place, about five blocks away from what might be called the hub of activity, which is the public dock, at the foot of Fourth. The sergeant went on.

"If Ernie Struthers decided, after he had been drinking for some time, to go and see Carlton Withers, his shortest route would be along Forest Road and down Third Street. That would take him right past the Eberley place. It seems most likely that Eberley saw him — perhaps he merely wondered what had happened to him earlier in the evening — and followed him."

Thuggy took over again. It was getting to be a cross-talk act.

"We think there was a confrontation. Eberley was not the sort of man to panic and lash out. If he was going to kill Ernie, you would expect him to do it carefully, but we think Ernie must have said something to him that so enraged him that, for once, he lost his cool. What it was, we don't know.

"He knocked Ernie out — we haven't found the weapon yet, but we will. Then he slipped into the Withers's workshop, found the set of pin punches, and stabbed Struthers in the kidneys with it. A simple, quick, sure way for someone

191

of Eberley's experience to commit a killing. There was not much blood — most of the bleeding was internal — but we have found traces on the lawn outside the door, despite the rain.

"Once he knew Ernie was dead, he searched the body and found what he was looking for — that blackmailing notebook. Either that, or he went up to Ernie's house, and found it there. The fact that he didn't destroy it suggests that he at once began to take steps to incriminate someone else, and realized that the notebook could serve exactly that purpose.

"When the autopsy indicated that Struthers had been hit on the head as well as stabbed, and that he had a considerable amount of alcohol in him, we began to reconstruct what might have happened. Frankly, for a time, we could make no sense of what we seemed to be finding."

"Because of the misdirection?" I wondered.

"Yeah. The stuff about the church, and the clipping. Obviously, when Eberley turned up the next day, just in time for the body to be found, he decided to make the most of the connection with the church that was suggested by the envelope.

"So, he planted the hat in the church to make the connection stronger. He could have done that, easily enough, in the hour or so when everyone was waiting around for the police to arrive from Silver Falls."

"Well, then, what about the tool set?"

"He removed that at about the same time, and deposited it in the lake — probably last night; it hadn't been in the water long — because he knew it would be retrieved by ordinary police investigation, and would seem to be one more tiny shred of evidence pointing to you."

My mind was, as the saying goes, in something of a turmoil. Hanson, my old friend, my hero, not only turned into a killer, but arranging to drop the blame on me. For Nora. There was that, at least. He had got into this horrible mess to protect his wife; it wasn't anything deliberately aimed at me.

"Nothing personal, Carlton," Hanson said softly, as if he

had been reading my mind. "You see, the detectives have at least some of it right. Nora was driving the truck and Ernie did take her place behind the wheel after the accident. It would have killed her to be convicted of a driving death," he explained, calmly. "For someone like Ernie, it was just a spell in jail. Everything else flowed from that.

"Ernie was blackmailing me; that is correct, too. But I didn't kill him because of that, although I certainly would have, in a rather less crude manner, if he'd kept it up. No, Sergeant Smollett's version is not so very far off. And if you want to know precisely what he said that so enraged me, Sergeant, I can tell you. It is not something I am ever likely to forget. He said, 'Well, Eberley, I see you've got your boozing under control. How about the Missus? She kill anybody lately?'

"But, Carlton, you must believe me when I say that I was sorry that I felt I had to land you with the crime. I never wanted to hurt you. It became a, well, practical necessity."

"How about me?" Dominic Silvio wanted to know. "Was the hit on the head I got a practical necessity?"

"Exactly," Hanson replied. "You see, I put Nora to bed that night" — another wintry smile — "as I so often do, but when I woke up about midnight, she was gone. I went out looking for her. I must have wandered up and down every street in the village and I was about to give up and go home, when, on my final trip down Third Street, I noticed someone moving about on Carlton's lawn. It was you, Mr. Silvio, and you were looking through Carlton's bedroom, ogling my wife in Carlton's bed. So I picked up a piece of oak — a windblown branch, in case you're wondering, Sergeant Smollett, the same thing I used on Ernie, they are never in short supply around here — and hit you. That would clear you as a suspect and point, once more, to Carlton," he finished, with a rueful smile.

Well, that seemed to be that, and I was just waiting for the cops to scoop up their man when Hanson made a sudden dart at the table in front of him, grabbed the pin punch — had the cunning rascal brought it along just in case? —

grabbed Hanna with one hand, whirled her about, and put the point of the punch close to her throat.

"Without wanting to appear melodramatic," he said, in a cold, calm voice, "I wish to point out that I can kill this young woman very quickly, and if anyone here moves, I will certainly do so. And now, if you'll excuse me, I believe we'll be on our way."

He began to back away from the table, dragging Hanna with him, and he appeared to be going to get clear away when, suddenly, from somewhere, there came a bellow of rage, a bellow so loud, so angry, so incoherently malevolent, that I was astonished to find that it was issuing from my own throat. I really was quite cranky. Not content with his role in the death of my parents, he had to go on and slaughter Ernie Struthers and the Rev., while trying to pin the blame on me; not satisfied with cold-cocking Dominic Silvio, who looked as if he might stand me a trip to California, not happy with trying to stage a public showdown, when the thing was getting out of hand, to make me panic, as I very nearly did, and make a run for it, this wily old thug was now about to make off with a girl for whom I had, as you may have gathered, formed an attachment. Something snapped, and I came out of my seat like a berserk bull. Startled, Hanson relaxed his grip for an instant and Hanna, never one to stand on ceremony, promptly drove her elbow into his midriff. I arrived about half a second later and hit Hanson across the bridge of the nose with all the violence that had been boiling around within me for some time. He went galley-west, the weapon clattered loose, and I clutched Hanna.

TWENTY-FIVE

THIS IS THE place, you're saying to yourself, where the hero-
ine flutters her eyelashes, murmurs, "My hero," in fluted
tones, and we get smooch, smooch, and the happy ending. I
was expecting something of the sort myself, and it would
have been all right with me. But we are wrong, both of us;
we reckon without Hanna Klovack, the most cross-grained
female to emerge on the planet Earth since Catherine the
Great handed in her sceptre. Not the eyelash-fluttering
type, our Hanna, nor the My Hero type, either. Instead of
sinking into my arms, she shook me off like a terrier shaking off a rat and yelped, "You big jerk, what did you do that
for?"

I ask you.

"Because, pinhead, the man was getting set to massacre
you."

"Oh, Carlton, don't be so dramatic."

"Dramatic?" I appealed to Smiley and Thuggy, who had
scooped up the dazed Eberley Hanson and were giving him
the arrest routine. "Was this man, or was he not, getting set
to massacre the young twerp?"

Smiley paused to think about it. "He might have," he
said, "but I don't really think so."

"There." Hanna was triumphant. "He just lost his cool
for the second time in his life. He couldn't go anywhere.
There are probably cops all over the place. Aren't there,
Sergeant Smollett?"

He nodded.

"See? There was no need to hit the poor man."

Poor man. You got that?

She went on, "Really, he was quite pathetic when you
come to think about it. The cops were onto him almost
from the start."

"They were? Then why did they throw *me* in the slammer?"

"Oh, well, not the Silver Falls boys. They were pathetic. But the Toronto cops. By the time I went to them with the stuff about the sunglasses, they were already running checks on Hanson and . . ."

"You told them about the sunglasses? I thought Hanson was doing that."

"Why should Hanson do that? He knew where the sunglasses came from. Ten to one, they were Ernie's. They were the very sunglasses he was wearing in the crash, I'll bet. Hanson got hold of them and put them in your place. He figured the cops would find them because he knew they would be coming out to your place with a search warrant, pretty soon. It was pure routine."

"So, when I took them over to him . . ."

"It queered the pitch. He didn't know what a diligent housekeeper you are" — significant lifting of eyebrows at this point — "and when you promptly turned them over to him, it must have put him out quite a lot. There was the whole weary job to do over; so he stuck you with the notebook, instead, and this time, the cops did the tidying before you could."

"That is quite incorrect," Hanson interjected.

"Oh, yeah, then tell us what really happened," Hanna challenged.

"I have nothing more to say until I see my lawyer."

"Suit yourself. It was also pretty pathetic, when you come to think of it, how he went around the church planting clues, like the hat and the Rotary pin and the *Lancer* pen, which his police experience must have told him were not going to be accepted for more than the time it took to check them out."

"Well, but, be fair, he was under a lot of pressure."

"Exactly my point. He was desperate. That's why he staged this little farce; he thought that if you didn't panic before, you would when he named you . . ."

"Well, I did."

"...and make a break for it."

"I would have, but I couldn't get my limbs to function."

"Anyway, when you told me about the sunglasses, I called Sergeant Smollett, here, and when Hanson hadn't bothered to say a word to him about them, it was pretty clear that something really fishy was going on."

"If the police were onto Hanson, why did they let him go ahead with this performance here?"

"Why not? If they refused, he might make a run for it, and somebody might get hurt."

"That's not quite it," Sergeant Smollett said. "The truth is, we were suspicious of Eberley, but we didn't have enough to justify a search warrant until one of our boys interviewed the witness who saw the Eberleys in Ernie Struthers's truck. That was late last night. We brought the search warrant out with us, and it seemed a useful thing to let him stage this little charade while we searched the place. There's a team over there right now, and my guess is that, among other things, they'll find that case with the sunglasses, and we'll find it belonged to Ernie Struthers."

"There," said Hanna again, with her irritating and triumphant grin. "When you think about it, for a former homicide detective, Hanson was really quite incompetent."

"He didn't look incompetent to me when he had that pig-sticker up against your throat."

"The trouble with you, Carlton," the young blot went on, "is that you think you're on television, and you're not. This is real life. Real life in Canada," she added.

That was a bitter blow. In the United States — and this is one of the things that makes that great republic what it is — the good guys behave like good guys, and the bad guys go down snarling and slashing; but in Canada, to be a good guy and rescue the fair damsel is to invite the contempt of the multitude. What a country.

Well, not all the multitude. Mrs. Golden made a fuss over me, and so did Dominic Silvio. "Nice work, kid," he said, and, with a wink, "We'll talk later."

Obviously, he still didn't know that I'd been canned from

the *Lancer*, and was no longer in a position where flying trips to California made much sense. However, I was speedily uncanned. Tommy Macklin, scuffing his shoes, and looking positively human, came shuffling up, stuck out his hand, and said, "Carlton, forget the crap about being fired. You're hired again."

"How about Hanna?"

A glower, a sigh. "Oh, all right. She can have her job back, too."

"With a raise?" This, needless to say, was Hanna talking, not me.

Another glower, another sigh. "Small raise," he said.

"Okay," said Hanna, and smacked me on the back. "See, Carlton, you've got to strike while the iron is hot."

The iron, in this case, was positively glowing. Tommy wasn't giving me my job back, or Hanna hers, out of boyish affection. We knew about the role he had played, or not, in the war. So did the Widow Golden, which of course meant that most of Bellingham County would have the story in about forty-eight hours, but that was not the same as having two journalists spreading the tale to the people who counted in Tommy's mind, viz., the rest of the trade. If he kept us on the payroll and under his thumb, we wouldn't rat; if not, we would. That was the unspoken deal that re-employed us.

"Great," said Hanna, "I'll just take a few shots before the police haul Eberley away. We can do a terrific feature for next week's paper."

I looked at Tommy; Tommy looked at me. More to be pitied than censured, our mutual looks said.

"Hanna," I told her, "there isn't going to be a feature for next week's paper."

"The hell there isn't."

"In the first place, the Toronto dailies will have it in about eight hours, and they'll pluck it clean. We'd be scooped on our own story."

"And in the second place," put in Tommy, "it isn't a *Lancer* kind of story. Murder. Blackmail. Drunken driving.

That's not the sort of thing our readers want with their morning coffee."

In this, as we know, he had his facts twisted. Murder, blackmail, and a dollop of booze and sex is just what our readers want, morning, noon, and night, which is why the weekly issue of the *National Enquirer* is always gone from the newsstand in Silver Falls long before the *Lancer*. But the readers who don't want all that juicy stuff appearing in the newspaper are Mrs. Post, our proprietor, and some of the advertisers. Moreover, the *Lancer* had been interested in an exclusive about sponsoring Hanson Eberley's investigation; it would be embarrassing to have to admit the paper had been working with the killer. Tommy didn't feel it incumbent upon him to spell this out.

"Well, my hat," Hanna exclaimed, "what kind of story do your readers want?"

Tommy smiled a secret smile. "Oh, I dunno." He gave me a little nudge. "I think we can come up with something, eh, Carlton? Something, for example, about a snazzy new condomimium development right here in Bosky Dell?"

"Well, uh . . ."

Hanna was on it like a swooping hawk. "Carlton? What is all this?"

"Um, nothing."

"You're going to do a story boosting this project, aren't you? I might have guessed."

That did it. "Sit down, Hanna. Sit down and shut up."

She did, too. Surprised me so much, I nearly forgot what I wanted to say.

"No. I'm not going to write a story boosting a condominium development for Bosky Dell."

Tommy began to wave his arms about, like a semaphore instructor who had forgotten to bring along his flags, and Dominic began to splutter. I silenced them with an imperious gesture, copied, as a matter of fact, from my VCR edition of Charles Laughton in *Mutiny on the Bounty*.

"I was thinking about it. We talked about it. But no, of

course not. Do you think I'd sell out my journalistic principles for a mess of pottage?"

Got her. She did, of course, think I'd sell out my journalistic principles for a mess of pottage, and so, until about thirty seconds before, did I. But the damn woman had gotten under my skin to the point where even a trip to California didn't seem worth having to explain to her why I was taking it.

"My hero," she murmured, and while she didn't flutter any eyelashes, she did give me a big kiss, although she rather spoiled the effect by saying, quite accurately, "I'll bet you would have, though, about a week ago."

The woman ought to be suppressed by official order. Tommy kicked up quite a stink, of course, and so did Dominic; but the condominium project was chancy, anyway, so that was the end of it, right there.

When we broke up the clinch and started to move off, we came up against Smiley and Thuggy. Thuggy was looking truculent, his favourite expression, while Smiley looked a trifle embarrassed.

"We aren't finished with you," said Thuggy.

"There's a bit of a problem," added Smiley. "The other murder."

"I thought we were all clear on that," I replied. "The Rev. must have found out, somehow, that Hanson stabbed Ernie, so he had to be killed, too."

"The trouble with that theory," Smiley told me, "is that, according to your statement in the matter of the Rev. Mr. Wylie's death, he called you about eleven a.m., and you went at once up to the church, where you found him dead."

"So what?"

"So," snarled Thuggy, "between nine-thirty and eleven-fifteen that day, Hanson Eberley was with us, first at his own house and then later at your place, while we were conducting our search."

"I didn't see him there that day."

"He slipped out the kitchen door when we saw you coming down the street. So, you see, we still have an unsolved murder."

"But why would I kill the Rev.?"

"That we haven't worked out, yet," said Thuggy, and Smiley explained, more kindly, "We're not saying that you did, Mr. Withers. We're just explaining to you that this matter is not yet concluded."

"Yeah, well, it damn soon will be," said Hanna, and her statement filled me with a nameless dread. The girl had obviously got it up her nose, and was seeing herself as a latter-day Nancy Drew, girl detective.

"Do me a favour, Hanna," I begged her, "let the cops do the detecting this time. We're all terrifically impressed with the way you solved the puzzle, but don't start plotting."

"Oh, as to that," she answered airily, "my plans are already in motion."

TWENTY-SIX

THE REST OF that day is a bit of a blur in my memory. Tommy Macklin said that, as we were back on the payroll again, Hanna and I should do some work — it was not, he said pointedly, five o'clock yet — so we went over to Silver Falls. Hanna's car had been left outside the office, but *Marchepas*, ever ready to surprise, thundered into life on command, and bore us in style to the *Lancer*. We arrived about four p.m. and I went to work on a column of Neighbourly Notes, while Hanna disappeared in the direction of her darkroom. Actually, she didn't emerge again until well after five, when she came tripping up the stairs from the street.

"Where have you been?" I asked her.

"Oh, I just thought I should run down and have a little chat with Belinda Huntingdon," she replied. And laughed. I did not like that laugh, and I was glad when she suggested that, instead of eating at the O.K., we should go over to her apartment for supper. Good, healthy food, it was, well-prepared, pretty revolting, come to think of it. Afterwards, we sat around listening to music for a couple of hours, and then I invited her to join me back at the Dell for a little fun and frolic.

"No, Carlton," she said, "that would only spoil things. You run along home."

"Spoil what?"

"You know. Things."

There was no moving her, so, after a while, home I went, *Marchepas* being still operational. It was after dark when I got there, and all the lights were out at the cottage, as usual, but I didn't care. I stumbled into the bedroom, donned the PJs, and crawled into bed. About fifteen hours of sleep, I figured, was just what a body needed about now.

Then I sat up and said, "Mrs. Eberley, we're going to have to stop meeting like this."

It was her. She. Whatever. In my bed, as before, clad in filmy night things, as before. The damn moon was shining, as before, and I could make her out quite clearly.

"Carlton," she murmured, giving me the old up and down, "how sweet of you to want to warn me."

"Um, ah, yes." Warn her? Warn her about what? Had the woman stripped her gears? All the tension, Hanson's arrest . . . no doubt that was it.

"This, um, warning," I said smoothly, clutching the bed-sheets under my chin, "did I give you any hint as to what exactly . . ."

"Oh, Carlton," she gave me a roguish push with her left hand, her right one being, I noted, behind her back. "*You* know."

I didn't, of course. So I kind of gawked at her, but made no reply. The situation was not covered, dammit, in Journalism 104.

The silence seemed to peeve Nora, for some reason. Her eyebrows drew together.

"Is this some sort of trick?" she wanted to know. "Did you get me down here under false pretences?"

Not knowing under which pretences I had got her down here — could I have invited her to drop in for a midnight chat and somehow have forgotten? — I continued my policy as before, to wit, a watchful silence.

For some reason, this ticked Nora off completely. Her voice went into the old, familiar screech.

"It is! It's a trick! It's some kind of blackmail scheme again! Well, I won't have it!"

Saying which, she uncorked the right arm, the one that had been behind her up to this point, and it was then that I noticed something different about her on this trip to my boudoir. She looked, well, a lot less sexy than before, a lot less appealing and a lot more, now that I came to check it out, a lot more knife-laden, than on that previous occasion. This looked like one of Hanson's hunting knives. There was, on the one hand, relief that it was not yet another of my Dad's pin punches that was going to be incriminated, and, on the other, a certain chagrin that it was not, apparently, because of my enormous sex appeal that she had come calling again, but with other, less friendly, motives in mind. We were facing what looked to be a very embarrassing moment when, suddenly, the lights went on and cops — it seemed to me there were about ten of them, but only two, as it turned out — came boiling into the room.

Behind them I heard a cheery cry, "Surprise!"

Klovack, again, riding to the rescue.

Nora gaped, then quickly reversed the knife and handed it to me, butt foremost. "Darling, I believe this is yours," she said.

However, the cops were having none of it, and Detective Thurston produced a pair of handcuffs, which he slapped on Nora. She didn't like it much. Then Sergeant Smollett phoned in a report. Very terse — "We got her," is all I heard. They were about to give us a merry good evening, when Hanna said, "Hey, wait a minute!"

"Ma'am?" he said, on a rising note.

"You're not going to just sail out of here," said Hanna, "not until we get the story. After all, if it hadn't been for me, you wouldn't have a collar."

Smiley looked at Thuggy, who nodded.

"I think maybe you have a point," said Smiley, and we all sat down. Thuggy, still holding onto Nora, sat beside me on the couch, and Smiley and Hanna occupied the two chairs.

I was just about to ask what in the name of tarnation this was all about, when the front door blammed open. The Widow Golden, alerted by the sudden burst of light and noise, had arrived, clad in a becoming chiffon robe. She quickly sized up the situation, then rushed out to the kitchen and began making coffee. It seemed a good idea.

"Okay, give," I said. "Hanna, you said something about 'If it hadn't been for me' — what's that all about?"

She was looking very pleased with herself. "You see, Carlton," Hanna explained, "as soon as the detectives here," thumb jerk towards Smiley and Thuggy, still on the job, and earning overtime, I'll bet, "made it clear that there had to be another murderer involved, I knew it must have been Nora."

"How did you know that? And, come to that, how did you come to be here?"

"I followed you out. Simplest thing in the world."

"Why?"

"Well, I had to be here. After all, I arranged this party."

"You mean, you knew that Nora was a killer, so you arranged for her to call on me?"

"Of course. Any idiot could have figured out that she had killed Wylie, once we knew it couldn't be Hanson. Well, maybe not you, Carlton, but any other idiot. It was the only explanation that made sense. If Hanson didn't kill the Rev., and you didn't, then Nora must have. You remember he saw her sneaking out of your cottage on Friday morning. She was there planting the blackmail book — that part of it wasn't Hanson at all? That right?"

The question was addressed to Nora, who nodded, slowly.

"But that was no reason to kill the Rev., just because he saw her."

"Yes, it was. The Rev. thought at first that Nora was there because of some extra-marital hanky-panky, but that explanation wouldn't hold up long. I mean, you weren't even there. He was bound to bring the subject up with you, and you were going to tell him that you and Nora were just good friends. Or, maybe, not so good."

"So, if he talked to the police, they would realize that she must have come here to plant the blackmail book?"

"You get a gold star."

"And the only reason for her to plant it there was to cover up a murder. Is that right, Nora? You killed the Rev. for Hanson's sake, just as he killed Ernie for yours?"

Nora grimaced, grimly. "You see, I knew that Hanson had killed Ernie, because the day you found his body, I found your Dad's tool kit, out in our shed. I never go in the shed, so Hanson must have thought it was safe there, but Jim Sampson came around to borrow the lawn mower because his is on the fritz. Hanson wasn't around, so I took him out to the shed. He got the lawn mower, but when he pulled it out, I saw something fall down, up against the wall. I went back in and there was the tool kit. I guess he'd picked it up at your place, just in case. At first I didn't know what it was, so I didn't do anything with it. But later I heard about the murder and put two and two together."

She looked up and me and gave a winsome sigh. "I knew that Hanson must have killed Ernie. Not that I blamed him a bit. If ever a person was begging for a pin punch in the kidneys, it was Ernie Struthers."

She sat there for a moment, thinking about Ernie Struthers. "He only agreed to take the blame for me for money, you know, Carlton." She put out one hand, and touched me, softly, on the arm. She said, quietly, "Oh, Carlton, I'm so sorry. That's why I came to see you the other night. I was going to tell you about what really happened the night your parents died. That and, well, perhaps other reasons. But mainly that."

I looked up at a movement beside me. It was Hanna, holding her nose. A person quite without the finer feelings.

Nora took my hand in hers, as she went on. "I was drunk the day of the accident. I was driving Ernie's truck. We were in town, at the hotel, Hanson and I, and we'd been drinking most of the afternoon. When we came out, and saw Ernie getting ready to drive home, we decided to leave our car — we used to have a car in those days, we sold it afterwards — in town and ride with him. So sensible, we thought." She laughed bitterly.

"But Ernie was drunker than we were. He didn't look it, but he was. We got in and started to drive home and the first thing you know, he ran right off the road and hit a fence post. He was out cold for a few minutes. So we changed places. Hanson doesn't like to drive, as you know, and after that business in Toronto, there was no way he was going to get behind the wheel when he'd had a few. It was just the natural thing for me to take over. And I did. And then, when we were almost here, oh, God, suddenly there was this other car coming right at us — I guess I veered right over the middle of the road — and there was this horrible crash. I never intended. . . ."

Her voice trailed off. "If you believe that malarkey, Carlton," came the cynical voice of young H. Klovack, "I believe I have a bridge I can sell you."

Nora looked up, timid and frightened. "Why, Hanna, why do you hate me so?" she said.

"Because you're such a bloody awful liar," Hanna replied. "Dry your tears, Carlton. The reason Nora came calling the other night was to plant Ernie's sunglasses on you. She obviously had something else in mind, too, but that was the main thing. Then, you turned up with the damn things — it was like that song, "The Cat Came Back the Very Next Day" — so she had to set you up again, this time with the blackmail book. Is that right? Or did Hanson handle the sunglasses?"

"No. I did all the planting," said Nora. She sounded faintly horticultural. "Actually, we had quite a fight about that. Hanson didn't know I was doing it, and when he realized it, after first the hat and then the Rotary pin turned up at the church, he was quite cross with me. He said it was amateurish, and would only get him into more trouble. He said all you had to do was to leave a little hint, here and there, and the police could be counted on to put it together.

"Hah! The police. He forgets I worked for the police for years, and I know why they call them 'leadheads.' So I paid no attention. I got the glasses out of Ernie's new truck. He must have held onto them for some reason and I found them there. The police were watching his house, of course, but the truck's away out back. They probably didn't even think about it."

Sergeant Smollett asked, "Didn't you realize what a risk your were running if somebody saw you in any of your expeditions?"

"What risk? I was covered for the night of Ernie's death — Hanson's police pal saw that I was, uh, indisposed that night — so, if somebody saw me, they'd just assume it was a little hanky-panky, and pay no attention. That was what I thought, anyway. Hanson didn't even know about it. He'd have tried to stop me, I'm sure.

"You know," she went on, very seriously, "that must have been the hardest thing of all for Hanson to bear, when it all started to unravel and all you people kept explaining in such a clever way all the dumb mistakes he had made. He didn't make them, I did. But he didn't say a word.

"Anyway, I didn't see a clear chance to plant the notebook until the Friday morning. Hanson told me they were bound to come out that day with a search warrant and they did. So, while they were all sitting around drinking coffee and talking about the case, I slipped out the back door and popped into your place, Carlton. I assumed you were at work; in any event, you weren't around when I knocked on the side door. So, I just slipped in and did it. I wasn't gone more than a couple of minutes."

I said I was impressed by her efficiency, and she gave me a vacant smile in return.

"But when Ephraim saw me leaving your cottage, well, he was the one person who wouldn't just let it go at that. He was bound to ask you about it, and he would learn that there was no reason — no sexual reason, anyway — for me to be there. That could lead to a very awkward situation, if he mentioned it to the police."

I asked, "Yes, but how did you know he'd seen you?"

"He told me. It worried him, you see, but he was not a very clever person, and the notion that there might be more to it than just hanky-panky never occurred to him. He thought you and I were having an affair; at least, that is what I gathered from his very broad hints when he telephoned last Friday morning, almost the minute I got home. He said he wanted to see me up at the church, to speak about what he called 'matters spiritual and physical.' When I pressed him, he told me he had seen me leaving your place. I told him I had been there to leave a note inviting you to dinner. I said you were in town at work, but he said your car was still in the drive, and he didn't believe me. I don't see how you can be a clergyman," she said petulantly, "when you don't have faith in people. Anyway, he said the only fair thing was for the three of us to have what he called 'a little chat.' Naturally, I agreed. I told him that I would come up to the church right away.

"The only thing I could think of was that I had to get rid of Ephraim, somehow, before he got hold of you. I knew you weren't at home, because I'd just been to your home, so that probably gave me a little time. I knew I had to kill Ephraim."

My flesh crept.

"Hanson had murdered for me, Carlton, don't you see? So I would murder for him, and that would make it even."

This was an equal rights killing.

She laughed, a small laugh, with no humour in it. "Poor Ephraim. Poor, poor, lamb. He thought it was his Christian duty to give me a chance to explain myself, and you to explain yourself. Which would not have done, Carlton. Would not have done at all."

She sighed. "He really was a nice man, if a bit of a simpleton. Hanson and the officers were still sitting around gassing, which is what policemen do most of the time, in my experience . . ."

"We were trying to draw Hanson out," said Detective Thurston, ruefully.

"And getting nowhere fast," added Sergeant Smollett.

"Well, while they were drawing Hanson out and drinking coffee, I went out the back door again. I took one of those things, punches, out of the package in the shed, put on gardening gloves, and went up to the church. When I got there, there was Ephraim, sitting in that box pew. I guess he thought that was a good place to talk things out, better than an ordinary pew. More discreet. So I just walked up, gave him my best smile, and stuck that thing in him."

She shuddered. "He jumped around quite a bit. In the movies, they always just fall down, but he clutched himself and gurgled and made horrible faces. It was quite unpleasant. Then he sat down, and I knew it was all right. He sighed, and then his eyes closed. I knew he must be dead. So, I left one of your pens there — there must be half a dozen around the house, here — and went back home and back in the kitchen door. The police and Hanson, they were still in the living-room, talking."

There was a silence, and then Hanna jumped in, "Weren't you taking a terrific chance that someone would see you kill Ephraim?"

"What choice did I have? When I told Hanson what I had done, he was quite shocked, I could see that. But he said he was sure it would be all right in the end. We thought it would be when you were arrested, and, since Hanson was helping the police, we figured that if it looked as if they decided Carlton couldn't have done it, we'd know right away. We'd have time to clear out.

"But you were let out on bail. Then, of course, Mrs. Wylie phoned yesterday, and told Hanson, not only that Ephraim had spoken to her about seeing me leave your cottage — which, I, personally, think was quite wrong for a priest to divulge — but that she had told the police about it. Well, we knew it was all going to come out.

"We only had one chance, and that was to panic you, Carlton. Hanson said you were the kind of person who would break and run. We thought," she said, in a perfectly calm, normal voice, "there was a pretty good chance the police would shoot you trying to escape."

"Sorry to disappoint you."

"Then, of course, when that didn't happen, and Hanson was arrested instead, I thought, 'Well, poor Hanson,' but I knew he would never tell about Ephraim. That was why I was so concerned, Carlton, when I got your note."

"My note? What note?"

"This one." She reached down into the front of her night-gown and extracted a slip of paper, which she laid in front of me. It was one of my memo pad pages, and it contained a short, cryptic message in that dotty little writing that comes off a computer.

It said:

Nora:

I must see you. New developments. Police suspect
another involved in Ephraim's killing. Come to my
place tonight.

Carlton.

Even I could figure out where this had to come from. I
waved it at Hanna.

"This is your doing."

Was she abashed? Of course not.

"You bet," said Hanna. "After this morning's little charade, I whipped that note up over at the newspaper, and
while you were busy writing drivel, I stuck it in an envelope
and drove over here and gave it to Nora. I told her it was from
you, that it was apparently something you didn't want to
say over the phone for fear of being overheard, but as I knew
that she was a good friend of yours, Carlton," — big rolling
of eyes, here — "I presumed it was something urgent and
private. I couldn't imagine what." Business with eyes again.
"I said I was sure you would tell me about it later, if it was
something I needed to know." She added, "And she believed
me."

Of course she did. Hanna has the clear gaze, straight-
forward manner, and innocent air that mark the really suc-
cessful liar. I was dumbfounded.

"So, you figured she'd read this note and come gunning
for me..."

"Not gunning, Carlton..."

"Knifing for me, whatever, and you didn't even warn
me?"

"That would have spoiled it," said Hanna, but then Smiley cut in, soothingly.

"There was never any real danger, Mr. Withers," he said.
"Hanna spoke to me on the telephone this afternoon, and
you have been under surveillance ever since. You see, we
came to the same conclusion that she did about Mrs. Eberley, but there wasn't any real hard evidence. So, if we could
get her to commit..."

211

"Mayhem on my body . . ."

" . . . herself in some way, perhaps verbally, perhaps, er, more physically . . ."

"You mean, if she had rammed me with that knife, you'd have a pretty fair notion that I wasn't the killer after all."

A small smile, the first since World War II, illuminated the face of Thuggy.

"There was never a chance of that happening. Mrs. Eberley is not exactly a trained killer, Mr. Withers, but she was in a desperate situation, and becoming somewhat, ahem, emotionally unstable . . ."

"Oh, fine. I was not to worry because she wasn't one of the Mafia, she was just a homicidal maniac. How," I asked Nora, "were you going to get away with killing me?"

"I never expected it to come to that, Carlton. I just wanted to know what you knew. I only brought the knife out when you got silly."

"But how was my death going to be explained?"

Smiley cut in, "My guess is that you were going to commit suicide."

"I was going to stab myself?"

Hanna said, "Why not? You were all out of pin punches. The police might be suspicious, might even be quite sure, but the evidence they had showed that Hanson couldn't have killed the Rev., but you might have. As before, Nora had to take the chance."

"After all that trouble," Nora said with a small shudder, "if you were going to undo all of Hanson's hard work, Carlton . . . well, you see that I had to stop that, don't you?"

Loopy to the gills, of course. The combination of booze, suspense, and life with Hanson under the constant threat of exposure had unhinged the poor creature.

So, the day wound to a weary close. The cops exited with Nora Eberley in tow, and the Widow Golden washed up the coffee cups, rolled her eyes, and made her ostentatious way to the threshold.

"Well," she said, "I guess I can leave you two alone." And she banged the door.

That left Hanna and self in the living-room.

"It was a set-up, this whole evening," I said.

"That's right."

"Like one of those Indian things."

"What Indian things?"

"You know, those Indian things. In India. With a goat."

"Ah yes. Where they tether a goat below the tree and wait for the tiger."

"Exactly. Nora was the tiger, and you cast me in the role of goat." I was sore as a boil. Two boils.

"But a nice goat, Carlton," Hanna said. "A cuddly goat." She gave me the eye.

"Say," she went on, "what are you going to do with your ten thousand?"

"My ten... holy smokes, I'd forgotten all about it." I thought about it. "To tell you the truth, Hanna, I don't think I can take the money."

"Why not?"

"Well, it was really Ernie's way of trying to square things, wasn't it? Of trying to say, 'Well, your parents are dead, but here's ten thousand dollars,' and it would be ten thousand dollars he had squeezed out of the husband of the woman who killed them. In the end, it would be blood money. I don't want it."

"That," she said, "was the right answer." She gave me another look.

"Boy, Carlton, you really do look a fright in those PJs."

"Then why," I said, reaching for the light switch with one hand and for Hanna with the other, "don't we take them off?"

So we did.